DEATH
CHECKED
OUT

DEATH
CHECKED
OUT

DEATH
CHECKED
OUT

A Larkspur Library Mystery

Leah Dobrinska

LEVEL
BEST BOOKS

First published by Level Best Books 2022

Copyright © 2022 by Leah Dobrinska

This novel is entirely a work of fiction. The names, characters and incidents portrayed in it are the work of the author's imagination. Any resemblance to actual persons, living or dead, events or localities is entirely coincidental.

Leah Dobrinska asserts the moral right to be identified as the author of this work.

Author Photo Credit: Photo courtesy of Beth Dunphy

First edition

ISBN: 978-1-68512-182-2

Cover art by Ana Grigoriu-Voicu

This book was professionally typeset on Reedsy.
Find out more at reedsy.com

For my kids. Always pursue the truth.

Praise for Death Checked Out

"Death Checked Out is one for the books! Leah Dobrinska's charming cozy debut expertly binds a library theme with a clever mystery and picturesque setting. You'll root for amateur sleuth Greta Plank as she wields her bookish knowhow both on and off the shelf!"—Kate Lansing, author of the Colorado Wine Mystery Series

"Death Checked Out by Leah Dobrinska welcomes cozy mystery readers to Larkspur, Wisconsin with open arms. Full of characters you can't help but love, *Death Checked Out* launches what is sure to be a memorable mystery series.

Greta Plank, Larkspur's perennially optimistic librarian, is a charming, modern-day Nancy Drew in Leah Dobrinska's cozy mystery debut. From the moment she ushers the reader through the doors of her Wisconsin library domain, Greta commands your attention and keeps it as she dives headfirst into solving her next-door neighbor's murder.

The town of Larkspur serves as the perfect cozy backdrop with a supporting cast of spirited characters that are all heroes in their own right. I didn't want any of them to be the killer because I enjoyed them all so much. But, oh, the mystery! So tricky and twisty—I found myself racing to the end to discover the big reveal.

Death Checked Out is a must for cozy mystery lovers; a true celebration of the determined amateur sleuth."—Sarah E. Burr, author of the Trending Topic Mysteries & Glenmyre Whim Mysteries

"Librarians Rock! Dobrinska's three dedicated and daring book protectors know how to ferret out clues and catch a killer. Leah Dobrinska's mystery, full of twists and turns in a lakefront Wisconsin town, is the perfect beginning to a new cozy series!"—Heather Weidner, author of the Jules Keene Glamping Mysteries & the Mermaid Bay Christmas Shoppe Mysteries

"A fabulous series debut, this fun mystery has it all—twists and turns, a library, a charming small town, great BFFs, and a hint of romance. *Death Checked Out* will keep you guessing until the very end!"—Christina Romeril, author of the Killer Chocolate Mystery series

"Cozy mystery fans will definitely want to check out this debut cozy mystery by Leah Dobrinska. *Death Checked Out* is a page turner full of intriguing characters and twists and turns."—Jackie Layton, author of the Low Country Dog Walker Mystery series

Chapter One

L arkspur Lane cut through the center of town like the spine of a storybook.

A fitting analogy, in Greta Plank's opinion, because four months into her tenure as director of Larkspur Community Library, she could honestly say that everything about this place was idyllic, which—given her recent history—was just what she needed.

She scooched her canvas tote up her arm, casting a fond glance back at the red-brick building that housed the library before taking off. She had a book delivery to make.

Ahead of her, neighborhoods and small businesses spread out from either side of the boulevard. *Like crisp pages brimming with fairy tales and happy endings*, Greta mused.

Larkspur Lane was a straight shot south to the lake. There, it teed into Lakeside Drive, which wound around the whole body of water. Greta walked in that direction, the sun winking at her through the trees. The leaves were starting to change, but they hadn't yet reached peak color. In a few weeks, Larkspur would be inundated with folks from all over Wisconsin and beyond who ventured north to enjoy the fall foliage and festivals. For now, greens were still mixed in with oranges and reds, forming a canopy over her head, and Greta had the sidewalk to herself.

She spotted Dolores Jenkins, who lived in one of the multi-colored cottages that sat on Larkspur Lane. Dolores was an active member of the Friends of the Library non-profit.

"Hi, Mrs. Jenkins!"

Dolores leaned on her broom and offered Greta a warm smile. "Greta, dear, you must call me Dolores, or I'm going to start getting offended. I know I'm no spring chicken, but 'Mrs. Jenkins' will forever be linked in my mind to my late mother-in-law, God rest her soul."

"Alright then, Dolores. Have a wonderful evening. Enjoy this beautiful weather."

"You as well, dear. You as well."

Greta strolled on, smiling to herself. She'd made a friend in Dolores, and it was a relief to be welcomed into the Larkspur fold. She knew all too well how it felt to endure gossipy gazes and shunned silences in a town she considered to be her home, and she had had enough of that to last a lifetime.

Greta didn't make it a point to dwell on that...or on *him*. It wasn't worth it. Besides, she wasn't even thirty yet. She had her whole future in front of her, and Larkspur was her new beginning.

Turning onto Lakeside Drive, she glanced at the lake on her left. The wind was generating tiny waves, and the reflecting sunlight made the entire surface shine like a collection of diamonds. Greta stopped and pulled in deep, contented breaths, inhaling the trademark aroma of early autumn in the Northwoods—minty pine, lake musk, and corroding aspen leaves.

A stiff breeze kicked up, whipping her tea-length skirt against her legs and blowing her strawberry-gold hair into her eyes. Greta fought against her curls, peeling hair away from her face before tugging her jacket's collar closer to her neck and hurrying on.

In five minutes, she'd made it to the home of Franklin Halloway. Greta skipped up the ramp to Franklin's front door, knocked once, and waited. If she looked to her right, she could just make out her roofline through the trees. Franklin's cabin sat closest to hers on the west side of Larkspur Lake, and equal parts pride and delight coursed through her veins at the thought of the friendship she'd struck up with the older gentleman.

Four months ago, when Greta first met Franklin, he hadn't given her the time of day. He had opened the door on her first visit only to shut it in her face before she could so much as say, "Hi, my name is…" But Greta was not to be deterred. She'd kept at him, and slowly, he warmed to her presence, especially when she offered to courier library books directly to him.

What could she say? She was not above bribing her way into someone's good graces with the promise of books.

After a few seconds, the rough sound of wheels rolling across the wood floor reached Greta's ears, and she turned as the door swung inward. Franklin sat in his wheelchair a couple feet inside the entryway, but the smile she had ready for him died on her lips.

Franklin's eyes blazed with disgust, and his voice was as frosty as a Wisconsin winter. "I understand what you're asking, but you don't seem to understand what I'm telling you!"

Chapter Two

I t took Greta a frantic moment to realize Franklin was wearing wireless earbuds and talking on his cell phone. He motioned for Greta to come inside, and she put up her hands to let him know she didn't want to intrude, but he beckoned her with a wave of his palm. She stayed silent and crossed the threshold of Franklin's cabin. The door clicked shut behind her.

Franklin held up one finger, signaling he'd only be a moment, before pushing himself in the direction of his living room. Greta bent down to offer Biff, Franklin's six-year-old golden Siberian tabby cat, a chance to sniff her. He was a handsome feline, with golden flecks adorning the tips of his brown-striped coat and piercing green eyes. He let out a low purr for attention, and Greta scratched him behind his ears.

Satisfied with her greeting, Biff batted at Greta's hand before darting into the kitchen.

Greta stood and followed Franklin down the hall, around the enclosed room where he stored his book collection, and to the living room, which looked out over the lake. Her cabin was almost identical to Franklin's, minus the accessibility features he had installed and his rare books room. She could only hope to have a book collection like his someday.

Franklin had stopped his wheelchair in front of the windows, and now he threw up his hands. "If I were to sell, then what? My property first, and pretty soon the whole lake? No. I don't think so. Good day, sir." He pressed a button on his phone, ending the call.

Greta held her breath and waited for Franklin to face her. His shoulders heaved up and down for several seconds before he turned and greeted her with a strained smile. Whoever he had been talking with, Franklin was not a fan. But that didn't narrow it down since he wasn't particularly close to anyone in Larkspur…except for her.

"Greta, thank you for coming. I'm sorry I was occupied when you arrived."

"Don't worry about it. I have the holds for you." She reached into her canvas bag and pulled out the books Franklin requested from the library.

"Excellent. I can't wait to dive in." He shuffled through the stack, pausing to read the back cover of *Crime and Punishment* before he met Greta's gaze. "These'll be great. Please, take a seat. Can you stay a minute? Can I get you anything to drink?"

"I can stay for a bit." Greta set her bag down and smoothed her skirt under her as she sat on Franklin's couch. "But I don't need anything."

"You're about the only person I know who doesn't need anything from me, Greta."

Greta waited for him to explain what he meant, but Franklin just steepled his fingers under his chin. His hair was streaked with gray, and he looked a little more out of sorts than usual. His forehead was creased with deep worry lines, and he stared straight ahead, but didn't seem to see what was in front of him. The man was temperamental, to say the least. But typically, Franklin was anxious for her to tell him all about her day at the library and any town happenings. He may not get out much, but he liked to keep tabs on Larkspur.

"Anything you want to talk about?"

Franklin looked up, startled, as if he'd forgotten there was someone else in the room with him. "Terribly sorry, Greta," he sighed. "I've got a lot on my mind."

Greta paused for a second and then decided to take advantage of the relationship she'd built with him to try to get some answers—even if she was being what some might consider nosy. "The phone call?"

"Yes. Among other things. Ed Kennedy was pestering me about my property. He wants to buy me out and develop this land."

"What?" Greta sat back. Ed Kennedy owned and operated Kennedy's Cozy Cottages, a resort on the opposite side of the lake. She'd met him several times over the course of the summer, and he seemed like a decent guy. What was he doing trying to poach Franklin's land?

"Don't worry, I'm not selling."

"I should think not! Why is he calling you?"

"My property is the closest to the main road. It would be best suited for a restaurant or a community center or something. I don't know. He was slippery as an eel, and I couldn't pin him down. I had to keep telling him no."

"Good that you did." Greta stood and patted Franklin's arm as she walked past him into the kitchen. "Let me get you a glass of water."

Franklin thanked her and slumped in his wheelchair.

She hurried to pour him a drink, and when she returned to the living room, he was staring out the windows overlooking his deck. Biff sat curled up in his owner's lap, and Franklin absently stroked the cat's iridescent fur. Greta followed Franklin's gaze. This was her favorite view. In the early evening, everything was so peaceful on the water. The hum of motor boats had faded with the warmth of summer, and now, just a couple pontoons dotted the lake. The water shimmered in the setting autumn sun.

Larkspur Lake was the town's crown jewel, and Greta still pinched herself every time she thought about how she'd managed to procure her own piece of lakefront property. A friend of a friend of her mother's was looking to offload his great-aunt's cabin, and Greta was in the right place at the right time. It had been a much needed win.

"Here." Greta placed a hand on Franklin's shoulder and handed him the cool glass.

Franklin took a sip and offered Greta a smile. "Tell me about the day at the library."

Greta returned to her seat on the couch. "Let's see. Someone in Karrington is hooked on Nancy Drew books. I wasn't sure, but today sealed the deal. This is the third week in a row we've had a hold request. It's from the same branch, and it comes in on the same day each week. The books being requested are sequential. First, it was *The Secret of the Old Clock*, followed by *The Hidden Staircase*, and this week, *The Bungalow Mystery*, which is such a good one." Greta closed her eyes as she tried to remember exactly how the plot unfolded. After a minute, she glanced at Franklin.

He stared back at her with an amused expression. "You love *Nancy Drew* the same way I love *The Hardy Boys*. That's how Biff here got his name. Did you know Biff is the nickname of a minor character in the series? He's a friend of Frank and Joe Hardy."

"I figured he wasn't named for the villain in *Back To the Future*. He's too sweet for that." Greta grinned at the cat. Biff happened to be the most easy-going creature on the planet, so it was hard not to love him.

When she first met Franklin's tabby, she was hesitant to get too close. Most cats made her sneeze. As a result, she hadn't spent much time around any felines. But thanks to Biff's hypoallergenic coat, the two got along just fine. Franklin had even given Greta a spare key so she could tend to the cat when he left town.

Franklin looked on with fondness as Biff hopped to the coffee table before abandoning them. He turned his attention to her. "Anything else of note happen today?"

Greta leaned back and thought over her day, sifting for something else she could share with her friend to keep Franklin in good humor. "Oh!" She sat up straighter. "I washed out two hundred cardboard milk containers for a community gardening project town hall is putting on. The school donated them, but Abby, Mayor Collins's assistant, asked me if I wouldn't mind getting them into proper shape to be used." Greta hid a grimace. She had found actual chunks of chicken nuggets in some of the cartons.

Franklin screwed his mouth to the side. "That doesn't sound like it's in your job description."

Greta slashed a dismissive hand through the air. "My job description is to be a public servant. I was happy to help." Honestly, on her quest to fit in, she'd do whatever it took to remain in the mayor's good graces.

"It's nice of you to try to help, but you need to be careful you don't get taken advantage of for your charity."

Greta frowned. She opened her mouth to argue, but Franklin shook his head. "It's one of the things I admire about you, Greta. Believe me. What

I wouldn't give for your heart. But I'd hate to see it come back to bite you. Even you can't cure everything with your kindness."

"Doesn't mean I can't try. Besides, this kept everyone happy. It was the least I could do."

Franklin issued an unconvinced snort. "Life is messy, Greta. I should know. I'm no stranger to messy situations." He sighed, glancing at the floor-to-ceiling bookcases on either side of his fireplace—the same ones Biff regularly scaled. "And what about you? Are you ever going to tell me what you're hiding behind your chipper façade? Your trademark happiness will only get you so far."

Greta blanched, her heart hammering a painful rhythm. All at once, she felt like she was a sampling of mold about to be put under a microscope in a high school science lab.

As if sensing her unease, Franklin cleared his throat. "Enough about that. Soon enough, we'll share all our deepest secrets with each other, but for now, let's take a page out of your playbook and talk about mostly happy things, shall we?"

Thankful Franklin wasn't going to press her about her past, Greta punched out a relieved breath, and the tension in her face slackened...until she registered Franklin's other comment. He was going to tell her more about some kind of messy situation of his own? What was that all about?

Greta quirked her brow at Franklin, but his face was closed off as he stared back at her, and not for the first time did she get the feeling there was so much more to learn about her new-ish friend. There would be time for that. "Alright then. What happy things do you want to talk about?"

Franklin's cheeks flushed, and he dropped his gaze. "I'd like Dolores Jenkins's phone number."

"Really?" She couldn't be blamed for the fact her voice rose an octave. It took everything in Greta not to jump up and squeal. Dolores was a widow, and the thought of Franklin trying to court her warmed her heart to no end. All her efforts to get him to come out of his shell and embrace the Larkspur community were finally paying off.

"Yes. I'd like to give her a call and see if she'd stop by in the next week."

Greta reached down and started shuffling through the contents of her bag. "How nice. I have her number saved in my phone if I could find the blasted thing." Finally, her fingers landed on the hard plastic of her phone case, and she lifted it out of the bag with triumphant gusto, slamming the back of her hand on the coffee table in her haste.

Greta shook out her wrist. In her clumsiness, she'd knocked some papers onto the floor. "I'm sorry. I'm such a klutz. Let me tidy up." She set her phone down and bent to collect Franklin's documents before Biff could use them as cat scratch toys. "Do you want these back here? Or should I put them by your desk?" They appeared to be business papers, and Franklin's home office was in the guest bedroom off the front of the house.

"I'll get them later." Franklin glanced toward the papers and gave a glib shrug. He looked back up at Greta. "But I'll take the phone number now."

"Franklin Halloway, did you just wink at me?" Greta beamed as she piled the documents into a stack on the coffee table. "You must have it bad for Dolores."

"I wouldn't say that. I haven't spent any time with her at all. I've seen her from a distance walking along the public access trail by the lake."

Greta typed quickly into her phone and sent Franklin Dolores's contact information. "There you go. Now you can get more acquainted with her. Promise you'll keep me posted?" It wasn't a question. She would pry him for details on this budding relationship until the cows came home.

"I promise."

"Good. I better be going. I told Josie we could hang out later. Iris ditched us for her boyfriend." Josie and Iris were her fellow librarians, and they'd quickly become close. Greta loved them like sisters, and since her own sister passed away when Greta was in her teens, she didn't say that lightly. Now, she smiled to show Franklin she wasn't offended by Iris's actions.

"Iris and Dean are pretty serious, then?" Franklin followed her to the front of the house.

"It seems so. Time will tell, I guess."

"Indeed."

Greta stopped when she reached the front entryway. "What do you have on tap this week?"

"The usual. Physical therapy, and I have someone coming over who's interested in buying one of my books." The lines in Franklin's forehead deepened.

"You don't want to part with the book? Which one is it?"

The two had spent many evenings discussing Franklin's books. He had a complete collection of James Bond first editions, including *The Man With the Golden Gun* in its first state with the rare golden gun embossed on the front cover. There were thought to be fewer than one thousand copies in existence. Franklin was also working his way up to the complete collection of the Harry Potter series—a later-in-life passion. He'd recently acquired a first UK edition of *Harry Potter and the Philosopher's Stone*.

"It's a copy of *Live and Let Die* by Ian Fleming. I have three different editions in my collection, so I wouldn't be sad to part with it, per se. But it's complicated."

Before she could ask why, Franklin pressed the button to open his door, and Greta stepped out of the way. She'd been bumped by it too many times to count.

Franklin may have warmed up to her over the past few months, and she might be chipping away at his reclusive tendencies, but that was her cue to leave. She'd ask about the book collector later.

Chapter Three

A few days later, Greta hummed a song about sunshine and tapped her pencil against the top of the circulation desk, which in their small library also doubled as the reference desk. Though she was hired as the library's director, she made sure to take her turn at the desk, as well. Being out on the library floor was the sort of work she was used to in her former role as the adult services librarian in Green Bay, and she loved it. Interacting with patrons—helping them solve problems—was good for her extroverted heart, and the methodical tasks of scanning in books and checking them out always soothed her.

Larkspur Library's computers were ancient, and their programs took forever to load, so Greta made a game of it, trying to guess how many verses of a given song she'd be able to sing before the screen she needed finally appeared.

After two verses of "My Girl" by The Temptations, a list of books popped up in front of her. Greta dropped her pencil and deftly navigated the screen, her eyes flitting over the list of hold requests. She would gather these titles from the shelves and ship them via courier to other branches in the County Library System.

Dolores Jenkins wandered by as Greta was about to fetch the books.

"Dolores! Hi! Can I help you with anything?"

"No, I'm just here to browse. I got a recommendation for a book I thought I'd check out."

"Nice." Greta pivoted so she was facing Dolores. "What's the title?"

"*The Guernsey Literary and Potato Peel Pie Society* by Mary Ann Shaffer and

Annie Barrows. Have you read it?"

"I have, and it's a great read. Who recommended it to you?"

"Franklin Halloway suggested it." Dolores absently patted her hair, a pretty blush dusting her cheeks. "I stopped in to see him last night."

"How wonderful!" Greta clasped her hands together over her heart, but she dropped her arms when she noticed Dolores's deer-in-the-headlights expression. The last thing she wanted to do was scare Dolores away from Franklin by being overly enthusiastic. "The book recommendation, of course," she hurried to add.

Dolores looked left and right before dropping her voice. "Franklin was pretty wonderful, too. I enjoyed my time with him very much."

Greta reached over the counter and covered Dolores's hand, pressing it gently. "That makes me so happy. He's a great man, and he has excellent taste in books. And company."

Dolores laughed a musical laugh. It was widely known Franklin didn't keep many friends in town besides Greta. And now, it seemed, Dolores.

"Do you have plans to see him again?"

Dolores nodded. "I'm going over there tomorrow evening. He wants to talk more about books and life, and I must say I'm looking forward to another visit."

Just then, a group of children and their parents trotted toward the desk. Some stopped and wanted to check out books, effectively ruining Greta's chance to get more details from Dolores.

Dolores stepped away from the counter and walked farther into the library as Greta greeted the crowd. Josie joined her. Together, they scanned books, distributed bookmarks and coloring sheets, and Greta pointed a wiggly toddler and his dad to the nearest bathroom.

After she said goodbye to the last patron, Josie tipped her chin to where Dolores was browsing a nearby shelf. "Did I overhear that we have a little geriatric romance brewing?"

"I hope so. Franklin asked me for her phone number. It's a big step for him."

"Nice. But what does that say about you and me? We're being shown up on the dating scene by a pair of sexagenarians." Josie's voice was jesting, but Greta couldn't mistake an undercurrent of moroseness.

She swallowed away the surge of panic that tickled the back of her throat anytime her relationship status was brought up and squished up her nose. "First of all, can we not call them 'sexagenarians'? It sounds weirdly erotic. Second of all, did things with what's-his-name go south?"

Josie had been casually dating a businessman who was staying at one of Ed Kennedy's rentals at the end of the summer. She hadn't mentioned him lately, and Greta had been waiting for an opening to bring him up.

"Yeah, *that* is over. Needless to say, he left Larkspur when his month-long business hiatus was over, and since then, I haven't gotten more than a few brief text messages from him."

Greta winced. While she'd all but given up on her own happily ever after, at least romantically speaking, she wanted it for her friends. Iris was well on her way, but Josie would take some work. "I'm sorry, Jos."

"No matter. At least I can focus on operation sexagenarian matchmaker."

Greta grinned, but, before they could discuss Franklin and Dolores any further, Iris emerged from the stacks and emitted a squeal of joy.

"Dean!" Iris all but skipped across the library to greet her boyfriend.

Josie rolled her eyes in Iris's direction before muttering under her breath, "Besides, I think one lovesick librarian is enough, don't you?"

Greta chuckled. "Oh, come on. They're cute."

Sidney Lawrence, Dean's assistant, sidestepped the embracing couple and shot a knowing smirk to Greta and Josie. "Young love, am I right?"

Greta returned Sidney's grin, even as Josie frowned.

"Josie. Greta, good to see you." Dean had his arm slung over Iris's shoulder as they approached the desk.

Greta cleared her throat and caught Josie's attention, glaring at her to stop being so obvious, before she faced Dean. "You, too. To what do we owe the pleasure?"

"I stopped by to see Iris and let you all know to expect myself and Sidney in the library a bit more in the coming month."

"Oh?"

"Our landlord is remodeling the whole office building. It's easier for us to be out of there entirely while his contractor does the work." Sidney hooked her finger through the strap of the computer bag at her side. "Good thing we can work from pretty much anywhere."

"That's right. When we aren't at client meetings, I figure we'll split time between here and Mugs & Hugs. You've got the reliable internet access we need. And Iris." Dean shot Iris a smile. "But the café has great coffee." He winked, and Iris swatted him.

"Of course." Greta laughed and took in the blissful glow on Iris's round face. "I'm happy we can be of service. That's what the library is for. Our wireless password is by all the computers, and if you need it, you can pay for printing right through your library card account. Holler if we can assist with anything."

"Thanks, Greta." Sidney left the counter and settled herself at one of the tables near the printer station at the center of the library. She retrieved her laptop, pulled her light brown hair into a top knot, and got to work while Dean lingered near Iris.

Josie disappeared into the librarians' office, and Greta synced the list of hold titles to the tablet affixed to the metal, three-tiered cart she used to collect books. She made her way to the children's corner, her full plaid skirt swishing around her legs as she efficiently gathered the books on the list. In the middle-grade area of the library, Greta paused and read the back cover of one of the Nancy Drew mysteries. She hugged the book to her chest, savoring the vanilla scent of its pages. The trademark yellow boards were faded, and the spine loose with age.

Adding it to her stack, Greta spent another five minutes methodically going through the adult fiction aisles, stopping to pull titles by Sarah Adams, Arthur Conan Doyle, Ursula Le Guin, Jenn McKinlay, and Marilynne Robinson and marveling at the eclectic pile of books she amassed.

When she wound her way back to the front desk, she accidentally bumped her cart into the corner of the counter and nearly sent all the books toppling. She sighed in relief when she managed to catch the stack, shooting a rueful glance at Dean and Iris, who looked on from where they still stood chatting

14

at the desk. As Greta began scanning the books, she couldn't help listening with one ear to their conversation.

"So, you have to work tonight?" Greta could picture Iris's pout from the tone of the question.

"Yeah, I have a couple client meetings lined up. What are you going to do?"

"Maybe I'll see if Greta and Josie want to get together. It's been a while."

Greta smiled to herself. She liked the sound of that. It would be nice to hang out, just the three of them, especially for Josie's sake.

Dean lowered his voice. "I can't help it if I want to hog my girl. Let me take you out tomorrow, okay?"

"Sounds great. I'm free."

Josie appeared at the office door. "Hey, Iris, can you help me with something back here?"

"Sure thing. Be right there."

Greta watched out of the corner of her eye as Iris turned back to Dean. "Duty calls. Call me later?"

"Definitely. Bye, babe." Dean winked before strolling over to Sidney.

Iris sighed like an infatuated teenager and stared after him before turning and hurrying after Josie's retreating figure.

Greta paused in her work to observe Dean for a minute. He was a handsome man. A couple years older than Iris. Probably in his mid-thirties and clearly successful. He wore cognac loafers with a pressed, black business suit, a fitting and professional outfit for Larkspur's one and only independent financial advisor.

As Greta was staring, she was startled to see Ed Kennedy pass into her line of vision.

Chapter Four

The resort owner strolled into the library, looking around until his gaze met hers. Ed approached the counter, and Greta's pulse jumped. He was an attractive man, too, but in a different way. While Dean was all straight-laced and business professional, Ed was ruggedly handsome, like a weathered outdoorsman. He also had about four inches on Dean's six-foot frame.

Ed was a master entrepreneur. No one could deny it. Greta had only seen it in action for one summer, but the resort business plan was brilliant. Families from all over Wisconsin visited throughout the summer and fall, and she'd been told he served a steady stream of ice fishermen, snowmobilers, and skiers in the off season. They rented out the clustered group of ten cabins to meet all their winter recreational needs.

While the traffic was great for Larkspur's economy, Greta certainly didn't like the thought of Ed trying to wedge other property owners out of their land.

"Ed, can I help you with something?" Greta stood up so he wasn't looking down at her, or at least not all the way down. She stacked the books she'd scanned into a pile so she was ready to take them back to the bins for the courier.

"Nothing major. I came to see if you guys had any extra fall programming brochures like the one I saw on the bulletin board over at Mugs & Hugs. I want to put them in all of the cabins and leave a stack in my office so the families coming to stay are aware of what Larkspur has to offer, especially with the fall festival coming up."

"Oh." Greta tugged her lips to the side. "What a great idea." She wasn't sure what she was expecting. A ploy for Ed to take over the library like he was trying to take over Franklin's house, perhaps? Greta mentally scolded herself. She was being unreasonable. "I'll print some out for you."

"Thanks. I'm going to look around for a minute. Can you set them up here for me, and I'll grab them when I check out?"

"Of course."

She pulled up the folder she had saved to the desktop with their promotional materials enclosed. Opening the fall programming flyer, she clicked print and hovered her cursor over the quantity, finally deciding on twenty copies.

She hoped that would be enough. At least it would tide Ed over for the first few rounds of visitors. He could always come back for more. When the printer stopped churning, Greta retrieved the flyers.

She was tapping them on the counter to even the edges when Josie wandered out of the office. "Iris and I are brainstorming holiday promotion ideas. We could use your input." She pointed to the papers in Greta's hands. "Are those the flyers for fall?"

"Yup. Ed wants them for the resort."

"Cool." Josie motioned toward the office. "Lend us your brainpower in there when you have a minute, would you? I'm running to the ladies' room."

"I'll be right there. I'm just going to make sure Ed gets these."

Josie nodded and slipped out, and Greta waited for Ed to return to the counter. When he did, Greta scanned his books before pointing out a couple of events of interest to him on the flyers.

"This is great. Thanks so much." He gave her a friendly wave and left, stepping to the side to allow Josie to pass on her way back into the library.

"Too bad he's trying to buy Franklin's land," Greta whispered when Josie joined her behind the counter. "That major, glaring dark spot aside, Ed is a very nice man."

Josie scoffed but planted on a smile when Dolores came by with a stack of books. Josie checked out the titles one by one, and Dolores scooped up her books and said her goodbyes.

She paused when she saw Dean and Sidney. "Dean, I'll see you this evening. I'm looking forward to going over my portfolio."

Dean glanced up from his computer. "Sounds good, Mrs. Jenkins. We're just finalizing some paperwork for the meeting. I'll be by around six thirty."

If that wasn't small-town living, what was? Nothing like seeing your evening appointment at the local library earlier in the day. The thought brought a smile to Greta's face, and a renewed sense of gratitude washed over her as she watched Dolores leave. She was so glad she'd ended up in Larkspur.

Dolores stopped in the hallway just outside the library door to chat with Chuck Sorenson, the chief of police. He was standing with a younger man dressed in well-fitting business attire. The man's back was to Greta, but his hair was jet black, a stark contrast to Chief Sorenson's salt and pepper coif. He turned, and Greta caught a glimpse of his profile—a sharp jawline and angular nose—which confirmed she had never seen him before. The three chatted for a minute longer before Dolores left, and the two men headed toward the back entrance of the police department offices. Both the police station and the town hall were housed in the same building as the library.

"Who's the new guy?" Josie, too, was observing the hallway through the wall of floor-to-ceiling windows lining the entire south side of the library.

"No idea. I thought maybe you knew him from around town."

"Nope, but I bet we'll find out sooner rather than later. That's the Larkspur way. Nothing is secret for long. I'll cover the desk if you want to go back and see if you can help Iris figure out a holiday game plan. Some of her ideas are a little out there. X-nay on the mistletoe-ay, mm-kay?" Josie made an exasperated face, and Greta snort-laughed.

"Say no more. I'll handle this. And hey. You, me, and Iris. Girls' night tonight at Mugs & Hugs. You in?"

"Of course, if Iris can spare the time."

"She can. I'll talk to her about it." Greta hurried back into the cramped office, anxious to keep the peace between her two friends.

After work the next day, Greta wished Josie and Iris a good night and took off across the parking lot. She had driven to work, but after her lunch break, she had decided to walk back to the library. It was a gorgeous afternoon with temperatures hovering around sixty degrees and the sun glowing overhead. Like a true Wisconsinite, Greta wanted to enjoy it while it lasted.

Now, she hustled down Larkspur Lane toward the water, her bellbottom corduroy pants rustling between her legs and her mule-shoes clicking on the pavement. She was anxious to get to Franklin's house and interrogate him about Dolores. It had been too late to bother him last night after her dinner with the girls.

She rounded the corner onto Lakeside Drive, and Greta welcomed the cooler breeze coming off the water. Power walking had caused her to work up a sweat. Her white button-up blouse stuck to her when she readjusted her bag, and she was thankful to see Franklin's house appear ahead. She slowed her pace and controlled her breathing. She needed to be efficient in her questioning of Franklin. She hoped he was in a talkative mood.

Greta walked up the ramp to his front door and was startled to see it open a crack. "Franklin?" She had never known him to leave his door ajar. Biff was well trained, but Franklin wouldn't risk his cat escaping. And, he wasn't one who welcomed neighbors with open arms. Maybe his automatic opener had malfunctioned, and the door latch was broken.

Greta pushed the door open a sliver wider and peered inside. "Franklin! Are you here?" She stepped through the entryway, pausing to listen for the familiar sound of the wheels of his chair on the floor. Nothing.

Greta shut the door behind her and took a tentative step inside. Biff shot toward her, and Greta exhaled.

"Hi, buddy." She bent down, still peering around for Biff's owner as he nuzzled her hand and trilled his hello.

Thinking Franklin might be out on the deck enjoying the beautiful day, Greta took a step in that direction, but she paused. He and Dolores were getting together tonight. What if she was already here? Greta didn't want to embarrass the fledgling couple. Then again, she'd made this intentional trip, and if Dolores wasn't here, she'd be wasting a perfectly good intelligence-gathering opportunity.

After a moment of deliberation, Greta decided to take a quick peek at the deck and, if Dolores and Franklin were together, she'd make herself scarce, pronto.

Leaving Biff to his cat tree, Greta zipped through the kitchen and dining room, around the rare books room, and into the living room. One glance out the windows didn't reveal Franklin or Dolores, but she did see an overturned pot near the stairs and adjoining ramp leading from the deck to the waterfront. Greta pulled the glass sliding door open, followed by the screen door, and walked outside to right the plant, inhaling the earthy scent of the early fall lake water as she went. Before Greta reached the upset pot, she glanced toward the shoreline and let out an involuntary scream.

Franklin lay in a heap at the bottom of the steps, partially covered by his wheelchair.

Chapter Five

Greta dropped her bag and threw herself down the steps toward him. "Franklin! Can you hear me?" When she reached her friend, Greta's stomach plummeted before shooting up into her throat and threatening to spill out her mouth. He was face down, and there was blood pooled around him. The library's copy of *Crime and Punishment* was flung off to the side. For a moment, she sat there, frozen, until her instincts kicked in. She tried to check for a pulse, but her own racing heart made her fingers tingly, and she couldn't get an accurate reading.

"Hold on, Franklin. I'm calling for help." She scrambled back up the steps, tripping on the top one and catching herself hard with her hands. Ignoring the shooting pain rocketing up her arms, Greta pushed herself back up and reached for her bag. She wrenched it open and dug around for her cell phone. Her fingers shook as she pressed 9-1-1. While she waited for the operator to pick up, she hurried down to Franklin. She had no idea what to do for him. Should she touch him? Move him? Move the wheelchair? Try to stop the bleeding? Her formal education in Library Science was about the furthest thing from nursing or the medical field, which was how Greta liked it. She much preferred the happiness and fictional world of books to the blood and gore of real-life medical emergencies. But she'd do whatever she needed to do to help Franklin.

The dispatcher picked up as Greta reached Franklin's side. "911 of Langlade County. Can I have the address of your emergency?"

Greta managed to get out Franklin's address and, before the dispatcher could ask her any more questions, she told him everything, unable to mask the terror in her voice.

"My neighbor fell down the stairs of his deck. He's lying here, and I can't find a pulse. He's bleeding. Oh God. Please send some help here." A sob escaped, and Greta clamped her free hand over her mouth. She couldn't tear her gaze from Franklin. If only she'd gotten to him sooner, maybe she could have helped. Maybe she could have prevented the accident. Had he gone to pick up the plant, and his wheels slipped?

Greta closed her eyes, queasy at the thought of Franklin careening down the full flight of stairs, helpless to brace his fall. In the distance, sirens wailed as the operator's soothing voice continued to talk to her through the phone.

"Help for your neighbor is on the way, ma'am. I want you to stay on the line with me until they arrive, alright?"

"Okay," Greta croaked.

"Ma'am, is the door open for officers and the EMTs to get in?"

"It's unlocked." Greta tugged her hand through her hair, anxiously gripping a clump of curls as she looked back at Franklin's immobile figure. "Tell them to come straight through the house to the back deck. And hurry, please."

Less than a minute later, running feet pounded above her.

"Down here!" Greta yelled.

The man she'd seen outside the library appeared at the top of the steps. He took them two at a time as he raced to her side and assessed Franklin, placing a hand in front of his mouth and a finger to his carotid artery.

The dispatcher disconnected the call just as the man from outside the library stood and faced her. His eyes were as black as his hair, and his clenched jaw accentuated the rigid angles of his face. If Greta was a betting woman, she'd say he sized her up in one look.

"Miss...?" The man raised his eyebrows in question.

"Plank. Greta Plank. Is he going to be okay?" More sirens blared. She hoped they were from an ambulance. She may not have been a medical professional, but she was certain Franklin had lost a lot of blood.

"Miss Plank, my name is Detective Mark McHenry."

Greta couldn't have cared less if his name was Abraham Lincoln. She wanted him to stop talking to her and help Franklin.

She tried to redirect his attention. "And Franklin?"

Detective McHenry glanced toward Franklin and shook his head once. Greta dropped her cell phone and covered her mouth with her hands.

"I'm sorry, Miss Plank. I'm afraid he's dead."

Greta's knees buckled, and she staggered backward.

Detective McHenry reached out to steady her. "Let's get you upstairs."

He slipped an arm around her waist and supported her as she stumbled back up the steps. He half-carried her into Franklin's living room, where she sunk onto his couch. Biff darted into the room and jumped up next to her. At the sight of Franklin's cat, Greta burst into tears, clutching hold of the feline for dear life. He whined as he pressed his head into her neck, obviously thrown off by the unusual activity and heightened emotion in the cabin.

"I'm going to go grab your bag and cell phone for you." Detective McHenry crouched right in front of her so he was at eye level. "Are you going to be okay here for a minute?"

Greta nodded numbly, and the detective left her to return to the deck.

When the front door banged open, Greta jumped, her eyes flashing toward the kitchen to find the EMTs arriving. At the sound of the stretcher's wheels screeching across the floor, Biff let out a warbled "yeow," hopping off her lap and, no doubt, expecting to see his owner. A fresh torrent of tears assaulted Greta.

Detective McHenry reappeared with her things. "Is there someone you can call, Miss Plank?"

Greta grabbed for her phone even as her limbs felt disconnected from her body. There was no way she wanted to break this news to anyone over the phone. Greta shuddered. "I'll be okay. I live less than a mile down the road."

"You shouldn't drive, even if it's only a half mile."

"I walked here, actually."

"Then I'll drive you home." The detective glanced out the large window. A group of police officers had congregated on the deck with the EMTs. "Give me one minute to talk to them." He walked back outside without waiting for a response.

Greta had started to shake the second she sat down, and she was having a hard time controlling the convulsions. Her gaze roamed around the living room, where she'd sat so often with Franklin the past few months. She couldn't believe she'd never again get to stop by his house on the way home from work to tell him about her day and drop off his next favorite book. Her mind kept short-circuiting.

Greta rubbed her face with her hands. This was all too much, and suddenly she was very anxious to get away from Franklin's house. She stood, her joints cracking in her haste, and wobbled on her feet. She would have fallen, but strong hands landed on her shoulders, holding her in place.

"Easy there." Detective McHenry moved to her side, cupping her elbow with one hand and reaching down to collect her bag with the other. "Let's get you home."

He guided her to the door until Greta stopped in her tracks. "What about Biff?"

"Pardon me?"

"Biff." Greta reached down and scooped up the ball of flecked gold fur as he tried to streak by. "Franklin's cat. I can't leave him here all alone. I'll take him with me and care for him until accommodations are made."

Detective McHenry didn't argue. He retrieved Biff's carrier from the kitchen, and Greta nestled the confused tabby inside, each of his anxious purrs like a papercut to her heart. She gathered his bowls, some food, and his favorite toys.

With Biff stowed, the detective led Greta out the front of the cabin, down the ramp, and to his vehicle. He opened the passenger side door to the unmarked police car parked at a crooked angle in Franklin's driveway, and Greta sat down. She leaned against the black leather, willing the worn material to warm her.

Detective McHenry deposited Biff and his supplies in the back seat before easing behind the wheel. His radio crackled, but as soon as the message was relayed—something about backup from Karrington coming to Larkspur, ETA seven minutes—he flicked the volume on the speaker down.

"Which direction to your house?"

Greta pointed down the road, and in less than two minutes, Detective McHenry pulled into her driveway.

"Thank you." Greta croaked the words out. It was as if she'd put her body through a marathon. The shaking had subsided, but exhaustion had set in, and she wasn't sure how she'd make it up her steps.

"I'll help you inside." Detective McHenry opened his door, retrieved the cat and her things, and strode to her side of the car to offer her a hand.

Now was not the time to be proud, so Greta took it and let him guide her toward her cabin. Her fingers wouldn't work on her keys, so Detective McHenry unlocked the door and pushed it open for her. Greta walked to the living room and collapsed onto her couch, staring straight ahead at the gallery wall of family photos. Kelly's smiling face leapt out at her, and Greta slammed her eyes shut.

"Can I get you anything? A glass of water? I'd like to ask you a few questions."

Greta fluttered her eyelids open and looked up, focusing on the man in front of her.

Detective McHenry was tall, and he filled her home in a way she wasn't used to. His brooding expression darkened the space somehow. She didn't like that he was here. Or the reason for his presence. She wanted to be alone, but Greta figured since she was first on the scene, he needed her statement. That's how it worked in books, anyway. She may as well get it over with.

"Water would be great. Glasses are to the right of the sink."

Detective McHenry disappeared into her kitchen.

Greta reached down and unlatched the door on Biff's carrier. He hopped out and tore around her living room, skittish in his new surroundings. The detective banged cabinet doors, and Biff yeowed nervously and jumped up on the couch, settling next to her. Greta methodically stroked his warm fur with one hand, letting her gaze drift back out over her deck and to the lake beyond.

Detective McHenry returned and handed her a glass of water. He took a seat across from her, and she looked into his onyx eyes.

"I understand this isn't easy, Miss Plank, but I need you to walk me through what happened."

Greta's throat was dry, and the water didn't seem to help. When she started talking, it felt like sandpaper coated her mouth. She explained to the detective how she'd gone to see Franklin after work.

"I found him at the base of the stairs next to the ramp." Her voice cracked, and Greta looked away from the detective, the hot threat of tears pressing painfully against the backs of her eyes.

Detective McHenry shoved a box of tissues in Greta's direction as she swallowed hard and worked to regain control of her emotions.

"And you're sure the front door was open when you arrived?"

"Yeah, which is strange because Franklin isn't super neighborly, but I figured he left it open by accident."

"And the plant on the deck. Was it on the ground when you got out there, or did you knock it over on your way to Mr. Halloway?"

"No, it was on the ground. That's why I was over by the stairs and ramp in the first place. When I didn't see Franklin outside, I was about to leave, but I thought I'd fix the pot. And then..." Greta's voice trailed off, and she took a swig of water to stop herself from crying.

"Can you shed any light on the book?"

"What book?"

"*Crime and Punishment.* It was near Mr. Halloway's body."

"Right. I saw it there." Odd, really. The more Greta thought about it, the more she couldn't figure out how Franklin could have been both reading and maneuvering his chair to right the disturbed plant. Unless he'd tucked the book into the side of his wheelchair before trying to tend to the gardening. Maybe he was on his way down to the lake to read near the water. Greta would never know. She gulped. "What did you want to know about the book?"

"Did you bring it with you today?"

"Oh, no. Franklin checked it out earlier this week. I dropped it off for him on Monday. I'm a librarian."

Detective McHenry stood and pocketed the notebook he'd been scribbling in. "Thank you, Miss Plank. I'll need you to stop by the police station to sign a formal statement, but it can wait until Monday. I'm going to go."

Greta moved to walk the detective to the door, but he held up his hand.

"Please, sit. Don't worry about me."

Greta slouched back, pulling Biff onto her lap and hugging him to her chest until he wriggled out of her grasp and dashed off.

"Miss Plank?" The detective faced her once more from the arched doorway in her dining room.

She dragged her gaze away from the floor and up to his face, blinking quickly to bring him into focus.

"I'm sorry for your loss." Detective McHenry studied her, his gaze piercing, before he took his leave.

Greta listened as the door clicked shut behind him, the simple sound reminding her of the end of a tape recorder. The end of a story. The end of a life.

Greta let her head fall back onto the couch, squeezing her eyes closed and praying when she opened them again, she'd find this was all just a bad dream.

Chapter Six

On Monday morning, Greta opened the door to Mugs & Hugs Café, anxious to get out of the rain, which fell in a steady drizzle. She'd spent the weekend trying to process the loss of her friend and making her cabin amenable to Franklin's cat. Now she was ready to fill her mind with something happy and her mouth with caffeine.

Mugs & Hugs was every bit as delightful as its name. The siding on the quaint building was a crystalline blue—like the color of the sky on a cloudless summer day. Inside, the walls were a combination of crisp white beadboard and cheerful yellow paint, which gave the whole place an airy, beachy vibe. Hanging plants cascaded in a neat row from above the giant picture windows that looked out onto the small parking lot and outdoor dining area. The honey-colored wood floor squeaked under Greta's feet as she walked inside and glanced around at the occupied booths and tables.

Allison, the owner of Mugs & Hugs, hurried from behind the counter and wrapped Greta in a hug. "Oh, G. I am so sorry. How are you doing?" She pulled back but kept hold of Greta's upper arms, staring at her and searching her face.

"I'm okay. Coffee would help."

"On it. Your drink is on the house today."

"You don't have to—"

Allison shushed her with a severe roll of her deep-brown eyes. "Of course, I don't *have* to, but I want to."

Allison spun around and began to prepare Greta's coffee before Greta could utter another word of protest, so she settled into a chair near the counter and off to the side of the register to wait on her drink. When Iris and Dean joined her a moment later, she offered them a half smile. "Morning."

"How're you holding up?" Iris's voice was full of concern.

"I'll be okay. The shock has started to wear off. Reality has set in. But I'll be okay," Greta repeated herself for her own sake, as much as for her friends'. She *would* be okay. The more she told herself so, the more it would ring true. "There wasn't anything any of us could have done."

Allison walked over with her drink before Iris or Dean could respond. "Here you go, girl. I added an extra pump of hazelnut, just for you."

"You're the best, Allison. Thank you." Greta took a deep breath of the buttery-scented coffee and a tentative sip of the steaming liquid, grateful for the care and concern of the town, even if it was a bit smothering. She'd moved from Green Bay, a much bigger city than Larkspur. She was still getting used to everyone knowing everything about everyone else, but Greta had to admit that there was some comfort in the close-knit community, too.

The rainstorm had turned from gentle shower to heavy downpour in the time it had taken Greta to grab her coffee, so she, Iris, and Dean wound up sprinting across the street to the library. When they made it to the entryway, they were soaked.

"What a way to start the week." Iris groaned. "I feel like a drowned rat."

"A cute drowned rat, though." Dean dropped a quick kiss on Iris's forehead, and she crinkled up her nose.

Greta swished her favorite skirt—one with green and blue buffalo checks, chosen to boost her spirits—back and forth to rid it of water droplets. She'd donned a warm, cream-colored sweater to match this morning, and it shielded her from the dampness of the rain.

The door opened behind them, and Josie entered. With one look at their saturated appearance, she deadpanned, "Haven't you guys heard of an umbrella?"

"Where's the fun in that?" Greta asked, a wry grin playing on her lips.

Iris only groaned again and headed for the bathroom, obviously anxious to freshen up.

"Glad to see you smiling, G." Josie shook out her umbrella, unlocked the library door, and the two walked inside with Dean on their heels.

Greta flipped the light switches, and the fluorescent lights overhead flickered on. "I'm still sad, but sadness won't bring Franklin back."

"It's still a hard loss, though," Dean said. "Don't hesitate to reach out if there's anything I can do for you, okay, Greta?"

Greta thanked him, and Dean ambled over to the table he'd staked out as his makeshift office and took a seat at one of the library's computers.

Josie turned to Greta. "Do you want me to handle children's story time this morning, or are you okay to do it?"

"I don't mind. It'll keep me busy, which is good." Greta dropped her bag and walked along the front counter, powering up each of the three computers. "I'm planning to read *Leaf Man* by Lois Elhert." She'd collected a bunch of leaves and was flattening them out underneath books.

"What a good choice." Iris joined Josie and Greta as the log-in screens appeared on the computers.

Greta left Josie and Iris behind the desk to open up for the day and wandered over to the children's area. With its colorful, kid-curated art adorning the walls, wooden toy train table, and the bin of cheerful stuffed animal puppets in the nearest corner, this was one of Greta's favorite spots. Unlike large branches with designated youth services and children's librarians, Greta, Josie, and Iris split the duties, and Greta always enjoyed spending time with their youngest patrons.

She made sure she had her low stool to sit on before arranging plenty of pillows in a half circle for the kids. She placed her copy of *Leaf Man* nearby. Once situated, she returned to the front desk.

Josie was propping open the door, and people started trickling in.

Thunder cracked outside, and Greta hurried into the office to find the old umbrella stand they used on rainy days. She rolled it out into the vestibule so folks would have a spot to store their rain gear. She saw several familiar faces come in from the inclement weather. Ed was holding the door for a group of people. After they entered, he followed them inside.

"Oh good, Greta. Hello. Say, I'm so sorry about Franklin." Ed paused, shaking his head. "It's hard to believe."

Greta thought so too, but a pit in her stomach formed at the idea of Ed swooping in to try to buy Franklin's property.

"Anyway." Ed straightened up and motioned to a group of people standing inside the doors, looking a little out of place. "I brought some guests over from the resort. They've been here since Friday afternoon, but I figured with the poor weather this morning, they might enjoy some indoor activities."

Greta pushed her worry about Ed aside and focused on the group made up of parents and young children. "We have story time starting in less than thirty minutes. Why don't you guys check out the library and join me in the children's area when you're ready."

One of the women slumped in relief as she walked by. "This is a lifesaver. The kids were going stir-crazy this morning cooped up in the cabins. I homeschool, and libraries are my secret weapon. So glad to find one we can tap into here, too."

Greta smiled and waited as Ed took his leave from the rest of the group.

After a brief interlude spent helping folks find materials and answering book-related questions, Greta took her seat on the stool in the children's area and reached underneath it, where she pulled out a small box. Inside was a bell. She rang it, and at the gentle tinkle, the children stilled.

"Okay, boys and girls. Please join me for story time."

The kids dropped the books and trains they were holding and plopped down on the pillows at her feet, staring up at her with wide, expectant eyes. Greta was always amazed what a little bell could do.

After everyone was seated, she spoke again. "Now, I have a very special story to read to you today, and if you're good listeners, I might even have a treasure for you to take with you when we're all done." Greta smiled as two little girls pressed their lips together and grinned at each other.

"What is it?" one boy shouted from the second row.

"We're about to find out!" Greta beamed at him. She loved kids and their unabashed excitement. "It's important you're all good listeners so you can see for yourself at the end of the story what the treasure might be."

The kids nodded solemnly, and Greta pulled out *Leaf Man* from behind her chair and began to read.

By the time she reached the final chorus, the kids were joining in with her.

"The End." Greta held the book to her heart. "Now, boys and girls." She took time to hold each of their gazes. "When you go outside, I want you to search for the Leaf Man. He might be blowing around Larkspur Lake or over by Kennedy's Cozy Cottages as we speak!"

The kids murmured to each other as Greta set the book under her stool. She bent in the opposite direction and reached for the bag of leaves. When she sat up straight, she was startled to see Detective McHenry leaning against one of the stacks near the back of the children's area, observing her.

Chapter Seven

The level of the kids' voices had risen, so she reached down and gently rang her bell again.

"It's time for the treasure."

One by one, the kids came forward, and Greta handed them a flattened leaf. They took it with reverence as their parents looked on in wonder.

"I hope you've enjoyed our story today. Come back and see us at the library, and be sure to hunt for Leaf Man when you go outside." Greta stood, and several of the adults softly clapped. Greta ducked her head to deflect their praise. She reached down to grab her book, and the stool tipped over. She righted it and stood, only to see Detective McHenry approaching.

"Miss Plank, may I have a word?"

Greta glanced around. Curiosity was evident in the parents' eyes. No doubt they were taking in the badge the detective wore on his hip and probably assuming the woman who appeared to be a sweet and innocent librarian had somehow found herself on the wrong side of the law.

"Of course." Greta pasted a smile on her face even as her neck prickled with the heat of embarrassment. The memory of being made a spectacle in Green Bay was all too fresh. "Let me check in with Josie and Iris."

She said a quick goodbye to the parents and offered the kids a wave before walking toward the circulation desk. "You guys alright here?"

Josie looked up from the computer as Iris walked out of the office. "All good. What's up?"

"I need to borrow Miss Plank. Have her sign her statement." Detective McHenry's curt voice made Greta flinch.

"Okay." Josie stretched out the syllables and peered at Greta. "You alright?"

"Yep." Greta widened her eyes and shrugged. She might as well get this over with. "Thanks for covering for me."

Greta followed Detective McHenry out the library door and down the hallway to the police station. Though the fluorescent lights were the same in this hallway as they were in the library, everything seemed dimmer the closer they got to the police station. Her shoes clicked on the linoleum floors in stark contrast to the quiet tread of Detective McHenry's soft-soled loafers.

The detective pushed open the door, held it with one arm, and with the other, motioned for her to enter. A small receptionist's desk was positioned straight ahead, though it faced the main entrance to the station, not the back door they'd passed through. Lori Lamponee, the woman who sat behind the desk, lived across the lake from Greta. She was a year-round cabin dweller, like Greta, and a member of the same quilting group as Greta's mom, Louisa. In fact, Lori had alerted Louisa to the library director opening earlier in the year, and Greta assumed she'd also put in a good word for her during the interview process. She liked the woman on principle.

"Hi, Greta." Lori shoved her readers on top of her pale gray hair and darted a glance to where Detective McHenry had headed down a side hallway. Lori looked back at her with question marks in her eyes, and Greta clenched her teeth, offering up an attempted smile that turned into more of a wobbly frown.

Lori's return smile was filled with encouragement, and Greta wondered if she could stop and beg for a hug from the matronly woman. But Lori shooed her along.

Greta turned and jogged to catch up with the detective, whose long strides were eating up the hallway. When Detective McHenry stopped on a dime and faced her, she collided with his torso. "Ope. Sorry." She took a giant step back.

The detective didn't acknowledge her clumsiness, instead motioning to what appeared to be a small conference room. "In here."

Greta walked forward and took in the space as Detective McHenry closed the door behind them. The cinderblock white walls were bare, aside from an old black clock hanging to the left of the door and a camera suspended from the corner of the ceiling. A red oak table with two chairs on either side took up most of the room. Detective McHenry walked around the table and took a seat, shuffling a few papers into a pile. He glanced up to where she stood.

"Please, sit." He motioned to one of the chairs opposite him. "I took the liberty of typing up your statement based on what you told me on Friday. Read it through. If it's acceptable to you, you can sign it."

Greta did as she was told. Her stomach rolled as she read through the account she'd given the detective. It was pretty straightforward, so she quickly signed the document and shoved it across the table. The sooner she could put this whole thing behind her, the better.

"Miss Plank, can you tell me more about your relationship with Franklin Halloway?"

Greta sat back in her seat, unease rising in her chest like fizz from an overflowing can of soda. "Why?"

The detective narrowed his eyes. "Because I'm trying to get a full picture of his life, and you seem to know him better than most in this town."

"Sorry." She held up her hands and spread her fingers in an attempt to show she meant no harm. "I'm just trying to understand how my relationship with him has anything to do with the accident. But if you need to know, I met Franklin four months ago when I moved to Larkspur. It took me a while to gain his friendship, though." Greta paused, smiling sadly.

"Did you two not get along at first?"

Greta chuckled. "Franklin didn't get along with anyone at first. He kept to himself, so I had to work to break through. But I think after he realized I wasn't going to take no for an answer, he gave up, and we've been friends ever since. Or, were friends, I guess." Greta's smile faltered.

Detective McHenry folded his arms, letting his hands rest in the crook of the opposite elbows and giving off an unruffled air. "If Franklin didn't get along with anyone, he must have had enemies, yes?"

"I don't...hey, wait a minute." Greta's mouth opened with a gasp. She

35

swore the temperature in the room dropped thirty degrees. "What are you not telling me?"

Chapter Eight

"Franklin Halloway's death was not an accident, Miss Plank."

"What?" A tingle ran up Greta's spine even as she worked to keep her voice smooth. "Are you saying you believe someone killed Franklin? If so, I'm afraid you've made a mistake."

The detective didn't blink. "The evidence is there. Now I need to figure out what happened. Can you think of anyone who would have wanted him dead?"

Greta's composure slipped. "For heaven's sake! This is Larkspur, Wisconsin. No one here would want anyone else dead. Franklin didn't have many friends, but he also didn't have enemies."

Franklin's phone call with Ed flashed through her memory, and Greta inhaled sharply.

"What is it?" Detective McHenry's gaze was on her like a laser.

She looked around the room to avoid his stare. Her words came out in an uncharacteristic rush. "Nothing. I'm sure it's nothing."

"Why don't you tell me what it is and let me be sure it's nothing."

She sighed, finally meeting his eye. "Fine. It's just when I arrived to visit Franklin earlier last week, he was on the phone. I could tell it was a heated conversation, and after he hung up, he confided he had been talking to Ed."

"Ed Kennedy of Kennedy's Cozy Cottages?" Detective McHenry produced a notebook from his pocket and jotted something down.

"Yes. Apparently, Ed had been trying to convince Franklin to sell his property. Something about wanting to develop it. I don't know. That's all Franklin told me. Oh, and he said he wouldn't sell."

"Okay. You visited Franklin earlier last week, correct? Is there anything else you can tell me from your time together? Anything seem different than usual?"

Greta thought back. It had only been a week since she dropped off Franklin's books. "Books."

"Pardon me?"

"He was going to be meeting with another rare book collector about negotiating a deal to buy one of his books." Greta crossed her leg over her knee. "I'm sure you've gathered Franklin had a pretty massive collection."

"The locked room in the center of his house tipped me off."

"Franklin was very particular about his collection."

"Is it worth money?"

Greta pressed her lips together. "Haven't you seen it?"

Detective McHenry blinked. "Answer the question, Miss Plank."

Greta drew back. "Sorry, I figured you would have gone through his things. But yes. Franklin's books are worth a lot of money. He had a complete set of James Bond first editions. Many of them are signed, and most of them are in their original dust jackets. At one point, he told me their worth was near half a million dollars. And that's not even the half of his collection."

Detective McHenry's eyes widened for a split second before he schooled his features. "You seem to have kept quite the record of Franklin's books yourself."

"I mean, I guess." It took a few extra seconds for Greta to register the insinuation. "Wait. Not in *that* way."

"Who else knows about these books besides you?"

Detective McHenry's rapid-fire questions were making Greta feel all sorts of off balance. She took a deep breath and thought for a minute. "Josie and Iris, the two librarians on staff with me. And I'm sure Dolores Jenkins does. Probably others, too. Franklin was in the rare books business. It started out as a hobby for him, back when he used to work in finance. But, after the accident, he lived off of the settlement. The insurance payout for the drunk driver who hit him and left him paralyzed was pretty massive. So, he managed his investments and bought and sold rare books. That's what he told me."

Detective McHenry didn't meet her gaze, and Greta wasn't sure what to think. She was trying to help him, and he wasn't giving her the time of day. He just sat, flipping through the pages of his notes.

Finally, after several moments of silence, Detective McHenry returned his attention to her. "Anything else you can tell me about Franklin's week? Did he mention other engagements or plans?"

"I asked him what he was up to for the week. Let me see." She cupped her elbow with one hand and tapped her chin with her fingers, trying to recall her last conversation with Franklin. "He told me he had his regular physical therapy appointment scheduled. And he mentioned the book collector." Greta paused. "I don't remember anything else. Oh, but I talked to Dolores, and she saw Franklin last week, too."

Detective McHenry made a quick note before meeting Greta's gaze. "Mrs. Jenkins showed up at Franklin's house on Friday after I returned from dropping you off."

Greta's heart clenched, and she waited for Detective McHenry to say more about Dolores, but he didn't. Instead, he flipped his notebook shut and stuck her with a hard look.

Greta shrank under his glare. "Is there anything else you need from me? Otherwise, I should probably get back to work."

"We're not quite done. I need you to tell me again what time you arrived at Franklin's house on Friday."

Greta's pulse skittered. She stood from her chair so fast it scraped backward. She cringed at the harsh, nails-against-a-chalkboard noise. "Do you think I had something to do with this?"

Detective McHenry stared her down until she repositioned the chair and dropped back into her seat. Once she was situated, he spoke. "Did you?"

"What? No! Of course not. Franklin was my friend. I would never hurt him."

"I need you to answer my question."

Greta pursed her lips. "Fine. I got to Franklin's house at quarter after five on Friday."

"And how did you get in?" Detective McHenry spun his notebook open again.

"The door was ajar. I called out, and no one answered."

"So, you entered anyway?"

"Well, yes. Like I've tried to tell you, Franklin and I are"—Greta pulled her top lip into her mouth and released it—"*were* friends. He wouldn't have minded."

"Seems a bit presumptuous to me, entering private property."

Greta smiled. "I don't know where you're from, Detective, but here in Larkspur, I've learned neighbors watch out for neighbors. I figured if Franklin had accidentally left his door open, he would appreciate me closing it for him."

Detective McHenry studied her. "If you were only going to close the door for him, remind me again how you ended up in the back of his property where his body was found?"

"I walked through the house thinking there was a chance he was out on the deck and couldn't hear my knock."

Detective McHenry grunted, but didn't sound convinced. "Can anyone confirm your whereabouts between the hours of noon and four on Friday?"

"I was at the library with Josie and Iris."

Detective McHenry froze with his pen perched above his notebook and slowly raised his head until he was looking at her. "The entire time?"

Greta swallowed, her mouth suddenly dry. How was this happening? She'd never gotten so much as a speeding ticket, and here she sat, being interrogated for murder. "Do I need to call my lawyer?"

Detective McHenry's gaze burrowed into her like a jackhammer, rattling Greta's insides. He didn't respond to her.

"What? It's a fair question. I'm allowed to ask it!" Greta's lungs seemed to have forgotten their primary function as panic overrode her usual sunny disposition.

"It's a fair question, yes. But also, one usually posed by guilty people."

"Or people who don't like being falsely accused." Greta spit the words across the table as she stood. "We're done here. I have been nothing but helpful, and I don't appreciate how you're treating me. If you want to talk any more, get a hold of my attorney. Lori knows her."

Greta turned on her heel and ripped open the door, craving the comfort and safety of the library.

She made it back out into the receptionist area, and Lori's head sprang up from her computer. Seeing the expression on Greta's face, her smile slipped. "Oh, hun. What's wrong?"

Greta was about to explain when the door to Chief Sorenson's office opened, and the chief ambled out.

"Greta. I am so sorry about your friend." Chief Sorenson walked over to her and took her hands in both of his. He was an older man with bushy eyebrows and a slightly oversized belly. Greta had liked him instantly, and they'd sat together at the mayor's monthly meetings all summer. "Detective McHenry informed me he met you. I'm sorry it had to be under these circumstances."

"Me too."

"Detective McHenry joins us from Chicago, as I'm sure he told you."

"Actually, no, he didn't." Greta didn't make eye contact with the detective as he came to a stop next to her. Greta wondered if he'd filled Chief Sorenson in on the direction he was taking with the case. She'd like to believe the chief would have her back. Then again, she hadn't known him for too long, so she couldn't count on it.

"I'm cutting back my hours, so we needed extra help," Chief Sorenson went on. "We're very glad Mark accepted the position. Who'd have thought his first week on the job, he'd be dealing with this Halloway mess. But, he's the best of the best, so I'm sure he'll get justice for your friend."

Greta forced her mouth into a smile even though her mind was reeling. "Franklin deserves that. Good to see you, Chief. Bye, Lori. I'll talk to you both soon." She pushed the exit door open, anxious to get the heck out of there.

"Miss Plank, one more thing."

Greta spun around to see Detective McHenry slip into the hallway behind her.

"What?" Her snappish tone was out of character, but she'd never been accused of murder before, so all bets were off.

Detective McHenry came to a stop in front of her and eyed her up and down. "It would be in your best interest and mine if you'd keep this investigation under wraps. The fewer people who know Franklin was killed, the easier it will be for me to do my job and get to the truth."

Greta gave him a disbelieving eye roll. He'd accused her of murder, and now what? He was asking for her cooperation? "Good luck."

Detective McHenry put his hands on his hips. "What's that supposed to mean?"

"Look, Detective. Again, I don't know how things work in Chicago, but here in Larkspur, population you, me, and the next guy, people find things out. I'd wager my friend Lori in there will mention something about Franklin in a casual conversation with her neighbors, and they'll bring it up to folks at the grocery store or the bank, who will, in turn, mention it at Mugs & Hugs the next day, and, well, you see where this is going. That's not even considering both Josie and Iris know I was with you for the past forty-five minutes, and they'll have their own form of interrogation for me when I get back. They're going to put it together that you're running with the idea Franklin's death wasn't an accident. And that you think I did it. It's only a matter of time before the whole town knows your hypothesis."

Greta was on a roll and, while she usually hated confrontation, Detective McHenry had gone and poked the bear of her pride. "Just so we're clear, I'll tell whomever I darn well please you think *I'm* a suspect. And I'll have you know, everyone in this town will have my back."

Even as Greta said it, her confidence faltered. She was still relatively new around Larkspur, and while she'd made a lot of friends, there was no telling how folks would react if she suddenly had the scarlet letter of a murder accusation pinned on her chest. It might actually be better for her to keep the detective's hypothesis quiet. But Greta wasn't about to let Detective McHenry see her sweat. She'd dealt with enough men who thought they were untouchably smart and above her, and there was no way she'd let herself be walked all over—not again.

She raised her chin. "Like I said, Detective, you can contact my lawyer if you want to speak to me further, but my advice is to take your investigation elsewhere. I didn't kill Franklin, and you're wasting your time if you continue to chase this ridiculous hunch. Besides, Franklin's death was probably just an accident."

Greta stalked toward the library, keeping her back straight and her head held high even as her heart hammered. The hairs on her neck stood on edge when Detective McHenry mumbled, "It certainly was not. And I intend to prove it."

Chapter Nine

"Tell me everything." Josie slid into the booth across from Greta at Mugs & Hugs.

When Greta had returned to the library after her meeting with Detective McHenry, she'd silenced her friends' questions with a "Not now" hiss before plastering on her best *everything's fine* expression and going about her work. But there was no way Josie was going to let her off the hook since they were now off the clock. Iris had left directly from the library for dinner with Dean, and Josie insisted Greta join her for a bite to eat at the café. Her friend had been patient all afternoon, but now it was time to pay the piper.

Greta looked around and waved to Allison, who approached to take their order.

"How was the rest of your day?" Allison came to a stop at Greta and Josie's table.

"Greta was about to tell me why she spent nearly an hour at the police station."

Greta rolled her eyes. "According to Detective McHenry, I'm not supposed to say."

"Screw that." Allison scooched into the booth next to Josie. She propped her chin up on her hand, using her fingers to twiddle with her dangling earring, which was shaped like a to-go cup of coffee. "Tell us everything."

Greta leaned forward. "Okay. Apparently, Franklin didn't fall to his death by accident."

Allison's mouth dropped open. "You're telling me"—she lowered her voice—"someone pushed him?"

"Something like that. I didn't get all the details. Detective McHenry is pretty tight-lipped."

"More like tight all over." Josie licked her finger and held it up to the air, making a sizzling sound effect.

"Josie!"

"What? I'm just saying what you're thinking. He is a fine specimen of a man."

"Really?" Allison looked between them. "He's attractive? Now we're talking."

"Seriously? We might have had a murder in our town, and you two are worried about the looks of the lead police detective? I haven't even told you the whole story." Greta wasn't sure whether to be amused or annoyed.

Josie twisted her lips. "So, he's the lead detective? Is he going to be around for a while?"

"He moved here from Chicago. Chief is cutting back on his hours."

Allison whistled. "Nothing like coming into the force with a bang. What did Detective McHottie want with you?"

Greta balled up a napkin and threw it across the table. "That's what I'm trying to tell you. He thinks *I* did it."

"Did what?" Josie's face was blank.

"Killed Franklin."

"*What?!*" Josie and Allison's collective outburst carried through the café.

"Shhhh." Greta glanced around, smiling and waving at the people who had paused their conversations and zoned in on the booth where the three women were sitting. When Greta swung her gaze back to Josie and Allison, she grumbled, "Would you two try to play it cool?"

"How are you playing it cool?" Josie practically shrieked. "Murder is a serious accusation. A bogus one, of course, but dang. What are you going to do? How did you leave it with Detective Dreamy?"

Greta let out a long-suffering sigh. "First of all, I hardly think the man accusing me of murder is dreamy. Second, I told him if he wanted to talk to me in the future, he needed to go through my lawyer."

Allison snorted. "Did you tell him your lawyer is your mom?"

45

Greta shot her an angelic smile. "No. But I'm sure he'll figure it out sooner or later, especially if he keeps after me." Her smile drooped. "I don't understand. I found Franklin, yes. But we were friends. I would never hurt him."

Josie tipped her head to the side. "There must be some reason the detective thinks you did it."

Allison glanced at Josie. "Can't you and Iris prove you three were together at the library the day Franklin died?"

"That's just it." Greta glanced over her shoulder before dropping her voice to a whisper. "I had lunch at home, alone, which means I don't have an alibi for a solid hour. Plenty of time to commit a crime. If I were a criminal."

"Which you're not." Josie's tone was firm. "What else did the detective say?"

"He asked me a bunch of questions about Franklin and his schedule. I told him about the phone call I overheard between Franklin and Ed and about an appointment Franklin told me he was scheduled to have with a book collector. He was going to see his PT and Dolores." Greta held up her empty hands in a shrug. "Not a lot to go on. And I still maintain Detective whatever-you-want-to-call-him may not be on the right track with any of this. There's no way there could have been a murder here. Right?"

Allison sat back, frowning. "I don't know. I mean, yeah, not a lot happens in Larkspur, and for the most part, it's a pretty tranquil place, but now that you mention him, Ed was in here talking pretty loudly on his cell phone the other day."

"People are allowed to talk loudly on their phones. No laws are being broken there," Josie said.

"I know, but I overheard him say 'I'll find a way. No matter what,' right before he walked out the door. What if he was referring to something having to do with Franklin?"

"Well, shoot." Greta rolled a curl of hair around her finger. "It could be nothing, but I've got to find out. I've got to clear my name somehow. If word gets out Detective McHenry suspects me, what will the town do? I don't want a cloud of suspicion hanging over me. Cindy Fields will have a literal field day with that."

Cindy Fields was the chair of the Library Board. She had been on the hiring committee, and Greta had gotten a seriously bad vibe from the woman. Between her perpetual scowl and her intention to keep the library in the Dark Age—think, silent at all times, fines enforced with no mercy, and the like—she and Greta could not have been more opposite. Greta knew she was on a short leash where Cindy was concerned. She imagined the woman was looking for any reason to call her appointment into question and get rid of her. It was part of the reason Greta had been working her tail off to do everything she could to prove herself. Cindy Fields was crazy intimidating, and she carried a lot of clout in the community. Town lore said her ex-husband had left her a lot of money in a messy divorce, and she was prone to use it to get her way in Larkspur. The library had been her pet project under the previous director.

When Greta came in and expressed her vision, she'd impressed Josie, Iris, and Mayor Collins, who had convinced the rest of the Library Board to give Greta a shot, but their recommendation would only get her so far. Cindy had a lot of sway in Larkspur, and if she latched onto her being a suspect in a murder investigation, Greta was terrified to think what could happen to her job.

"I don't know, G. Shouldn't you leave all this to the cops?" Josie tapped the straw she was fiddling with on the weathered wooden table before glancing at Greta.

Greta crossed her arms, surprised Josie, of all people, would give her any pushback.

Josie smirked. "I know. I know. I had to play the rational part for a second, but I'll gladly help you nab the bad guy and make sure ol' Cindy doesn't mess with you. What do we do first?"

Greta grinned and leaned in. "I need to talk to my mom and tell her what's going on. Then, we should use your connections around town. You guys know this place a lot better than some newbie detective. Heck, even I do. We can use that to our advantage. No one will suspect a couple of librarians."

"Good plan." Allison stood up and adjusted the scarf she had tied around her choppy pixie cut. "I'll keep an ear open, and if I hear anything helpful, I'll let you know. Now, what can I get for you?"

Josie and Greta placed their order—large bowls of Allison's homemade tomato parmesan soup and grilled cheese sandwiches—and Allison left for the kitchen.

"I can see your wheels spinning. What's your plan?" Josie asked.

"I might make a visit to Kennedy's Cozy Cottages sometime soon. See what kind of feel I get around there. I made friends with several of the guests this morning, so I could disguise my visit as a trip to see them and bring them something from the library."

"Like books," Josie teased.

"Actually, yeah. I could bring a variety of titles to the office for Ed. Allow him to keep them there in case anyone forgot their beach read at home. It could be a three-week rotation, like regular checkouts, and he could either drop them off and pick up new titles, or I could bring another batch. We could also leave him some guest library cards so his tenants could come and browse if they want something in particular." Greta warmed to the idea even more as she talked about it. She loved the thought of getting books into more readers' hands.

"That's sort of genius. Gosh, I'm brilliant."

"You? It was my idea!" Greta scoffed but couldn't keep the smile from her voice.

Knowing she had Josie and Allison on her side settled Greta. Her equilibrium restored, Greta mentally brushed off the yuck of the day like she would the dust from an old hard-covered book. It would all be okay. It had to be.

Chapter Ten

The next afternoon, Greta was busy shelving books in the nonfiction section when movement in the hallway caught her attention. Dolores approached from the direction of the police station. Greta left her cart where it was and hurried out to meet the woman.

"Dolores." Greta opened her arms, and Dolores stepped into a hug.

Dolores's brown hair was pulled back off her makeup-free face. She wore jeans and an oversized sweatshirt and looked in stark contrast to her usual put-together self. When she leaned out of the hug, she offered Greta a gloomy smile. "Hi, Greta, dear."

"Dolores, I am so sorry for your loss."

"Yours, too, Greta. Franklin was closer to you than any of us around here. I'm sad." Dolores's voice caught.

"Franklin will be missed." She squeezed Dolores's arm, glancing behind her toward the closed door of the police station. "So, what brings you by?"

"Detective McHenry called me. He wanted to talk to me about Franklin."

"Really?" Greta did her best to mask her apprehension. Did the detective tell Dolores he suspected Greta? What was his angle?

"I don't quite understand why my relationship with Franklin matters, but I answered his questions. I wish Chief Sorenson would have been around. I'd have been more comfortable with someone familiar."

Greta understood that. Detective McHenry wasn't the easiest person to talk to, with all his posturing and stony stretches of silence. "What did the new detective ask you?"

"He wanted to know how long I'd been seeing Franklin. What the extent of our relationship was. What we talked about. Why does any of it matter, though? Franklin fell and died. What do I have to do with anything?" Dolores threw up her hands, but, before her arms even had a chance to drop back to her sides, understanding dawned in her eyes. "Wait a minute. That detective doesn't think Franklin fell, does he?"

"I'm afraid not."

Dolores sucked in a breath. "So what? I'm a suspect?"

"I'm sure he just brought you in to try to fill some of the holes in the story. It's no secret Franklin kept to himself. Detective McHenry had me in there for almost an hour yesterday asking questions to try to get a better grasp on his life."

Dolores jammed her hands into the pocket of her vintage Larkspur Lancers sweatshirt. "I don't like any of this."

"Me either. Trust me. I'll keep you posted if I hear anything, though. You do the same, okay?"

Dolores said she would. "Will I see you at Franklin's funeral on Thursday?"

"Of course. I wouldn't miss it."

"Okay. You take care now, Greta."

Dolores took her leave, and the urgency to get to work on Franklin's case settled on Greta like the weight of water after a deep dive, crushing the air out of her lungs. She needed to figure out what happened to Franklin so she could close the book on this whole mess and put it behind her.

At the end of the workday, Greta checked in with Josie and Iris. "Plans for tonight?"

Iris strung her purse across her body. "I'm headed to Dean's place."

"I've got yoga and a date with Germavitis, the new streaming series about the icky microorganisms on literally everything." Josie looked elated.

Greta recoiled. "Sounds dreadful."

Josie just laughed. "What about you?"

"I'm heading to Ed's cottages with some books. I'm going to drop them off at the office, take a peek around, and see if I can catch any of our friends from story time yesterday."

"Why are you bringing books to Ed?" Iris furrowed her brows.

"It's part of a great plan I came up with." Josie ushered her out the door and shot Greta a pointed glance over the top of her head, mouthing "call me" before turning back to Iris. "I'll tell you all about it."

Greta was relieved Josie understood she didn't want everyone privy to what she was doing. Sure, Iris was one of her best friends, but at this point, she hoped to keep her operation close to the vest. No need to arouse any suspicion, and if they told Iris, she would tell Dean, and who knew who he would tell. He talked to a lot of people on any given day.

Greta lifted a pile of books up from the shelf under the front counter. She'd accumulated quite the stack over the course of the day—everything from children's picture books to adult fiction to a couple of Nancy Drew and Hardy Boys books, for good measure. She considered the latter a small homage to Franklin.

Greta eyed the stack, knowing full well she wouldn't be able to fit all the books in her usual canvas tote. She shoved as many as she dared into her bag and looked around for something else she could use.

"Ah-ha." She grabbed for an empty courier box. "Check me out, being resourceful." She spoke out loud to the quiet, empty library. She put the remaining books in the box and wedged it on her hip. Flipping off the lights with her index finger, she pushed the door to the library open with her backside. When she turned forward again, she came face-to-face with Detective McHenry.

"Oh!" Greta's hold on the box slipped, and it slid down her body. She scrambled to get a better grip. "You startled me."

"It looks like you could use a hand." Detective McHenry reached for the box.

Greta scooted away from him. "Nope. I've got it. Thank you anyway, though." She didn't particularly like the idea of taking help from the man, and she didn't want to prolong her time in his presence for fear he'd start trying to weasel some sort of incriminating information out of her.

"Suit yourself." Detective McHenry motioned for Greta to go ahead of him.

After locking up, Greta limped down the hallway, weighed down by the box and bag of books and probably looking like a cow in labor.

With some maneuvering, she managed to knock open the outside door and squirm her way into the parking lot, clinging to the last wisps of her dignity.

The early-evening sun was warm on her skin, but the air held the telling chill of fall. Greta pressed the unlock button on her key fob, and her car locks clicked open. She propped the box up on her trunk, opened the door to the back seat, and shoved her canvas tote all the way to the far side before lugging the box onto the seat with an *umph*.

"See? All set." Greta dusted her hands and shot Detective McHenry a triumphant glance, refusing to act embarrassed.

He stared at her, his face void of expression. "That's a lot of books."

"I'm running them over to Ed's cottages." The second the words were out of her mouth, Greta silently cursed her incurable need to fill silence with blabber. There was no good reason to let the detective in on her plans.

"Ed checked out all these books?" He rotated his gaze to the box in the back seat of the car.

"N-no. Not exactly. We've been in discussion about ways to enhance the experience of his guests. If they get bored in inclement weather, they might appreciate a book to read. That's where the library comes in. I'm dropping them off."

Greta hoped her spiel didn't trigger the detective's Spidey senses. She thought she'd sold it well, and it was the truth. Sure, she was using the books as an excuse to snoop, but she also hoped they'd come in handy for Ed's renters.

"Quite the service. Do you provide book drop-offs for everyone in town?"

"I do whatever I can to help whomever I can." She crossed her arms, not appreciating the detective's condescending tone. "Where are you off to on this fine evening, Detective?"

"Actually, I was going out to Mr. Kennedy's cottages myself."

Greta stopped her lips from parting. Barely. Was he planning to go to Ed's before he ran into her? Or was he going to Ed's now in order to keep tabs on her? She wasn't sure.

Before she could say anything, Detective McHenry marched across the parking lot toward one of the unmarked cars. He got in and took off.

Greta shook off her surprise and climbed into the driver's seat of her car. This might be her first bit of good luck. If Detective McHenry was going to question Ed, she could try to eavesdrop on their conversation and learn something more about what happened to Franklin. For all Detective McHenry pried her for information, he certainly was less willing to offer any in return, and Greta hated being left in the dark. It went against the nature of her job—librarians knew things, and what they didn't know, they knew how to find out.

Greta pulled out of her parking spot and drove toward Larkspur Lake. At the tee in the road, instead of turning right to get to her house, she made a left turn and followed the curve of the lake. It glowed in the evening sun, the light reflecting off the water and shining broad columns through pine tree trunks and branches.

Ahead, off the side of the road, were Kennedy's Cozy Cottages. The resort was nestled in the pines lining the lake. Four of Ed's ten cottages sat directly on the water, and the other six buildings were mixed in between the trees.

Greta parked in front of the small office building behind the detective's cruiser, opened the door, and stepped out, a quick glance acclimating her to her surroundings. She took a deep breath of piney air and smiled. She had a plan.

With several grunts, she managed to get the box of books and her bag out of the back seat. She hobbled over to the door to Ed's office and nudged it open with the corner of the box.

Detective McHenry stood across from Ed's desk. When she entered the space, he arched an aggravated brow in her direction. She ignored it and flashed a smile. "So sorry to intrude. Hi, Ed!"

"Greta! What a surprise." Ed made a move to help her with the box.

"I've got it." Greta hoisted it up onto a small table in the corner of the office. "I'll come back and chat with you about some library programming and things Josie and I brainstormed for your guests. I see you're tied up at the moment."

"Okay. Great." Ed shifted his gaze between Detective McHenry and Greta, grimacing as he motioned toward the detective. "I-I'm not sure what this is about, but I'm sure it won't take long."

Greta's heart tugged with a hint of sympathy for Ed, who was obviously uncomfortable in the presence of law enforcement, but she bottled it up. She couldn't let her emotions get in the way of finding out the truth about his dealings with Franklin.

"No worries." Greta kept her tone light. "Why don't you come and find me when you're finished up here. Your grounds are so beautiful. I'll enjoy them while I wait."

Greta gave a finger wave and turned to leave as Detective McHenry stared her down, skepticism pooling in his eyes. Undeterred, Greta held her head high, started humming a happy tune, and let the door slam behind her. She walked down the path to the lake, intentionally cutting directly in front of the office so if either Ed or the detective was watching, they would see she left.

Reaching the water's edge, she paused for a second. The tangy smell of cool sand hit her nose, along with a hint of smoke, but the lakefront beach was deserted. A group was congregated by the firepit in front of one of the cabins a stone's throw down the shore.

Taking one last survey of the lake, Greta stole her way in the opposite direction. She clutched her book-filled tote to her side as she circled back and hurried toward the office, coming at it on the far side and hoping to sneak under the window she'd seen open behind Ed's desk.

As she approached the small office building, she slowed her pace. She wouldn't be able to accomplish anything if her panting gave away her position. Greta crept forward and crouched beneath the window.

"I don't know what you're implying." Ed's voice cut the crisp, fall air like a knife.

"I'm not implying anything, Mr. Kennedy." Detective McHenry's response came slicing back. "I'm asking you to tell me about your contentious relationship with Franklin Halloway."

Chapter Eleven

Greta pinched her lips together to keep quiet. This was exactly what she came for.

"Contentious? Who told you I had a contentious relationship with Franklin Halloway?" Ed's tone was strained, and Greta wished she could see his face. She had a knack for reading people's expressions, but she didn't dare peek in through the window.

"I have it on good authority you were trying to buy his property from him, and he didn't want to sell. That must have made you pretty upset."

Greta held in a scoff. That was rich of Detective McHenry, referencing her as 'good authority' when he all but accused her of murder yesterday. Was this how all criminal investigations were conducted? Pitting sources against sources and suspects against suspects until a crack appeared big enough to shine a light of truth through?

"What are you getting at?" Ed sounded confused. Whether it was an act or not, Greta couldn't be sure.

"Where were you the afternoon of September fourteenth, Mr. Kennedy?"

"Whoa, whoa, whoa." Ed's voice grew shriller with each word. "Franklin died on September fourteenth, right? Why do you need to know where I was?"

"Answer my question, Mr. Kennedy, and I'll tell you." Detective McHenry's voice was hard as ore.

A flock of birds suddenly decided now was a good time to begin their evening calls, and Greta groaned, leaning closer to the window to try to pick up Ed's response. As she did so, her canvas bag full of books swung forward on her arm, and before she could stop it, the bag slammed into the exterior wall of the office, connecting with the siding and issuing a resounding *thunk*.

"What was that?" Detective McHenry displeased tone carried outside.

There was shuffling as the two men moved closer to the window. Greta cursed under her breath, ducked down, and dashed for her car, running along the side of the building as fast as she could in a bent-over position, lugging the traitorous books all the way. Once she had rounded the corner, she stood upright and slowed her stride. She cast what she hoped was a discreet glance toward the front office window.

Detective McHenry was staring out it directly at her. Their gazes connected, and Greta's stomach lurched, adrenaline balling itself up and firing around her insides like a pinball.

Greta smiled and waved, tucking a flyaway curl behind her ear as casually as she could. She turned away from the window and dropped her bag to the pine-needle-covered ground, pretending to rummage around inside of it for something. She breathed through her nose, counted to ten, and willed her heart rate to slow as she exhaled. When she looked back at the office building, the detective was no longer at the window. She slumped against her car. "Okay, Greta. Think. What next?"

The door opened, and Detective McHenry stalked out.

Greta bolted upright, smoothing down her skirt. She shot him a jaunty smile and did her best to appear the picture of innocence. "All set?"

He grunted, climbing into his cruiser without a word. He made a y-turn on the gravel drive before driving off toward the police station.

The man wasn't one for pleasantries, that much she understood, but if Greta could convince him she was innocent or that Franklin's death was just an accident, perhaps for her next project, she'd set to work chipping away at his cantankerous disposition.

First things first, though.

Greta waited for Ed to come outside and find her. After a couple minutes passed, she decided to take matters into her own hands. She hoisted her bag back onto her shoulder and walked inside.

Ed was sitting at his desk, rubbing his temples.

Greta knocked gently on the doorframe. She let concern seep into her voice. "Is now an okay time?"

Ed looked like Detective McHenry had put him through the ringer, but he offered her a tight smile. "Of course. Sorry I didn't come get you. I'm glad you came back. Please, sit. Tell me about your idea."

Greta launched into an explanation of her plan. She'd gotten pretty good at this pitch since discussing it with Josie and, inadvertently, Detective McHenry. By the time she finished, Ed's smile actually reached his eyes.

"Brilliant. What a cool service to offer to our guests. I could even include it in our promotional materials. A sort of a 'we've got everything you need and more for complete relaxation, including your next favorite book' type message."

"Wonderful." Greta reached into her bag and deposited the remaining books she'd brought from the library onto the table. "I talked to Josie, and we could be on a three-week rotation with books. One of us would be happy to swing by to grab your returns and bring you new titles. Or, if you're in town, you can pick them up."

"Sounds good to me. Why don't you give me your number so I have it, and I'll text you. You can share my contact information with Josie and Iris, and we can play it by ear as we get going with this."

Greta rattled off her number, and Ed entered it into his phone. "I'll text you so you have mine," he said.

"Sure." While she waited for a ping alerting her of his message, Greta straightened the stack of books and tried to figure out a way to turn the conversation to Franklin's death. She wanted to figure out the extent of Ed's business with her late friend. Where did it start, and where did it end? But she didn't want to be obvious in her questioning and risk arousing Ed's suspicions.

Her phone vibrated, and Greta decided not to push her luck tonight. At least now she had a reason to keep tabs on Ed. With one last glance at the books, she smiled and made to leave. "I'll create a text message group for us, and we can figure out a plan of attack for returns and exchanges going forward."

"Thanks again." Ed rose from his chair and followed her to the door. "You changed my mood with this idea."

"Oh? Did Detective McHenry give you a hard time?"

"Something like that."

"Well." Greta dangled her now-empty book bag from her pointer finger. "I'm glad I could help. You better be careful, though. Once word gets out you're offering free books with every stay at Kennedy's Cozy Cottages, you might be inundated with reservation requests."

"We're already so inundated with reservation requests I'm looking to expand."

"What?" In her shock, Greta let her bag slip from her finger, flinging it in front of her. She scrambled to pick it up. "I mean, wow. I didn't realize business was so good." She hadn't expected him to be so open about it. "What are your plans?"

"Nothing definite, yet." Ed glanced out over the lakefront property. "But I'm working on it. I'm hoping to have more to report soon."

"Can't wait to hear about it." Greta forced a smile. "Bye now, Ed." She pushed open the door and walked back to her car, her hands significantly lighter but her heart laden with the news that Ed was, indeed, trying to grow his property holdings. Could his desire to expand and buy Franklin's land have driven him to murder?

Greta swallowed hard as she got behind the wheel. She squinted back at the office, but Ed had disappeared from the front door.

Greta took the long way around the lake to her cabin, giving herself time to puzzle over what she'd learned. Or hadn't learned. Considering her neighbors as suspects didn't sit well. In fact, it was in direct contradiction to the permanent glass-half-full outlook she'd vowed to keep since everything happened with Kelly, and again more recently, with her ex-boyfriend in Green Bay. But she couldn't ignore the facts on her quest for the truth, and if she wanted to shelve all these bad feelings for good, she needed answers.

The sun dipped lower in the autumn sky, casting an orange glow over the water, and she cracked the windows of her car, even though the temperature was dropping. When she rounded the bend, a strip of properties came into view, one of which was Josie's home. Her friend's car was in the driveway, and on the off chance Greta could catch her after yoga, and before she started watching the terrible-sounding germ show, she pulled in. Josie appeared on the front porch.

"Did you miss me?" She rested her arms against the rail as Greta climbed out of her car.

Greta laughed at her friend's dry delivery. She and Josie couldn't be more opposite. Greta was all sunshine and good times, and Josie was all sarcasm and germ shows. They were the definition of opposites attracting. "I always miss you, Jos. I was on my way home and saw your car."

"Come in for a minute." Josie disappeared through her front door. She had swapped her usual black, pencil-cut pants and sleek blazer for black leggings and a crew neck sweatshirt.

Greta followed Josie inside. "How was yoga?"

"Great." Josie opened her refrigerator and pulled out two bottles of water. "I'm all loose and bendy." Josie handed one to Greta before she tucked a strand of her short hair behind her ear. "How did it go at Ed's?"

Greta perched herself on one of Josie's barstools and took a swig of water. "For starters, I ran into the detective before I left the library."

Josie elevated an eyebrow.

"He was on his way to the cabins, too. He wouldn't tell me exactly why, but I figured it was to question Ed. So, I hatched a plan to eavesdrop."

"Look at you, Nancy Drew." Josie grinned. "Did you find out anything useful?"

Greta gave her head a quick shake. "I was almost made. Detective McHenry is on to me."

"What did he say?"

"Nothing. He glared at me and left." When she thought about it, she probably looked more guilty in his eyes now, but Greta didn't want to dwell on the detective. "Anyway, I didn't hear Ed's response to the detective questioning him about his alibi for the time of Franklin's death, but after Detective McHenry left, Ed did say he's planning to expand his business. He didn't say exactly how but says he has ideas in the works. Speaking of ideas, he loves the library books idea I pitched to him. I'm going to give him your phone number."

"Is that necessary?"

"Well, yeah. To coordinate book drop off and return and stuff. It's no big deal. I don't picture Ed as the type of guy to start texting us at random."

Josie narrowed her eyes. "Unless he's a psychopathic killer, and we're next."

"Well, gosh, when you put it like that..."

Josie held up her hand. "I'm kidding. It's fine. But for real, could Ed have done it?"

"I don't know, but he's the only suspect I've got, other than myself." Greta twisted her lips. "So, we have to keep him on the list. I need more information, and I have an idea of where I can get it."

"What are you thinking?"

"My mom needs to give her friend and fellow member of the Langlade County Quilting Club, Lori Lamponee, a call."

Josie whistled her approval. "Now we're talking. What did your parents say when you told them about the whole debacle?"

Greta fiddled with the cap from her water bottle. "They were outraged on my behalf. My mom, bless her heart, wants to rip the detective to shreds. I honestly think she hopes he calls so she can lay into him."

Josie laughed. "I want tickets to that show."

Greta smiled before turning serious. "I need to see if she's up for some meddling of her own, though. She may draw the line with aiding and abetting a potential criminal, even if I am her daughter."

"Doubtful. Also, it's not meddling if she's merely checking in with a friend."

"An excellent point. I'll get out of your hair and call her."

Greta drove the rest of the way around the lake and pulled in her detached garage. She lugged herself inside, exhaustion hitting her body even as her brain was still working a mile a minute. She made quick work of changing into sweatpants and a thermal Henley. Biff eyed her with interest as she pulled on her rubber bottom slippers, grabbed her cell phone, and wandered out onto her back deck, careful to tug the screen closed behind her. "I'll just be a minute, buddy."

In response, he darted off to the corner of her living room where she'd set up a sequence of cardboard boxes and stacks of heavy library school textbooks to serve as a makeshift cat playground.

Outside, the cold air bit at Greta's face, warning of the coming change in seasons. Pretty soon, she'd have to put up her dock for the winter and stash her stand-up paddleboards in the basement. She walked across the deck to where she had them leaning against the outside of the cabin. Greta ran a hand over the smooth fiberglass and epoxy resin. She still hoped to squeeze in a few more days out on the water. She might have been clumsy as all get out on land, but in the lake, she was as graceful as a mermaid.

Greta leaned on the deck rail, looking out over the water. She scrolled through the contacts in her phone and hit her mom's number.

"Hey, G."

Greta smiled. "Hi, Mom. How's it going?"

Greta's parents, Dale and Louisa, lived about an hour away in the small town of Churchill, where Greta had grown up and where her mom was the town's only lawyer. "Oh, we're fine here, dear. The real question is, how are you?"

"No worse for the wear. Have you heard from Detective McHenry?"

"No, not yet." Her mom's voice was laced with disappointment.

Greta hid a laugh. "That's probably a good thing."

"If you say so. What's up?"

Greta broached the idea of her mom talking to Lori with as much tact as one could muster when asking for help wringing information out of an unsuspecting potential source. "I don't have any idea what to do next to figure this thing out, and I'm sure Lori is privy to some of the information on Detective McHenry's investigation."

"Say no more. We have a quilting group gathering here in town in about an hour. I'll corner Lori and see what I find out."

"Seriously?" Greta had expected a little pushback.

"You betcha. I suppose I should probably try to stop you from pursuing this, but I'll leave the caution to your father."

As if on cue, her dad called out in the background. "What you guys should do is leave this to the professionals. The truth will come to light."

Greta couldn't help but smile at her dad's protective streak.

"Oh hush, Dale. I don't trust the detective as far as I can throw him."

"Louisa, you haven't met him!"

Greta crossed the deck and walked through the sliding door as her parents bickered.

"Well, nothing harmful will come from talking to my friend Lori tonight." Her mom's voice grew louder as she turned her attention back to Greta's call. "Sorry, dear."

"No problem. And thanks, Mom."

"I've always got your back, G. One of your parents needs to step up." Her mom's teasing lit earned a harrumph from her dad.

Greta grinned. "I'm glad I can count on you."

"Absolutely. You leave it to me."

Chapter Twelve

The next morning, Greta stared out the exterior library windows that faced the front entrance to the police station. There was a line of people out the door. "What are they all doing?"

Josie walked over and stood next to her. "No clue, but we haven't had this much foot traffic since we offered unlimited free sno-cones in June."

Greta groaned at the memory. "Our worst idea ever. Sticky fingers and library books don't mix. Hey, there goes Ed." Greta stood up straighter as, sure enough, the resort owner walked across the parking lot and joined the group of people waiting outside the police station.

Iris bustled in. "Good morning. Quite the crowd outside, huh?" She made her way behind the desk and dropped her bag and her jacket before coming to stand beside Greta and Josie. "What's new?"

"Not much. Just trying to figure out what's got half the town knocking on the PD's door," Josie said. "You know what? I'm going to find out."

She headed outside. Greta and Iris watched through the window as she reappeared in the front of the building, inserting herself into the group who welcomed her with waves and, from the looks of their wagging mouths, a flurry of conversation.

"Good. I'm sure if anyone can get answers, it's Josie." Iris walked to the circulation desk and clicked on the home screen of the computer in front of her.

Greta followed. "While we're both here, there's something I wanted to chat with you about." Greta told Iris what she learned from Detective McHenry at the beginning of the week and her resolve to get to the bottom of things, figuring she may as well come clean now, before the library got crowded for the day, or Iris found out some other way.

Iris's eyes grew wider and wider as Greta told her story and shared her plans to dig deeper into the case.

"You've got to be kidding." Iris's mouth hung open. "First of all, murder in Larkspur!? That's wrong on so many levels. And you being a suspect is preposterous. I don't like this."

"I know, but I want justice for Franklin, so I'll do whatever it takes. And it'll all work out. I'm sure of it, so don't you worry." Greta walked around the front of the desk toward the stacks. There were some open stands that needed to be filled with books. She often positioned titles from the top or bottom shelves in facing stands. It helped them to circulate.

By the time she finished facing books, Josie was back behind the circulation desk.

Greta saddled up to her. "So, what did you learn?"

"Someone started a rumor there was foul play involved in Franklin Halloway's death. No one seems to be able to pinpoint exactly where the news sprouted from, but everyone wanted to hear it from the police themselves. Several people were in line waiting to share *relevant information*." Josie made air quotes.

Greta leaned in and dropped her voice. "Did you find out anything helpful?"

"Nope. You've figured out how people in this town are. We're a clan of busy-bodies. Everyone is arguing their less-than-warm run-in with Franklin from a year ago is relevant." She chuckled. "I almost feel bad for the detective. He'll be stuck taking people's statements all day."

The light bulb lit up in Greta's head.

Josie pointed at her. "Why are you making a face?"

"I have a guess as to where the rumor started." Greta whipped out her phone and typed a quick message. This had her mom's name written all over it.

"It's all pretty far-fetched, though, isn't it?" Iris asked. "There's no way Franklin was actually killed."

With a nod of her head, Greta silently informed Josie that Iris was now in the loop.

Iris swiped at a crumb on the circulation desk. "I mean no one would intentionally hurt anyone else in Larkspur. We live by a certain code around here."

"I want nothing more than to believe that, too, but—" Greta was interrupted by the vibration of her phone in her hand. She glanced down and scanned the message from her mom. "It's like I thought." She held up her phone for Josie and Iris to read the message.

Mom: Yes, I saw Lori last night. Had a good conversation with her. Some other members of the sewing squad may or may not have overheard us. I tend to raise my voice when I'm incredulous, you know how I get, G. ;) Call me later tonight after work. I'm in court all day, but I have more details about the case you should hear.

Iris sucked in a breath. "Sounds ominous."

Josie chewed her lip. "I wonder what Louisa knows."

"Your guess is as good as mine." Greta locked her phone's screen and stowed it in her pocket. She glanced at the clock. It wasn't even nine a.m.

It was going to be a long day.

"Dean!" Iris hurried out from around the counter to greet Dean when he strolled in the library's entrance with Sidney.

"Hi, babe." Dean leaned forward and kissed Iris's forehead. "Busy place here today."

Iris jutted out her bottom lip in a pout. "All these people are stopping at the police office giving tips and information about Franklin Halloway's death. Isn't it awful?"

"I'm not sure I'm following. What sort of details?" Sidney asked.

"The police are working under the assumption Franklin's death wasn't an accident." Greta walked out from behind the counter, pushing a cart to retrieve the books she needed to pull for the hold shelf.

Sidney gaped. "You can't be serious. Franklin seemed perfectly normal when you saw him, didn't he, Dean?"

The cart Greta was pushing lodged itself on the lip where the floor changed from linoleum to carpet squares. She jolted to a stop.

"You saw Franklin last week?" Iris asked. "I had no idea."

"Yeah. I had a routine client meeting with him. It's still hard to imagine not working with him anymore."

"I completely forgot you were his advisor." Greta straightened out the cart. "When was your meeting with him, then?"

She had been mentally putting together a snapshot of Franklin's final days, but she'd failed to consider Dean may have been one of the last people to see Franklin alive. Hopefully, he had more information to help eliminate her as a suspect.

"It would have been Thursday night. I remember because I had a jam-packed evening. I met with both Franklin and Dolores. I didn't tell you after he passed, Iris, because I was afraid you'd worry about me." Dean dropped his chin to his chest, and Iris wrapped him in a hug, her petite frame dwarfed in his embrace.

"You can tell me anything." Iris leaned back and looked up at him with glassy eyes before aiming them at Greta. "Promise me you'll be careful. I don't like the thought of you getting mixed up in this. Especially if there's a murderer around town."

Dean shot Greta a questioning look. "Wait? Are you running your own investigation, Greta?"

"I wouldn't call it an investigation. I'm merely keeping my ears open."

"Even still, that could land you in danger." Iris stepped toward Greta, as if she was ready to defend her from any and all bad guys.

"Don't worry about me. I'm, like, the least reckless person I know." Greta hoped her joke would lighten the mood, but Iris's lip quivered.

"That's half the problem! You're too nice. You could be taken advantage of by someone who wants to hurt you."

"Nah. We've got her back." Josie came to stand next to Greta with a pile of books that needed to be shelved.

Greta clapped her hands. "See? Everything's going to be okay. I promise. But now, back to work. The books wait for no one."

Chapter Thirteen

By the end of the day, Greta was dying to talk to her mom. She'd tried her cell at three, but it had gone straight to voice mail. The same thing happened at four. Now it was pushing five, and Greta drummed her fingers on the circulation desk.

"Why don't you leave the closing up to us?" Josie suggested. "You're not going to be much help anyway."

Greta glanced around the nearly vacant library. "I'm sorry I'm so preoccupied."

"It's fine. Go. Keep us posted." Josie made a shooing motion with her hands, and Iris shot her a thumbs up.

"You guys are the best. Thank you." Greta grabbed her coat from the office and looped it over her arm, tucking it into the crook of her elbow before heading out into the parking lot. She was getting behind the wheel of her car when her cell phone rang. She nearly dropped it in her rush to answer.

"Mom! Hi."

"Hi, G. What a day!"

Greta pulled out of her parking spot and navigated toward her cabin, trying not to bark with impatience at her mom's small talk.

"...And Mr. Bernard was in court again. I swear he's had to appear four times in as many years. You'd think the man would figure out he's not allowed to catch so many bass—"

"What a guy." Greta cut her mom off with feigned interest in the notorious rouge fisherman from Churchill. "Mr. Bernard still can't seem to grasp the fishing limit, can he, after all these years? Listen, I've been waiting on pins and needles. Tell me what you heard from Lori."

Greta sat in her parked car in her driveway and waited for her mom to get to the good stuff.

"Right." Greta pictured her mom settling into the high-back swivel chair in her office. "Lori was all too willing to tell me everything she could about the case. It's shaken her up, to be honest. It doesn't sound like Detective…what's his name again?"

"Mark McHenry."

"That's it. Mark. It doesn't seem like he's very understanding of the fact Lori and the rest of you there in Larkspur aren't as used to dealing with murder as he is."

"It is a murder for sure, then?" Greta's heart sank. She'd been expecting the news, but until having it confirmed, she'd held out a sliver of hope maybe Detective McHenry had it wrong.

"Definitely murder. Official cause of death is strangulation. Lori overheard Detective McHenry filling in Chief Sorenson immediately after returning from the scene. He noticed ligature marks when he assessed the body. It seems someone strangled Franklin. Whoever did it shoved him down the stairs to make it seem like an accident."

Greta pulled her cardigan tighter around herself. "Could have fooled me."

"Well, the coroner wasn't fooled. He came out with the official cause of death already on Monday. Chief Sorenson told Lori it confirmed what Detective McHenry already knew. Apparently, the man has seen enough foul play to recognize it."

"What's the detective's story, anyway? Did Lori say?"

"He came from Chicago. I guess after he interviewed Detective McHenry, Chief Sorenson told Lori the man was looking for a fresh start in a smaller community. She didn't get anything else out of the chief about the new guy."

"Hmm." Greta pondered the minimal information at her disposal pertaining to the detective's past. Had something bad happened in Chicago? Was Detective McHenry forced to leave the city? Maybe they had that in common. She shook off the thought, not wanting to go there in her head. Greta returned her attention to her mom.

"Anyway. I told Lori she should tell the detective how she was feeling. Communication is key, after all."

"And what did Lori say?"

"The detective is being pressured by Mayor Collins to solve the case quickly, so it doesn't interfere with the fall festival next month. Lori told me she wanted to prove herself to Detective McHenry. He tasked her with some research to speed up the investigation. Apparently, they're having a hard time tracking down the book collector you told the detective Franklin was meeting with."

"That's weird. How hard can it be to find an appointment Franklin had? He kept everything written on his calendar in his office." Greta had seen the desk-sized calendar herself on several occasions.

"I guess this appointment wasn't on there." Her mom's voice faded.

"And?" Greta leaned her head back against her seat, fearing where her mom was going with this.

"And, according to Lori, Detective McHenry hinted he thought you were making it up to throw him off your scent."

"That's ridiculous. Why would I lie?"

"Lori doesn't think you did, dear," her mom soothed. "Which is another reason she's all the more determined to figure out who this guy is. The other factor at play here is that Franklin's email account was deleted."

"Seriously? By Franklin or someone else?"

"The police aren't sure. Either way, Lori wasn't able to check his recent email correspondences to see if he'd been in touch with any book collectors. The detective is working to try to restore access, but there's no telling how long that'll take. Lori did say they have a record of a series of calls to Franklin from a hospital in Karrington. So, she's working on tracking down whoever made them."

Greta frowned. "Why would a book collector be calling from the hospital in Karrington?"

"Not a clue."

Greta filed that away. Her mom had given her the next step. She was a librarian, after all. If there was one thing she was good at, it was ferreting out information. She'd start compiling a list of potential suspects based on their book-collecting profiles online.

She massaged her temple. "Alright. Anything else I should know?"

"That about covers it." Her mom paused, and when she spoke again, she sounded almost gleeful. "So, was there a pretty big crowd at the police department this morning, then?"

"I'd say so. Half the town turned out. How'd you pull it off?"

"You know the sewing squad. Our members are from all over. A couple of them, like Lori, come from Larkspur. I figured they would take our conversation and spread it like wildfire, and to ensure that happened, I let slip you were a suspect."

"Mom!" Greta pressed her palm to her forehead. "I was trying to keep my name out of the conversation. What will people think of me?"

"It was a calculated revelation." Her mom's tone was nonchalant. "Besides, my friends were indignant on your behalf, naturally. I suspected they'd give the new detective a piece of their mind one way or another. From the sounds of it, they told their friends and neighbors, and he had quite the busy day today."

Greta couldn't argue with her there, and she was grateful for her mom's connections. Larkspur and Churchill were only an hour's drive apart, and the crossover between the small towns might just work in her favor if her reputation was thrown into question—more so than it already had been. Greta pulled her lips into her mouth and worked her jaw before speaking again. "Okay. Thank you for digging into this some more for me. I'll let you know what I learn."

"You better. The only reason I'm helping you with this is because I trust the head on your shoulders, G. I gave your dad a hard time about being overly cautious, but I mean it. I expect you to keep us posted, and if this takes a turn toward danger, you need to remove yourself entirely. Do you hear me?"

"I'll be fine, Mom. All I'm going to do is start researching this evasive book collector. No harm will come of that. Thank you for caring so much. I'll be in touch."

71

Evidently satisfied with the answer, her mom hung up the phone.

Greta stared out her windshield at her still-dark cabin. She was burning to get started with some research, and she made the split-second decision to go back to the library. She would accomplish much more with the databases there and would be far less distracted than she would be at home.

After checking on Biff, she made the drive back into town. Greta hesitated when she let herself into the now sleepy municipal complex. She was sure there was a police officer on duty somewhere in the bowels of the building, but all was quiet on the library end as she used her key and unlocked the glass doors. The space seemed especially eerie, with dust particles illuminated by the late-day sun. Greta's gaze darted around the open circulation desk area and through the stacks of books. The printer in the middle of the space kicked on, recalibrating itself, and Greta flinched. The hairs on her arms stood at attention, and for a split second, she questioned her decision to come back to the deserted library. But then she gave herself a mental shake. She was perfectly safe. This was her place of employment—her happy place. There was no need to jump at shadows.

Greta marched into the library and took a seat at the research table where Dean and Sidney had set up shop for most of the week. "Alright. Book collectors based in Wisconsin, here I come."

Greta wasn't sure how much time had passed, but it was now completely dark outside. All she had to show for her efforts was a lengthy list of book collectors' names mentioned in different rare book society membership indexes, but without any filtering factors, trying to narrow down the names would take all night.

Greta leaned back in the old wooden chair and stretched her arms over her head. At some point during her research, she'd tugged the chain cord on the desk lamp. The dim glow emanating from beneath the emerald glass shade was the only light in the space.

A clunk sounded from somewhere in the back of the library. Greta froze in her seat, her eyes darting toward the non-fiction section. "Hello?"

Chapter Fourteen

G reta stood, her legs quivering as she grabbed for her cell phone and tapped on the flashlight. The narrow beam lit up the floor in front of her, and she pointed it at the stacks, taking a steadying breath. "Is anyone here?"

She took a hesitant step forward. The floor creaked, but not under her. The sound seemed to come from near the far wall of the library. Greta had the total body sensation of knowing she wasn't alone—her throat went dry, and her limbs felt hot and cold at once. Who else was here? Had they been here since she arrived? The thought caused beads of sweat to form on her hairline.

"I'm sorry. The library is closed," she called out. "If you need assistance or a place to stay, I would be glad to help you."

Greta tiptoed forward, keeping her light in front of her. She strained her ears, listening for any sign of movement. Was someone else breathing nearby? Or was her brain playing tricks on her? Her blood raced through her veins as she made it three-quarters of the way down the non-fiction aisle. There was a book in the middle of the floor, and she bent to retrieve it—a biography of Bernie Madoff. She hadn't read it herself—Ponzi schemes and nefarious criminals weren't her jam—but she'd placed the book in a stand just the other day, hoping it would get snapped up by an intrigued patron. Had it tumbled to the floor on its own, or did someone knock it off the shelf? Greta set the book back in the open stand and continued down the aisle.

Reaching the end, she held her breath and peeked around the corner. The perpendicular corridor was empty. At the end, there was a closed door that led to the hallway that joined the library to the mayor's office and the police department. Fighting not to dwell on the tingling of nerves at the base of her neck, Greta strode forward and tried the handle. As she expected, it was locked. They never used that exit. Greta kept the key in her office. This was so weird.

Just then, Greta heard the sound of the library's front door latch click.

"Hey, wait!" Her curiosity outweighed her fear, and she bolted back in the direction of the circulation desk. When she made it to the front door, there was no one around. Greta shoved open the door, glanced left and right, and ran out the exterior doors of the municipal complex.

The parking lot was deserted. Across the street, the small outdoor eating area in front of Mugs & Hugs was half full, upright space heaters cozying up the night air. A man walked his dog down the sidewalk a half block down, but nothing looked out of place.

Greta did one last scan of the area, her skin prickling with her adrenaline. She swore someone was watching her, and she couldn't get back inside fast enough. She turned and nearly ran smack dab into Detective McHenry.

"Oh! Detective. My apologies. You startled me."

"Miss Plank. What a surprise." Detective McHenry's voice was cool as he stepped to the side. "What are you doing here?"

Greta narrowed her eyes, forcing herself to stand even straighter. "I work here."

"At this hour?"

Even in the dim light, Greta didn't miss the suspicion splayed across the detective's face. She debated how much to share with him. In the end, the heebie-jeebies at knowing she hadn't been alone in the library spurred her to tell Detective McHenry what happened.

He looked past her. "You're sure there was someone in here?"

"I swear I heard the door latch open, but I was at the back of the library, so I couldn't see who it was."

"Show me where you were and what happened."

Greta flipped on the overhead lights and led him around the library, retracing her steps. "I was just getting ready to leave when I heard the noises," she explained after they returned to the front entrance. "It was probably just someone who needed a warm place to spend the night."

McHenry grunted. He strode toward the windowed wall and stared out into the darkened hallway.

Greta took the chance to quickly close the browser window she'd been using and power down the computer before he could see what she'd been researching. No use raising his hackles or getting Lori in trouble for letting slip that the police were looking for the book collector.

He spun around. "That doesn't explain why they felt the need to run away when they did. Why not just take you up on your offer to help them? I'm going to have an officer pull the video footage from the building's security cameras. See if we can get anything off of them. But if anything else ever feels off, don't hesitate to reach out to me, Miss Plank."

"Thank you. I will." Greta smiled, slinging her bag over her arm.

With Detective McHenry in the library, everything felt much less spooky. She was sure there was a perfectly reasonable explanation for what had happened, and she doubted she'd have issues going ahead. Still, she appreciated that the detective didn't blow her off or dismiss her ordeal as nothing.

He *was* good at his job—at least when he wasn't accusing her of murder. Which reminded her...

"Long day?" She shot him an innocent look.

Detective McHenry actually laughed, and Greta had to force herself not to gasp. She'd never seen the man show any shred of emotion beyond stoic, indifferent, and accusatory. His face completely transformed when he wasn't scowling, and Greta didn't hate it.

"You could say that. I'm assuming you had something to do with the stream of people who came by to see me today? They were all quick to inform me of your innocence."

A scrape of heat worked its way up Greta's back. "I had nothing to do with the crowds." She didn't dare tell the detective that, while she might not have been behind his eventful day, her mom most certainly was. "But I'm guessing the news of Franklin's murder got out then?"

The smile evaporated from his face. "I'm afraid so."

"What did you learn? Anything?"

Detective McHenry just stared at Greta.

"What? It was worth a try." When the detective's face remained impassive, Greta fought an eye roll. She motioned toward the door. "I'll be going now."

Chapter Fifteen

Greta hurried into Mugs & Hugs the next morning. Once again, the sky was dark, and the air hung heavy with rain. The café door rattled shut behind Greta, and she tried to shake the dampness from her bones.

Allison rushed up to her and pulled her into an empty alcove off to one side of the café. "Okay, spill."

Greta blinked. "Spill what?"

"Tell me everything about your heated conversation with Detective McHot Face last night."

"What are you talking about?" Greta's voice came out in a hiss. She looked around, relieved to see everyone else was occupied. She waved to Sidney, who caught her gaze from a table by the front window, before turning back to a smirking Allison.

"Don't play coy. I saw the two of you practically nose to nose just outside the library doors." Allison's eyes twinkled. "Out with it."

Greta sighed, sinking into the chair at the table tucked into the niche. Allison sat opposite her, staring at Greta expectantly.

"I wish I had more to tell. Detective McHenry caught me in the library after hours."

"Juicy."

Greta snorted. "Hardly. I was finishing up some research and getting ready to leave." Greta quickly filled Allison in on what her mom had found out and then on the events that transpired at the library that led to her running into Detective McHenry.

Allison grimaced. "That's creepy. And you didn't make any progress with the book collector, then?"

"I'm afraid not. I'm not sure what to do next."

"You'll figure it out. Are you going to the funeral today?"

"I am." Greta swallowed, trying to loosen the sudden constriction in her throat.

Allison gave her a sympathetic look, her warm brown skin glowing with kindness as she stood. "Hang in there."

Greta offered her a weak smile, and when Allison returned to work, she squeezed her eyes shut and willed her thundering pulse to quiet.

The last funeral she'd attended was her sister's, and she'd died almost ten years ago in a snowboarding accident. Kelly had been out with some friends, and they were riding in and out of a wooded area. From what they could piece together from her friends' accounts, Kelly hit a tree and died instantly. Losing her had rocked Greta's world.

She dragged in a ragged breath, images of the hospital waiting room where the doctor told them the news formed in her mind as if it had happened yesterday. She could still hear her mom's sobs.

Greta focused on breathing in through her nose and out through her mouth, giving herself a mental pep talk until her heart stopped racing.

You can do this. Think happy thoughts. Everything will be okay.

After a couple minutes of repeating the mantra, Greta's mind settled. She rose and made her way to the counter to order her drink. As soon as Allison handed it over, she took a slow sip of the steaming liquid, and her resolve strengthened. There was nothing like a shot of caffeine for fortitude.

Sidney's head popped up from her computer as Greta walked past. "Hey! Can you sit for a minute?"

Greta blew into the opening of her to-go cup lid. "Actually, no. I've got to run to the library. I'm only working a half day today before I head out for Franklin's funeral."

Sidney's eyes fogged over, and she frowned. "That's right. Dean will be there, too." She glanced over Greta's shoulder, checking their surroundings, before lowering her voice. "Have you found out anything more about

Franklin's death? Anything to prove your innocence?"

"I'm still working to piece things together. The lead detective doesn't hold me in high esteem, which is a bummer. Hard to get any information out of him."

"He's new to town, right? What's his deal?"

"I'm not sure yet, but Chief Sorenson has nothing but good things to say about him."

Sidney stuck up her nose. "I don't care what the chief has to say. If the detective is accusing you of harming your friend, he's got a screw loose. There's obviously some mistake."

Greta felt her spirits lift with Sidney's support. "I'm trying to give him the benefit of the doubt, but he's not making it easy." She motioned to Sidney's computer. "I should let you get to work and get my butt to the library."

Sidney waved, and Greta left the café.

That afternoon, after stopping by her cabin to change into her black skirt and a sweater and refill Biff's food bowl, Greta walked into the funeral home for Franklin's visitation.

"Welcome." A funeral home attendant offered her a somber smile. "Please, come in. Since Franklin's parents are deceased, and he was an only child, there are no family members to greet today."

Greta's stomach knotted when she realized Franklin didn't have any living relatives. Who organized his funeral? Should she have done more? She never put it together he was actually all alone in the world. He rarely spoke of his family. She once heard him refer to his mother as "mumsy" and Greta thought it was the most endearing thing. She'd asked him about the term of endearment, but he ignored her and changed the subject. Anytime she tried to get Franklin to open up about his family, he'd done the opposite and all but closed down. Eventually, Greta stopped asking.

A lump formed in her throat. She should have tried harder to learn more about him—beyond books and the day-to-day. She should have dug deeper.

"We'll hold a brief memorial service in about an hour. Go ahead and mingle, pray, and share memories with others in attendance." The funeral home attendant bowed his head and moved on to speak to the next guest.

Dolores approached from across the room with a woman who appeared to be around Greta's age. Greta reached out to give Dolores a hug, grateful to see a friendly face. "How're you doing, Dolores?"

"Been better." Dolores dropped her gaze. "This is so sad. This is my daughter, Stacey. She drove up from Wausau to be with me tonight. She teaches eighth-grade language arts there."

"It's nice to meet you." Greta and Stacey shook hands before Greta turned to Dolores. "Any idea who put this service together?"

"Not a clue."

"Me either. I wish I would have known. I figured he didn't have much for family, but I assumed there would be at least a distant relative or someone to take care of things."

Dolores's eyes filled with tears. "We never got to know each other well enough to get to family talk."

Stacey pulled her mom into a hug and held her while Dolores cried silent tears.

Greta looked away to give her some privacy and took in the rest of the people in attendance. She identified a scattering of folks from around town. Franklin's physical therapist was there. Tony, if Greta remembered correctly. There were two men in particular whom Greta didn't recognize. One stood on the far side of the room dressed in a brown tweed jacket and wearing black-rimmed spectacles. His face was partially covered in a scraggly beard. The other was younger and cleaner cut. He wore a dove gray suit and black tie. He appeared much more approachable than the disheveled man, probably because he, too, was actively looking around. His gaze connected with Greta's, and he offered her the sort of subdued smile that was appropriate for the occasion. She returned it until her attention was caught up by Dolores, who pulled back from Stacey and grabbed a tissue.

Greta placed her hand on Dolores's shoulder and gave it a comforting squeeze. "I'm sure Franklin valued the time you did have together."

Dolores dabbed her nose. "I know I did."

"Pardon me."

Greta looked up and found herself staring into the blue eyes of the man in the gray suit.

"I don't mean to interrupt." He held out his hand. "My name is Liam Shark. I'm Mr. Halloway's attorney. I couldn't help but notice you appear to have been friends of Franklin?"

Greta clasped his hand. "Greta Plank. I'm the director of the library in Larkspur, and I was Franklin's neighbor." Greta glanced at Dolores, who was still trying to compose herself. "This is Dolores Jenkins. She was a friend of Franklin's, as well. And Dolores's daughter, Stacey."

"I'm so sorry for your loss." Liam looked between Greta and Dolores, his gaze coming to rest on Greta. "I hope the memorial service will help to give you some closure."

Greta motioned around the room. "Was this your doing?"

"I set up the service, yes. Franklin designated me as his executor when I took over as his attorney last year."

"Were you and Franklin close?" Dolores wiped her nose with a tissue one last time before stowing it in her coat pocket.

"We had a typical attorney-client relationship. He wasn't one to overshare, but we got along well enough. He appreciated my organization. He entrusted me with his will."

Greta gasped before tucking her mouth in on itself. She wasn't quick enough to stem her outburst, and Liam tilted his head in question.

"I sort of forgot Franklin would have a will. I mean, of course, he would, but I didn't even consider it. His death was so sudden," she added by way of explanation.

Dolores grabbed for her hand and pressed it, and Liam's eyes gleamed with sympathy. "Of course. And we typically don't deal with the will until after the funeral or burial. One thing at a time. But, I'm glad to have met you." His attention lingered on Greta for a beat before sweeping to Dolores. "Both of you."

When Liam said goodbye, Greta tracked him as he worked his way across the room. As he passed by the front door to the funeral home, it opened. Dean walked in...followed a moment later by Detective McHenry.

Chapter Sixteen

"What's he doing here?" Dolores sounded defensive.

Stacey followed her mom's line of sight. "Who *is* he?"

"Detective Mark McHenry of the Larkspur Police Department. He's in charge of Franklin's case. I'm not sure why he's here." Greta waved to Dean, who started in her direction, and because she had terrible luck, her gaze then connected with Detective McHenry's. Her pulse jumped, and Greta fought the urge to stomp her foot. All she wanted to do was mourn the loss of her friend, and now she had to do it with a suspicious detective looking over her shoulder.

"Hi, Dean." Greta forced a smile when he made it to her side, but she was distracted by Detective McHenry. "Ugh. He's coming this way. Would it be too much to ask for him to leave us alone, just today?"

"Amen," Dolores agreed.

"Is this the same detective who questioned you?" Stacey asked her mother, and Dolores bobbed her head up and down.

"He questioned me, too," Greta said. "I'm high on his list of suspects."

Stacey pulled herself up to her full height. "He told Mom not to leave town. Come on, let's go over there." Stacey put her arm around Dolores and steered her toward another group of mourners.

Greta was about to follow, but a tap on her shoulder stopped her. She turned to find Detective McHenry giving her his ever-present glower.

"Miss Plank." He slipped his hands into his pockets. "We meet again."

"Detective McHenry, I didn't expect to see you here."

"Just paying my respects." Detective McHenry's gaze left hers and roved around the room.

Greta shot Dean a look, but he shrugged.

Out of habit, Greta started talking to fill the void in the conversation. "They're going to start with the service soon. See the man over there?" Greta pointed her chin toward Liam, who was talking to Tony, the physical therapist, and both Dean and Detective McHenry followed her gaze. "He's Franklin's lawyer and estate manager. Have either of you spoken with him?"

"Liam Shark, yes." Detective McHenry's tone was anything but genial. "He's the keeper of Franklin's will, and he's taking his merry time with it." He rolled his inky eyes.

Greta bit the inside of her lip. Could Liam be stalling the will disclosure on purpose?

"I'm sure he has his reasons." Dean's comment rang diplomatic, but Greta was determined to pull on this thread.

"Liam told me they like to do one thing at a time, first the funeral, then the will. Is that not typical?"

Detective McHenry continued to study the room. "Depends. He has to take the will to probate court to get it validated, and afterward, he technically has three months to notify any beneficiaries. Typically, it doesn't take the full ninety days. It shouldn't, anyway. I'm anxious to get my eyes on the will in case there's something in it that'll help with the investigation. After he takes it to court, it becomes public record, so I'll be able to view it. Of course, I'll attend any will reading Liam holds to watch people's reactions."

Greta stared at him until Detective McHenry swung his focus back to her. He arched one brow.

"Do you seek out trouble everywhere, then?" she asked.

"Sort of in the job description."

"Pity. You might get farther by being nicer, you know." Greta shot him a smile, but he didn't bite.

"Not in my experience."

Her smile fell. "Okay, then. Why did you give Dolores a reason to believe you think she's guilty?" It was one thing to come after her, but to come after one of the town's matriarchs was quite another story.

Detective McHenry didn't even blink. "I never said I thought she was guilty. I asked her the same questions I've asked everyone, and I'll see where the investigation takes me."

"I can tell you Dolores is innocent, and you could save yourself a lot of trouble if you started looking at suspects other than her."

"Suspects like you?"

Greta clenched and unclenched her fists at her sides, willing her blood pressure to return to a healthy level. "I resent that."

She had half a mind to think Detective McHenry was only there because he was following her. Was that why he'd been at the municipal center last night? Had he been tracking her? The thought of that made her stomach do a tuck and roll.

Detective McHenry just tipped his head to the side and remained silent. The man was infuriating.

"Okay. Okay. Greta, we should find a seat." Dean placed his hand on her back, his apprehension with the rising strain in the conversation evident in his darting expression.

Greta turned away from the detective, allowing Dean to lead her to the chairs. She didn't know what she had to do to convince Detective McHenry of her innocence, but she'd figure out a way. For now, she needed to regroup.

She took a deep breath and panned the crowd for Dolores and Stacey. The man in the tweed jacket was leaning against the far wall, looking uncomfortable and out of place. Greta empathized with him, in all his awkwardness.

"You know what? I'll be right back."

"You okay?"

"Yep. I see someone I want to speak with."

Dean said he'd find her for the service and peeled off to talk to someone else.

Greta made her way to the opposite side of the room. She hated the effect the detective had on her. It was as if her world dimmed after each of their encounters. If she could just do something to counteract it, she'd feel better. Her plan was to strike up a conversation with the man in the tweed coat, whoever he was. Maybe she could brighten his spirits as well as her own.

She was almost to his side when a bell tinkled. Greta stopped and turned to the source of the sound as everyone in attendance quieted. The man walked away and took a single open seat.

She sighed. It was the thought that counted.

"Ladies and gentlemen, if I could please have your attention." Liam stood front and center. "I'd like to start by saying a few words. I'll open the floor, and I'd encourage anyone who is comfortable doing so to share memories and stories about Franklin." Liam adjusted the microphone in its stand attached to a podium. The reverberations echoed throughout the room. "Let's begin, shall we?"

Everyone filed to a seat. Greta spotted Dolores and Stacey and, grateful to put some distance between herself and the detective, slid into a chair in their row. Dean joined her a second later. She tried to relax, but her insides cartwheeled, and her breath came in shallow bursts.

The next thirty minutes were spent in recollection of Franklin. As individuals shared, Greta was able to put names to faces. A couple folks had made the trip from Franklin's childhood hometown in central Iowa.

Tony spoke about Franklin's work ethic and his dedication to his health, even after being dealt a rough hand.

The doctor who had treated Franklin after the automobile accident left him paralyzed stood and spoke about the attitude Franklin had when he found out he would never walk again.

"I told him, 'Mr. Halloway, I am so sorry.' And Franklin, well, he nodded, thanked me, and turned his head to face the other side of the room. Our conversation was finished, and I figured he wouldn't want to have anything to do with me ever again. Not only was I the surgeon who couldn't do anything to bring his mobility back, but I was also the voice he would always hear in his head telling him he couldn't walk." The doctor paused, collecting himself.

Greta pulled at her skirt, anxious to hear what came next. Franklin never told her much about the accident beyond the cause—drunk driver—and the outcome—a wheelchair.

The doctor continued his speech. "But the next day, I was doing rounds, and I glanced into Franklin's room. He was propped up in bed, face still bandaged from the accident, and he waved me in. I entered and waited for him to speak first. 'Thank you for telling it to me straight. I'll be okay.' That's what he said to me. Now, of course, the mental and emotional ramifications of paralysis would take their toll on Franklin. I understood as much, but his simple declaration of thanks and the assurance he'd be okay had me believing him. We kept in touch. Mostly via email over the years. It's safe to say Franklin was more than okay. He had a home he loved and had hobbies he enjoyed. He commanded his space, from what I could tell. I'm only sorry I didn't get up here to visit him before he passed. May he rest in peace, and may he be an example to all of us of making lemonade out of lemons."

The doctor sat down, and Greta swallowed the knob in her throat, a sharp pain behind her eyes a sign of the tears she was fighting. Here she thought she was Franklin's only friend. Turns out, he had a lot of people who loved him. Greta's heart warmed, and then broke open. He was taken too soon. She swiped at the tears trickling down her cheeks as Liam invited any remaining guests to share stories.

Greta raised her hand, and Liam motioned for her to come forward. She walked to the front of the room and took the microphone before she could second-guess herself.

"My name is Greta Plank. Franklin and I were neighbors, and we both loved the lake and books. Even though we knew each other for just a few months, I considered Franklin a great friend, someone I could always talk to, and who looked out for me like a father figure. I will miss him terribly."

Greta's throat closed up then, and she handed the microphone back to Liam. She walked quickly back to her seat as images of Kelly's funeral flooded her vision, blurring with her tears. Detective McHenry's gaze was heavy on the side of her face. He was undoubtedly analyzing her words to try to pin guilt upon her. Greta shuddered. She shouldn't have said anything at all.

No.

Franklin was her friend. She was not going to let Detective McHenry and his faulty hypothesis dictate what she would or wouldn't do to honor his life. Still, Greta couldn't make out Liam's last few words over the pounding of her heart in her ears.

A minister approached the front of the room, and Greta closed her eyes as he prayed for eternal rest and perpetual light to shine upon Franklin. When the group echoed his "Amen," Greta blinked, relieved to find her composure returning. People stood and started mingling.

"What a beautiful memorial." Dolores leaned back in the chair next to Greta, gripping Stacey's hand.

Stacey agreed. "It was a lovely tribute. I would have liked to have met Franklin myself."

Dolores choked up again, and Greta dropped her gaze, fearing one glimpse of Dolores crying might send her along the same path.

Dean bid Greta goodbye and told her he would see her at the library soon. Greta watched him leave, and when she turned to Dolores, she caught sight of Liam. He smiled and made his way toward her. Behind him, Detective McHenry stood scowling, but Greta ignored him.

Greta placed her hand on Liam's forearm when he reached her side. "Thank you for pulling this all together for Franklin."

He dipped his head at her appreciation. "It's the least I could do. As we all heard today, Franklin was an exceptional man." Greta's eyes misted, and Liam cleared his throat. "I know this isn't really an appropriate time, but I've got to think Franklin wouldn't mind me asking."

Greta met his nervous gaze. "Go on."

"I was wondering if you'd like to get dinner with me at some point."

"Oh!" Greta took a slight step back. She hadn't dated in over a year—not since everything went to pot with Nathan, the two-faced liar. She tried to blot out a flash of renewed anger and humiliation at the thought of her ex and returned her focus to Liam, who stared uncertainly back at her.

"Um, sure," she said. Her response was more dictated by her desire to avoid awkwardness and keep everyone happy than anything else, and Liam visibly relaxed, so...mission accomplished?

They made quick work of exchanging personal phone numbers before

Greta said her goodbyes and left the funeral home, making an effort not to make eye contact with Detective McHenry.

She drove back to Larkspur in silence, the events of the day on a loop in her brain, making her dizzy. Finally, she pressed a button on her steering wheel and spoke into the voice-controlled speaker. "Call Mom."

Calling Mom, the machine parroted. The phone rang twice before her mom's cheery voice picked up on the other end.

"Hello, G."

"Hi, Mom."

Immediately, her mom's voice filled with concern. "What happened?"

"What? What do you mean? Nothing happened."

There was a pause on the other end of the line. "You're sure? You don't sound like yourself."

Greta let out a shaky breath. Leave it to her mom to have her all figured out from the tone of her voice and two simple words. Moms are something else.

As she drove toward her cabin, she told her mom everything: how she was sad she'd missed out on so much time with Franklin and about Liam asking her out. "I'm okay. I guess I just...I don't know. I needed to talk. It's a lot, the ongoing investigation into Franklin's death. And the funeral just reminded me of Kelly."

"That's understandable. Her death is going to stay with you your whole life, and it's going to sneak up on you in different ways at different times. It's no surprise funerals are especially hard."

"Does it happen to you, too?" Greta's question came out a hair above a whisper.

"My grief has ebbed and flowed over the years, too, honey. As a parent, burying a child is a nightmare. One you never get to wake up from. But your father and I have learned to cope. We remember all Kelly brought to our life, and we keep in mind she wouldn't want us to stop living because she's gone."

Greta sighed, turning onto Lakeside Drive. The rain had stopped, and the sun was fighting its way through the clouds. "I just hate when things aren't happy, and this is very much something I can't make happier."

Her mom chuckled. "Being cheerful is a great gift, G. But you also have to let yourself feel real feelings, too. You like to keep things all tidy and wrapped in a nice little box because it makes you feel in control, but life is messy. More like a package that's ripped open or split at the seams with its contents spewed everywhere."

Greta pulled into her driveway. "That's quite the visual. Not sure I like it, but I'm home now. I just needed someone to talk to. Thanks for listening. Give Dad my love, okay?"

"Call anytime. We love you. Oh, and keep us posted on Liam."

Her mom sang Liam's name, and Greta rolled her eyes. She should have known she was opening herself up to teasing by mentioning him. Then again, it was a small price to pay for the accompanying wisdom and comfort. She'd just have to set her mom straight some other time. "Yeah, yeah. Love you, too, Mom. Bye."

Greta ended the call with the button on her steering wheel. She grabbed her bag and walked into her house. She scooped up Biff and headed straight for her deck. The sun was hitting the water at a perfect angle, sending glittering sparkles across the trees on the far side of the lake, magnifying their changing colors. Pumpkin orange and corncob yellow leaves were like highlights against the brown branches to which they clung. Greta let the slightly sugary scent of the air tickle her nostrils as she took in the scenery, silently stroking Biff's coat.

From her memories of Kelly, she let her mind bounce to Franklin and then to Liam Shark.

Franklin's attorney *did* seem like a nice man, but what had she been thinking, agreeing to go out with him? She hadn't been thinking. She'd been panicking. Because she was nowhere near ready to date. She didn't know if she'd ever be ready.

Greta groaned. "What am I going to do, Biff?"

In response, the cat wiggled in her arms, so she turned and slid open the door, setting him down inside. He whizzed off toward the kitchen. Greta went to follow, but her gaze caught on the roof of Franklin's cabin through the trees.

She hadn't told Franklin what had happened with Nathan. It was too humiliating. Still, if Franklin were alive right now, he'd be barking at her to not be a baby and to go and have a nice time with Liam. After all, he'd chosen the man as his estate manager. If that wasn't a ringing endorsement, what was?

Greta paused and turned over the idea of a date in her mind, looking at it from all angles—trying to give it a fair chance. For Franklin's sake.

Nope. Still not working for her.

But maybe she should think about it differently. What if she didn't think about it so much as a date but as part of the investigation? Because if she could get Liam talking about Franklin, she might learn something relevant to the case. After all, who needed romance? She had a mystery to solve.

Chapter Seventeen

The sun shone all day Friday, and Greta's mood was lighter as a result. She pushed through the library doors at the end of the workday and walked into the parking lot with Iris and Josie.

"Who's up for one last early morning paddleboarding adventure?" Greta spun around and walked backward to face her friends.

Iris shivered. "Won't the water be freezing?"

Greta grinned and couldn't help but tease her friend. "The goal is to stay out of the water."

"Very funny. Just because you grow leaps and bounds in the coordination department when you're around the lake doesn't mean the rest of us do."

"Are you in or not?"

"Not. Sorry." Iris screwed up her mouth, not sounding sorry at all. "I'm going to sleep in and grab breakfast with Dean."

"Okay. What about you, Josie?"

"I'll join you. Can I use your spare board?"

"For sure. Meet me at my house at six thirty?"

Josie agreed, and Greta cheered. "I've been itching to get out. I'm glad the weather is going to cooperate." She held her hand up, shielding the sun from her eyes, but letting it warm her face.

"Anyone want to grab a bite at the café?" Josie asked.

"Now?" Iris faced Josie.

"No, next week Tuesday," Josie deadpanned. "Yes, now, silly. I could go for a sandwich."

Greta nodded. "Sounds good to me."

"Why not?" Iris said.

The trio changed course and headed across the parking lot.

Mugs & Hugs was packed. Since it was Friday night, folks were decked out in purple and black, the school colors of the Larkspur Lancers.

"Is it a home game tonight, Mr. Williams?" Greta asked an older gentleman who she recognized as a library regular. He was slowly making his way through Tom Clancy's backlist.

"Indeed, it is. Should be a good contest. Mapleton has a solid team this year, but we have their number."

Greta shot him a thumbs-up. Her dad was the varsity coach in Churchill growing up, and she enjoyed football. Greta made a mental note to get to a game or two yet this fall. She wanted to support some of the student athletes she'd met during the summer reading program.

They settled into a booth, and Allison waved at the trio from behind the counter where she was manning the cash register. A group of teenagers in purple hoodies were selecting pastries from the glass case Allison kept heartily stocked with an assortment of mouthwatering baked goods. A young waitress placed water glasses at the table, promising to be back to get their food orders shortly.

"So." Iris leaned over the table, resting her elbows in front of her. "Dean is talking about building a new house and moving in together."

"What? When? Where? How do you feel?" The questions cascaded from her lips, and Greta had to clamp her mouth shut before she gave Iris any more of the third degree.

Iris grinned shyly. "I'm not sure. There's no definite plan yet, but he's looking into purchasing lakefront land. It's sort of sooner than I expected, but it all feels so right."

"That's great." Greta kicked Josie's shin under the table. "Isn't it, Jos?"

Josie grunted upon contact and glared at her. Greta stared pointedly back, expanding her eyes and giving an imperceptible nod in Iris's direction, willing her friend to say something.

Josie sniffed. "I don't know, Iris."

Greta wanted to groan, but then Josie reached across the table and put her hand on top of Iris's. "It's your call. You should make sure you're completely comfortable before you jump into anything."

"I know, I know." Iris swirled her straw around her drink.

Greta relaxed her rigid posture. *Crisis averted.*

"Nothing's happening immediately." Iris took a swig of water. "He brought it up the other night, and I got all those butterflies in my stomach."

"What are these butterflies you speak of? It's been so long since I've experienced them, I assumed they'd gone extinct." Josie laced her voice with longing.

"Same here." Greta chuckled, even as her mind flew to Liam. While he didn't give her butterflies, she couldn't deny she was anticipating their time together with great interest—at least since she'd hatched her intelligence-gathering plan. She hadn't told her friends about it yet, and it didn't seem like the best time to turn the attention onto herself, so Greta refocused on the conversation and Iris. "We support you. Whatever you decide. It's good to see you happy. Is Dean taking good care of you?"

Iris blushed. "He's been nothing but a gentleman."

"Good." Josie squeezed Iris's hand before letting go and reaching for her glass.

Allison appeared next to their booth. "Hey, you three. Sorry. I finally snuck away. I swear teenagers these days cannot make a decision."

"It's because all of your cookies are amazing. I have a hard time choosing, too." Greta licked her lips, and it wasn't even for show. Allison made a white chocolate peppermint cookie that was the stuff of goals and dreams. Then again, her peanut butter delights were equally as wonderful. "What's new with you?"

Allison tugged at the red and white polka-dotted scarf she had tied like a headband, glancing left and right. "I heard something. Well, I saw something."

Greta's ears perked up to rival her taste buds. She scooted over on her side of the booth and patted the bench. "Do tell."

Allison tossed a glance toward the register before sliding in next to Greta. "Ed was in here earlier today, and he wasn't alone. He was with a woman."

"Did you recognize her?" Josie asked.

"I've never seen her before. And I know most everyone around here."

Greta couldn't help but smile at the truth in Allison's words. She'd been in town for less than six months, and even she knew that anybody who was anybody passed through these doors. Allison was definitely a reliable source.

"Anyway, at first, I thought she was a tourist or someone staying at one of his rentals. But she was dressed to the nines. Her pantsuit fit her perfectly. She had chestnut-colored hair, blown out and everything. And I heard them talking. The café was pretty empty at the time, so even though they were speaking in hushed tones, I could still pick up bits and pieces of what they were saying."

"Eavesdropping. Nice." Josie grinned.

"Darn right. Town news isn't going to find itself out." Allison smirked. "Anyway, I could tell what they were talking about was stressing Ed out more than it was this mystery woman. He kept darting his gaze around to make sure they weren't being overheard. Very fishy. The vixen did a lot of the talking. At one point, she stared him down and said, 'If you can't close, I'm out. You know the deal.' And Ed hissed back, 'I can close. The plan is working, you have to give me a little more time.' Then the woman glared at him before standing abruptly. 'You know the deal,' she repeated again, and she walked out."

Greta had sucked in a breath and was holding it, hanging on Allison's every word. Now she exhaled. "What did Ed do?"

"He sipped his coffee for a couple minutes before standing up and leaving. That's all I got." Allison put her palms down on the table, pushing herself out of the booth to stand. "So, let me know if you make anything out of it. I've got to get back to work. Soon, I want details from you about where your"—she whispered the word—"investigation is at."

As she watched Allison walk away, Greta chewed on what she'd learned from her. Was Ed trying to close on Franklin's house? Could his conversation with this woman have been about the new development he told Greta about?

94

"So." Iris interrupted Greta's thoughts. "What are you going to do next?"

"I've got to get more information about Ed." Greta drummed her fingers on the table. "What is he up to?"

Josie tapped her temple, looking pensive. "And who's the mystery woman."

"Exactly."

"How do you plan to get this information, though?" Iris looked apprehensively between Josie and Greta.

"Not sure. I'll come up with something," Greta said.

"Better you than me." Iris shrank in her seat. "All this mystery business has me on edge. Why can't people be nice?"

Greta smiled. "People are nice. Larkspur is like the poster town of Midwest Nice. But I can't sit on this knowledge and not do anything about it."

"I suppose not," Iris said begrudgingly, and judging by the wrinkles puckering her usually smooth forehead, she didn't like any of it.

"You focus on Dean and leave the mystery to me." Greta wiggled her eyebrows.

Iris's features immediately smoothed, and her face took on the distinct glow of puppy love. "Deal. But I'll help you in any way I can."

"Me, too. What's your plan for Ed?" Josie asked.

Greta looked up at the one-of-a-kind clock hanging behind the counter. Allison had fashioned it herself out of an old China plate and a clock kit. The delicate blue and yellow flower pattern sat softly behind the harsh black hands of time.

"It's only six o'clock. I might run over to the resort and poke around a little before I head home for the night."

"Wish I could join you, but I've got that virtual continuing ed class tonight, and the library is paying for it. I can't miss," Josie said.

"And I promised my parents I would come and see them. I've been MIA lately, so I don't want to reschedule on them again." Iris's eyes held a nervous glint. "I don't like the thought of you going alone. What if you get caught?"

Greta waved her off. "I'm not doing anything wrong. Besides, who's going to catch me?"

Chapter Eighteen

Twenty minutes later, Greta had polished off her dinner—homemade chicken salad on a buttery croissant with a side of sweet potato chips—and was in her car, making the short drive to Kennedy's Cozy Cottages. She hadn't quite figured out what her reason for being there would be, but she was hoping if she could sneak around unnoticed, she wouldn't need to answer to anyone.

With the idea to stay hidden in mind, she drove past the main entrance that led to the cluster of cottages and pulled over to the side of the road fifty yards beyond. There was a decent-sized patch of grass in one spot before the line of trees started. If she kept her car parked here, it would be masked from anyone who may be in the office. She could only hope if Ed was leaving for the night, he'd turn left out of the resort and head toward town rather than right and discover her car.

Greta cut the ignition and sat back in her seat. "Okay, think," she muttered to herself as she sorted out what she was trying to accomplish. She needed information on Ed's mystery woman and on the deal the two of them had. What did Ed need to close on, and what had he told the woman was supposedly working?

Greta opened her car door and pressed it shut with only a dull snick. She glanced up and down a deserted Lakeside Drive and blew out a breath. "You've got this."

She was going to be the queen of self-talk by the time this whole ordeal was over.

She set off and backtracked into the woods toward the resort. Her low-heeled ankle boots weren't ideal for this sort of detective work, but at least she wasn't wearing a skirt. The slacks and chunky, cable-knit sweater she'd donned this morning were proving to be a good pick.

Greta walked among the trees until the tiny office came into view. There was a small clearing between the wooded area where she stood and the building. She'd have to cross it and hunker down outside the window on the backside of the office and either listen in or, if Ed wasn't around, take her chances trying to sneak inside. Greta hoped to overhear or find something incriminating, but a flurry of doubt pummeled her with the sudden force of a snow squall. This was a long shot, and a big part of her felt crazy for even trying. She debated turning around and heading back to her car. No harm, no foul. But leaving now wouldn't accomplish anything, and she'd made it this far. She may as well see her plan through. What was the worst that could happen?

Greta glanced toward the water. A few families were milling around. Children played in the sand while a couple older kids fished from the end of one of the docks. For the most part, everyone was looking away from Greta and the office.

Putting her head down, Greta scurried to the side of the building. When she got to the window, she crouched underneath it, thankful it was open. Sounds of a conversation drifted outside.

"Of course, you can." Ed's voice was instantly recognizable.

"Thank you so much, Mr. Kennedy." It was a woman who responded. "I hoped you'd have a solution. I was beginning to get desperate."

Greta's heart pounded. Could it be the mystery woman Allison had seen? Could she have lucked out and stumbled over to the office in time to find out something helpful to the investigation? There was no way Greta could chance standing up and looking into the window to see if the woman matched the description Allison had given, so she stayed put and opened her ears.

"Go ahead and take the paddleboat outside cabin number four. Are you familiar with where it's located?"

"Two cabins beyond ours, right?"

Greta wanted to slump into the building, but she refrained. This was no one special, just one of Ed's renters. She listened as Ed gave instructions, and the woman assured him her family would return the paddleboat to its original position. The door on the front of the office building slammed, and footsteps crunched along the red gravel road leading down to the beach. Greta said a silent prayer Ed would leave the office and assist this woman, but after a few seconds, only the woman came into view. She had blonde hair, which confirmed what Greta had already deduced. This was not the woman from Mugs & Hugs. Worse yet, Ed had stayed inside.

Greta tried not to be too disappointed. She had just gotten there. She settled in—as much as one could settle in when holding a crouched, squatted position—and waited for something, anything, to happen.

Thirty minutes later, Greta's quads burned, and she had nothing to show for it except the knowledge Ed sang Nineties rap to himself when he was alone...badly and off-key.

From what Greta could gather, he was doing paperwork. Greta changed her position to try to relieve the strain on her legs, but her knees cracked, and to her, the sound seemed as deafening as a crash of thunder. She stilled, afraid Ed would come outside to investigate. When he kept singing, she relaxed. Greta decided to give it twenty more minutes, and if nothing happened, she'd turn in for the night.

The air around her had cooled significantly since she arrived, and the sun was nearly set. The clear, dark sky above would be full of stars tonight, and Greta couldn't wait to get home and see their reflection on the lake. The darkness made Greta breathe a little easier. If anyone looked at the side of the office, hopefully, she'd appear as one of the many shadows.

A ringing phone made Greta jump. It sounded so shrill against the backdrop of crickets chirping and leaves blowing in the night breeze.

"What now?" Ed's low voice was harsh, sizzling through the open window.

Greta leaned closer. After a brief pause, Ed spoke again.

"Look, Miranda. You're pushing too hard." Another pause. "Yes, I know the deal. As I told you earlier, I'm working on it, and I'll have the money.

Don't you worry. It's only a matter of time. But I cannot have you causing a scene in town. I don't want to meet again. Inserting ourselves prematurely won't go over well. You—"

The caller named Miranda must've cut Ed off because he stopped speaking. Greta held her breath.

"No, no, no." Ed's voice bellowed out the open window after a minute. "You don't understand how things work in small towns. These people are sensitive about this place and its inhabitants."

A shadow passed in front of the window, and Greta ducked lower, trying to make herself invisible.

"I can't push things any further than I already have right now. You're going to have to be patient. I will be in touch with *you* as soon as I have something."

Greta waited, but Ed didn't say anything more. He must've hung up on Miranda.

The lights inside the office flicked off, and Greta tucked her head into her neck, doing her best impression of a turtle when she sensed Ed at the window she was crouched beneath.

"No good, anxious, busy body," Ed grumbled.

Greta remained motionless as the window snapped shut. A couple seconds later, the front door slammed, and a car engine started up. A hint of exhaust fumes hit her nose, but Greta didn't dare move until Ed had driven away. She wanted to cheer when he pulled out and turned left. He didn't come past her side of the office, and he wouldn't discover her car. She stood to her full height then, cautiously stretching out her legs. She'd be sore tomorrow. Did she dare try to break into the office and see if she could find out more about Miranda?

Before she could give it another thought, a figure came tearing around the back side of the office.

"Found you!"

Chapter Nineteen

G reta shrieked and jumped back.

"Oh." The voice sounded disappointed, almost deflated. "You're not Owen."

Greta cleared her throat as her eyes took in a young girl in front of her. She appeared to be around ten years old. "No...no, I'm not."

"Who are you?" The girl took a step closer, peering up at Greta. Her hair was in pigtails, and she wore black sweatpants and a dark-colored sweatshirt.

"Uhh." Greta stalled before deciding to tell the truth. "I'm Greta. The town librarian."

The girl looked her up and down. "Whatcha doing here?"

Greta would have smiled at the question had she not been terrified somehow, this was going to get back to Ed. Thinking fast, she started in on an excuse. "I was actually stopping by to see if Mr. Kennedy needed any books replenished. We have a partnership with him here. He has sort of a traveling library."

The girl reached up and tightened her ponytails, first on the left and then on the right. "Oh yeah. I picked up a book when we got here this afternoon. *Holes*. But what are you doing *here*? Like behind the office. We're playing Ghost in the Graveyard."

"A great choice." Greta applauded both the girl's book choice and yard game selection. She and Kelly used to spend countless summer weekends tromping around with their cousins after dark, playing Ghost in the Graveyard, Kick the Can, and Spud. A pang of sadness at the thought of Kelly hit her hard, but Greta ignored it and smiled. "I was out for an evening stroll, and I came from this direction. I hadn't made it around to the front door yet when you came along and accused me of being Owen."

The girl frowned, and Greta could practically see the gears turning in her head as she tried to determine the plausibility of Greta's story. Finally, she pointed at the road. "I saw Mr. Kennedy leave a minute ago, so you missed him."

Greta chucked her closed fist in front of her body and tried to sound disappointed. "Just my luck. I guess I'll stop back later, then. I'm going to get on with my walk." She turned to go, heading directly toward the road. No use trying to break and enter with an audience. "Thanks for your help." Greta stopped and shot a smile over her shoulder. "Good luck finding Owen."

The girl waved and slunk off into the night. Greta puffed up her cheeks and let out a long breath. Nancy Drew, she was not.

"Wait a minute, let me get this straight. Your cover was blown by a ten-year-old playing Ghost in the Graveyard?" Josie stopped paddling beside Greta. The two stood side by side atop the glassy water the following morning. True to her word, Josie had arrived at Greta's house at six thirty. The librarians were in yoga leggings and long underwear tops. Neither had any intention of actually getting in the chilly lake water, but the view from the paddleboard couldn't be beat.

"How was I supposed to know the kids would be out playing? And I have to give it to the girl. She was stealthy. I didn't even hear her coming."

Josie snorted and dug her paddle into the water again. "If she was that sneaky, she definitely didn't buy your excuse for being behind Ed's office after dark."

"Don't remind me. Let's hope she forgets all about it or, at the very least, doesn't have an opportunity to mention it to Ed."

They paddled on in silence, and Greta relaxed. The calm of the early morning was one of her favorite things, especially this time of year when the brilliant colors of the trees were mirrored in the still surface of the lake. All of the cabins lining the shore were dark, and they had the entirety of the gleaming water to themselves.

Josie tipped her chin up to the sun. "So, who do you figure this Miranda person is?"

They were paddling past Franklin's empty cabin, and Greta forced herself to stare straight ahead. Knowing Franklin took his last breath on the adjacent deck made her shiver.

"Not sure. I tried to research her when I got home last night, and I came up with a couple options. There's a Miranda who is an up-and-coming property developer in Milwaukee and a Miranda who is an accountant in the Green Bay area. From their LinkedIn pictures, both have dark-colored hair. Those were my two top hits."

"Wow. Impressive. Now if we could figure out which one it was, it might give you an idea of what to do next."

"I'm going to text pictures of both women to Allison to see if she can ID one of them as the Miranda who Ed was with. If, in fact, it was Miranda, which I'm just assuming."

Josie laughed. "You are all in on this, aren't you?"

Greta shot her a look, ready to defend herself, but Josie's face was etched with approval, not mockery, and Greta's comeback died on her lips. "I am. It's in my nature to try to figure things out."

"You can take a girl out of a library, but you can't take the library out of the girl," Josie quipped.

"Something like that. Mostly I want to see justice for Franklin. And I'd like to protect my reputation." Greta gave her head a rueful shake. She did not need her name smeared. She'd had enough of that at the last library she worked at.

Josie paddled ahead. "Your reputation is safe. Look at all the folks who came to your defense at the police station."

Greta warmed at the knowledge that the Larkspur faithful had her back, but then she frowned. "But you know who wasn't there?"

Josie pretended to gag. "The notorious Cindy Fields."

"The one and only. I haven't seen much of her lately, and that worries me. I'm afraid she's up to something."

"Let's not stress about that right now. If she comes out of the woodwork, we'll squash her like an ant."

"Brutal," Greta chuckled.

"I don't have time for that woman's games." Josie tossed her hair out of her eyes. "But back to the matter at hand. I'm sure you're right about Miranda being the same person Ed was seen with at the café. I doubt he's messed up with two different women for two different reasons. It's most likely the same issue."

"That's what I figured, too."

They paddled along for a couple strokes. Greta relished the undulation of the water beneath her board. Everything was tranquil in the early morning until Josie lobbed out a question, displeasure clear in her voice.

"What's your honest opinion about Iris moving in with Dean?"

Greta blew out a breath, trying to figure out a way to be diplomatic. "It isn't necessarily what I would do. Not so soon into a relationship, anyway. But I'm happy for them. I guess when you know, you know, right?"

Josie plowed her paddle into the water. "I don't like it."

"So I've gathered," Greta said dryly, but if Josie caught her tone, she ignored it.

"I just don't get it. It all seems rash to me. I don't know. I guess I'm cynical."

"Hey, it's okay." Secretly, Greta agreed with Josie. At the same time, she liked seeing Iris happy, and who was she to judge the course a romantic relationship took? She was no expert. "All we can do is support her as her friends. You said as much last night at dinner. I'm proud of you."

Josie grunted. "Only because you kicked me into gear. Literally."

"Well, someone had to. Iris needs affirmation. She likes when we approve."

They approached the far side of the lake. Greta saw a couple people milling around Ed's resort. A group of kids was crowded around a firepit, trying to stoke the embers left from the night before into more of a fire. She wondered if one of them was the elusive Owen.

Josie sighed. "She probably likes Dean because of all the attention he showers on her."

"Are you jealous?"

"Of Iris's relationship with Dean? Heck no." Josie shook her head so swiftly she almost lost her balance on the board. "Dean is so not my type. He's way too smooth."

Greta watched Josie out of the corner of her eye. "But?"

Josie gave an almost imperceptible lift of one shoulder. "But like I've said before, a relationship, in general, doesn't sound so bad."

Greta had her thoughts about relationships and how bad they could turn out to be, but she kept that to herself, choosing instead to lend a supportive voice to her friend. "It'll happen for you, Jos. I just know it. In the meantime, let's try to keep the peace with Iris, shall we?"

"Fine. You're right."

They passed the docks by Ed's resort and came up on Josie's cabin.

"Look at your gorgeous mums!" Greta praised. Josie had them positioned in multi-sized terracotta pots around her deck. "Your house looks straight out of a magazine."

"I do what I can."

Greta laughed. "Want to race back to my side of the lake? No skipping the cove."

"Let's do it!" Josie bent her knees and shoved her paddle farther into the water, propelling herself forward.

Greta grinned and followed. "Hey, no fair. You got a head start!"

They flew across the lake. The wind blew through Greta's hair, tangling her curls. The cool spray of water against her legs was invigorating, and Greta took a mental picture of the morning. These were the sort of days she lived for—the reminder that even though she'd been dealt a rough hand a time or two, there was still so much good, so much beauty to be had.

By the time they reached the cove south of Greta's property, her arms burned from their quick sprint around the latter half of the lake, but the rest of Greta's body strummed with happy energy. She was grateful for a morning spent doing what she loved. She hadn't realized how much she needed a break from thoughts of Franklin's death, debates over Ed Kennedy's dealings, and the steely stare of Detective McHenry until she had this reprieve. It was good for her soul.

"I'm beat." Josie slowed her strokes as they came around the bend of the inlet.

Greta's cabin appeared ahead, and beyond it, Franklin's.

Movement in the windows of Franklin's home caught her attention. "Did you see that?" Greta sunk her voice to a whisper even though they were still eight hundred meters from Franklin's house.

"What?" Josie looked at Greta.

"There's someone in Franklin's cabin."

Chapter Twenty

"Are you sure?" Josie's head snapped to where Greta was staring.

Greta didn't take her attention off the bank of windows overlooking Franklin's deck, waiting to see if her eyes were playing tricks on her.

"There."

Josie sucked in a breath. "I saw. What do we do?"

"Come on." Greta dug in again and paddled forward, water splashing up behind her.

"What? Where are you going?"

Greta didn't answer, trusting Josie would follow her. She paddled to her dock but slowed her strokes before she made it there and steered toward the sand bank on the near side of it. When her paddle connected with the sandy bottom of the lake, she jumped off into the ankle-deep water. Greta didn't want to risk being seen out on the dock. She pulled her board onto the sand and dropped her paddle. "Hurry up. Maybe we can see who it is."

"Shouldn't we call the cops?" Josie kept her voice low, but Greta sensed her apprehension.

"No time. I don't have my phone. Do you?"

"No," Josie grumbled.

"It'll be fine. We're just going to look. I don't want to miss out on catching a glimpse of whoever is in there."

Not daring to take the visible public access trail, she picked her way through the clump of woods separating her property from Franklin's with Josie hot on her heels. Greta stopped at the edge of Franklin's lot, trying to hide herself among the trees.

"We can't go up the stairs to his deck. We'll be seen," Josie whispered into her ear.

"I know." Greta chewed on her lip.

There was only a small strip of grass on the side of Franklin's house closest to them. It was flanked on one side by an extension of the thicket they were standing in and on the other side by the deck and the cabin. It was a steep hill up to the street-facing side of the property.

"We're going to have to climb up the ravine and go around from the front to try to spy on whoever it is. Let's not engage. If the person in there killed Franklin, they're dangerous."

"Peachy," Josie deadpanned.

Greta choked out a nervous laugh, suddenly wishing she would have opted to go to her cabin for her phone so she could call the police.

But, no. It would be fine. They could do this. They weren't really *doing* anything. Just observing.

"Let's go." Greta crouched down and left the cover of the trees. She half-ran, half-walked up the steep embankment on the near side of Franklin's house. Greta kept one eye on the living room windows, praying whoever was inside wouldn't glance out and to the right.

About two-thirds of the way up the embankment, Greta slipped on a patch of mud and lost her footing. She threw an arm out to try to regain her balance, but she couldn't stop her fall. She let out an involuntary yelp as she landed hard on her knees, sliding back down the hill.

"What are you doing?" Josie scolded in a whisper, trying to sidestep Greta's floundering figure while at the same time reaching out to grab her.

Greta clawed at the muddy ground, hoping she wouldn't slip lower and back into view of the window. "I didn't try to fall! You know I'm not particularly coordinated and—"

At the sound of the front door creaking open, Greta pinched her mouth shut. She and Josie looked at each other, anxious gazes colliding. Greta's heart hammered. Would the intruder come around the side of the house to investigate her scream and find them there? They stared at each other until the sound of a car engine split the otherwise quiet morning air.

"No! They're getting away." Greta struggled to get to her feet, but when she pulled on Josie's arm, she took her friend down with her. They were no match for the narrow space of grass and mud. Greta groaned. "Sorry."

Josie delicately stood back up, wiping her muddy hands against her shirt. "It's fine. Are you okay?"

"Yeah." Greta finally got to her feet after a couple tries. "Nothing's hurt but my pride."

"Come on, we're over halfway up. We may as well keep going and take the road back to your house."

They slowly picked their way up the rest of the hill. When they made it, there wasn't a car in sight.

Greta put her hands on her hips, facing the cabin. "Whoever was in there left the front door open."

"Should we shut it?"

Greta thought for a minute. "Why don't I stay here and keep watch. You head back to my house and grab a cell phone. We'll call the police, tell them what happened, and let them come in and survey the scene."

"Good idea. You sure you're okay here by yourself?"

Greta waved her off. "We spooked whoever was in there. I doubt they'll come back."

"Alright." Josie started for the road.

Greta walked over to Franklin's front porch and leaned against the railing to wait. In less than ten minutes, Josie drove up.

She parked and got out, handing Greta her cell phone. "I used this to call the station."

Greta took the phone, trying not to smear the screen with her mud-coated hands. "Are the police on their way?"

"The officer on-call patched me through to Detective McHenry, and he's going to drive right over. I took my car because I figured we might want to make a quick escape." Josie winked, and Greta bit her teeth together, squishing up her nose and turning her mouth into an exaggerated frown.

"What did he say? Was he mad?"

"You can ask him yourself."

A large pickup truck pulled up, and Detective McHenry stepped out. He wasn't driving the cop sedan she associated with him, so Greta figured the truck must be his personal vehicle. She doubted she'd be earning herself any brownie points with the detective by being the reason he was working during off hours. But there was nothing for it. Here she was. And here he was. Greta pasted on her most innocent smile as she stood next to Josie.

"Ladies." The detective slammed his truck door and strode toward them. "Care to fill me in?"

"Detective McHenry! Great to see you again." Greta went with a sugar and sweetness approach, which made Josie snort next to her, though she made a valiant effort to hide it with a cough.

The detective grunted as his eyes scanned the premises. He was clearly not amused. "What are you doing here? Returning to the scene of the crime?"

Greta ignored his insinuation and tried to sound chipper. "To be honest, I wasn't expecting to be here. I just sort of fell into this mess."

Detective McHenry's gaze whizzed to her, and he took his time surveying her from head to toe. "Clearly."

A rush of heat spread up Greta's neck. She'd almost forgotten that she likely looked as if she'd mud-wrestled a pig and lost, but she cleared her throat, refusing to cower. "Yes, well. I'm not sure what Josie told you, but we were out paddleboarding when we saw someone moving around in Franklin's house. We tried to come around the front of the house to learn more, but we were too late."

"So, you didn't see anything?"

Greta had to work to keep her voice even. "I *said* we saw a person walking back and forth in front of the windows, but we were too far away to make out anything specific."

"A vehicle drove away, but we weren't close enough to see the make and model or who was driving."

"Right." Greta picked up the story again, thankful Josie didn't mention her fall as the reason they didn't make it in time to learn anything more. No use revealing she was a graceless oaf who couldn't put one foot in front of the other on dry land. Not to mention giving Detective McHenry another reason to chastise her. "By the time we got up here, all we saw was a cloud of dust and the open front door," she finished.

The detective glanced between the two of them before marching up the steps to the house.

Greta looked at Josie, who hitched up her shoulders. They followed the detective, sprint-walking to keep up.

"What are you doing?" Greta asked.

"I'm going inside to see if anything was disturbed."

"Can we join you?"

Detective McHenry turned on a dime, and Greta skidded to a stop. Josie was right behind her, and there was almost a domino situation.

The detective shot Greta an *are you kidding me?* look, but Greta wasn't going to go down without a fight. "Only because I might be able to more quickly figure out what's out of place. I was one of the last people to be here, after all. Which is something you keep reminding me about." Greta batted her eyelashes. She did have Franklin's spare key, so she could come back on her own time and poke around, but she'd rather go inside with the detective and see if she could learn anything new.

"Fine. But don't touch anything, got it?" Detective McHenry changed courses and walked back to his truck. He fished out some booties—the same kind a person puts on over their shoes if they're walking through an open house. "Here, put these on so you don't track any dirt in. We don't need anything confusing our forensic people."

"Yes, sir." Greta saluted him before taking the booties from where he held them.

Detective McHenry stared at her, his expression unchanged. When he turned away from them, Greta and Josie gawked at each other, quickly slipping on their makeshift shoes.

Detective McHenry pulled a pair of gloves from the pocket of his jacket and put them on before touching the door handle. "We'll get someone over here to fingerprint again." Greta could barely make out the detective's mumbling until he raised his voice. "Don't touch anything unless you want to strengthen my case against you."

Greta resisted sticking out her tongue at Detective McHenry's back. She longed to ask what, if anything, the previous round of fingerprinting had turned up, but it was a stroke of luck he was letting them come inside with him as it was, and she didn't want to risk him changing his mind.

The two friends walked in silence behind Detective McHenry. Greta glanced into the kitchen. Everything looked the same as it had when she showed up here and found Franklin dead. She shivered at the memory.

The detective glanced back at her. "You saw someone moving around in the living room?"

Greta and Josie nodded, and the trio walked ahead. When the hallway opened into the living space, they fanned out. Again, nothing looked out of place to Greta.

"By the way, have you talked to Dean?" Greta asked.

"Yes." Detective McHenry had his back turned to her.

Greta waited to see if he would say more, and when he didn't, she prompted him. "And? Did he shed any light on Franklin's last few days? I heard he had a meeting with Franklin."

The detective slowly pivoted and glowered at Greta.

She lifted her palms, creating a barrier between them. "Forget I asked."

"Jeesh. We'll keep our intel to ourselves if he's going to be so dismissive," Josie said under her breath, but Detective McHenry's gaze rocketed to her.

"Your intel?"

Greta's cheeks flamed. Next to her, Josie met the detective's eyes. Her friend, bless her heart, had a much better poker face.

Detective McHenry doubled down on Greta, isolating her with his intense stare. "Are you attempting some sort of amateur investigation?"

Greta forced herself to appear relaxed, even as her heart raced. She reminded herself she had done nothing wrong, and, taking a page out of the detective's own playbook, she merely stared at him.

Detective McHenry's jaw pulsed, but Greta didn't give him a chance to reprimand her or ask further questions. She started spinning around in a slow circle, taking in the room and looking for anything out of place.

Greta had seen the intruder walk back and forth in front of the window twice before he or she disappeared. The person must've either sat down out of sight of the windows or gone into a different room. Greta's gaze settled on the door leading to Franklin's rare book room.

"There." She pointed to where the door stood ajar. "Did your people leave that door open?"

Detective McHenry followed Greta's gaze, and his whole body tensed. "No. That room was locked. Based on the value of Franklin's collection, it made sense to keep the books secure." Detective McHenry walked over to the door and used his gloved finger to prod it open.

Greta had been in Franklin's rare books room on a couple of occasions, but not recently. She was anxious to see it, so she hurried to follow the detective. He stepped inside and triggered the motion-activated lights. He looked up, taking note of them. "It's chilly in here."

"Climate controlled." Greta wrapped her arms around her chest and ran her hands up and down to preserve heat.

"Helps prevent bookworms and keeps the books from falling victim to humidity and the elements." Josie slid inside behind Greta.

Detective McHenry walked into the room and looked around. "Like I told my people when we first came in here, it's not what I expected."

Greta took in the metal shelves and the file folders filled with plastic-protected dust jackets. "What did you expect?"

"I don't know. I guess something more like a library. Wood shelves, a warmer feel."

"Sounds like your perception was influenced by *Beauty and the Beast*."

Josie chuckled at Greta's assessment, and Detective McHenry opened his mouth to retort, but stopped when Greta held up her hand. "It's a common misconception, but actually, wooden shelves are terrible for books, especially rare books. The acid from the wood can seep into the pages causing permanent damage."

Detective McHenry ran a preoccupied hand through his dark hair and offered Greta a slight nod before sweeping his gaze around the room again. "Do you see anything out of place in here?"

There was a metal viewing table in the center with nothing on it. Shelves lined the walls. Franklin had placed tags in appropriate places, so particular collectibles were easy to identify. Greta walked over to the line of books denoted with the James Bond symbol. Franklin's James Bond collection was his pride and joy.

"Franklin told me the book collector was coming over to discuss buying a copy of *Live and Let Die.*" Greta paused and looked through the Ian Fleming titles.

Detective McHenry stood next to her and scanned the books. "I see two *Live and Let Die* editions here."

"Two." Greta closed her eyes, trying to remember word for word her conversation with Franklin about this book.

"What is it?" Detective McHenry asked as Josie joined them.

"If I'm not mistaken, Franklin told me he had three copies of *Live and Let Die.*"

Josie let out a whistle. "So, either Franklin changed his mind and decided to sell, or the person who was here today stole a copy?"

"I'll have to cross-check our records. We made notes about every book in here when we inventoried the house." The detective pinned them both with a look. "There's another scenario to explore."

Chapter Twenty-One

Greta and Josie glanced at each other and back at him, waiting for Detective McHenry to explain.

"Will I find this book on your property, Miss Plank?"

"What are you talking about?"

"Answer the question."

"No. Of course not. That's absurd."

"Is it?" Detective McHenry didn't seem convinced.

"Do you think we staged this whole thing?" Josie blurted out.

Detective McHenry dropped the corners of his lips, making his mouth into a shrug, but instead of answering Josie's question, he faced the door. "Let's go." He walked out of the rare books room and turned, standing with a grim expression on his face, waiting for them to follow him into the living room.

"Whoa, whoa, whoa." Greta was not about to let Detective McHenry off the hook without explaining himself, and she certainly wasn't going to let him drag Josie into this mess. She marched out and stopped right in front of him. "Josie was with me the entire time."

"Yeah, so then she's your accomplice or an unknowing alibi. Did she actually see the person inside the house?" Detective McHenry directed his question to Josie.

Josie shot daggers back at him. "As a matter of fact, I did, and I don't like what you're implying."

"Josie had nothing to do with this." Greta's voice was all pitchy, but she didn't try to smooth it out. She was vibrating with frustration. "We're trying

114

to *help* you. Isn't there more of a chance the killer was here and fled when he heard me and Josie outside? From where I'm standing, an actual intruder being here seems much more likely than us going through the trouble of setting this scene up and calling you. Besides, I was the one who told you the book was missing. Why would I do that if I was harboring it?"

"Criminals do stupid things all the time."

Greta took a step back. "Did you just call me stupid?"

"He did. And he called you a criminal, neither of which are true." Josie stood shoulder to shoulder with Greta and crossed her arms over her chest. "Look, Detective. I trust Greta with my life. Before you go accusing us of staging a crime scene,"—Josie paused and looked skyward—"which is so preposterous, I can't even." She looked back at Detective McHenry and pointed at his chest. "You better do your job and check with everyone on the lake who saw us out paddleboarding this morning. They'll confirm our story."

Greta barely refrained from pumping her fist and yelling, *Yeah! What she said!* She had never been more grateful for Josie's loyalty and logic.

Detective McHenry stared Josie down before turning his gaze back to Greta. "We'll see. Don't leave town, Miss Plank. I have your prints all over the crime scene and on the book found near Franklin's body."

Greta recoiled. She sputtered, trying to come up with something to say to defend herself, but she wasn't quick enough. The detective plowed ahead. "And if you are attempting to conduct any form of your own investigation. Stop it right now. Leave it to the professionals before you get yourself into any more hot water. I mean it."

Greta stared at Detective McHenry for a beat before turning without a word. Josie followed her to the driveway, where they slid into Josie's car.

The second their doors slammed shut, Josie turned to face Greta. "What, in the name of all that is good, was *that*?"

Greta leaned back in her seat. "I can't do anything right with him. I try to be helpful, and he turns it on me. He's impossible." Greta worried her lip. Her fingerprints linking her to the scene made the case against her stronger than she thought. Granted, she was sure her mom could create reasonable doubt—Greta had been at Franklin's house and handled the book earlier in the week, after all. But still.

"He was pretty outrageous. I was honestly waiting for him to say he wanted to come and search your house for the book. How could he have matched your fingerprints to the scene, anyway?"

"I was a ride-share driver to make extra cash in college. They fingerprinted us before we were hired so I'm sure I'm in the database. I never thought my temp job would come back to bite me."

Josie snorted but narrowed a conspiring gaze at Greta. "On a different note, if we can get beyond the whole 'you're a stupid criminal' malarkey, it's obvious Detective McHenry totally has the hots for you. I was watching him watch you."

"You can't be serious." Greta cut a glance at Franklin's house, half expecting to see Detective McHenry leering at them from the window. Josie was out of her mind to suggest he had any feelings for her other than borderline disgust.

"Oh, I'm dead serious."

"Josie!" Greta palmed her forehead.

"Sorry. My bad. Too soon. But, I mean it. There's some major romantic tension going on between the two of you. The way he looks at you..." Josie stopped and fanned herself.

"He's looking at me to try to make me crack so he can pin a murder on me." Greta tapped her head against the headrest three times, trying to think. "Now, if you're done being ridiculous, we need to figure out who the book collector is. I have this weird sense the collectible is at the heart of this whole crime. Why else would someone risk breaking back in to Franklin's house?"

"I don't know. But why wouldn't the killer have grabbed the book after he offed Franklin?"

"He panicked? He couldn't find the code to the rare books room and was afraid of being found out while searching for it, so he came back today? There are lots of explanations." Greta chewed her lip. "Whatever the reason, we need to figure out who has the missing book."

"Okay. You came up with a list of some names of collectors the other night, right?"

Greta sighed. "It's less of a list and more of an essay. It's going to be hard to narrow it down."

"Let's divide and conquer. We can work on it in our spare time at work."

"Good idea. I also want to talk to Allison and get an ID on the mysterious Miranda. I'm not ready to give up on that angle yet, either. A trip to either Green Bay or Milwaukee might be in our future."

"Detective McHenry told you not to leave town," Josie reminded her.

Greta wrinkled her nose. How could she have forgotten? "Ugh! What are my rights here? Do I honestly have to stay in Larkspur?"

"I could go on your behalf," Josie said, and Greta glanced over to see her eyes twinkling. "I don't mind getting my hands dirty. Besides, I'd be happy to do something to help the case. Even though Detective McHenry told you to leave it alone, I know you, and there's no way in heck you're leaving the investigation up to him."

Greta smirked. "You've got that right. Let me see what I can get out of Allison, and we'll figure out a game plan."

Chapter Twenty-Two

On Monday morning, Greta fluffed her hair over her ear as she paced back and forth behind the circulation desk.

She'd sent Allison the photographs of the two Mirandas she'd researched, and Allison identified one as the mystery woman she'd seen arguing with Ed. Greta was thrilled to have a solid lead but dismayed she couldn't go meet this woman herself. She didn't dare push her luck with Detective McHenry, so Josie was on the case.

The woman's name was Miranda Cash, and she was a property developer in Milwaukee. From Greta's research, she'd learned Miranda acquired and funded all sorts of different ventures across the state.

"Alright. I'm outside her office. Can you hear me?" Josie's voice came through wireless earbuds Greta was wearing and attempting to keep hidden with her curly hair. The library's employees had a no cell phones while on the job policy, but even Greta, who prided herself on following the rules, could admit this was a case of desperate times calling for desperate measures. Josie had risen at the crack of dawn to make the three-hour drive to Milwaukee, and she was about to meet Miranda Cash—with Greta listening in.

Greta snuck into the office. "I hear you loud and clear. You feeling okay about this?"

"Piece of cake." The car door creaked open and slammed shut. "This building is impressive. I'd say Miranda Cash has done well for herself. You think she'll buy my cover story that my small-town newspaper sent me to interview her?"

Greta and Josie had schemed up a plan to have Josie pose as a reporter come to collect information on a rumored new development set to take the Northwoods by storm.

"We are going in kind of blind." Greta poked her head out the office door. No one was at the desk, so she stepped back inside. "But we know something's brewing, and everything we've heard points to Ed being the one who is trying to keep this under wraps, whatever it is. So, if you present her with that information, she might bite and use this interview as a way to put even more pressure on Ed. Hopefully, we'll learn something about him, or her, in the process. A clue as to why Ed might have wanted Franklin out of the picture."

Greta pinched the bridge of her nose. It was a stretch. The only thing tying Ed to Franklin was one heated phone exchange. Hardly a slam dunk. Out loud, she spoke, forcing her words to convey confidence. "It's worth a shot, right?"

"Um yeah. If it wasn't, I wouldn't be here."

God bless Josie. If her friend thought this was a fool's errand, at least she was keeping it to herself.

"Alright. I'm going in. I'm going to stick my phone in my purse. I'll talk to you after."

"Good luck." Greta paced the small space in silence, listening as Josie introduced herself to the receptionist, giving the fake name they'd concocted of Josephine Vale. When asked if she had an appointment, Josie played it cool by saying she was in the area and hoped to catch Miranda before the rush of the day.

Greta wanted to cheer. So far, the story Josie was spinning was believable, and that bolstered Greta's confidence.

The receptionist directed Josie to the waiting room, and Greta stepped out into the library and showed a pair of young moms the children's area. Iris was covering the Monday morning story time, set to begin shortly.

Greta had gone back and forth on it but ultimately decided to fill Iris in on the Miranda Cash mission, and she was glad she did. Just because Iris was dating Dean shouldn't mean Greta treated her any differently. It was exactly what Greta had been trying to tell Josie. Besides, it was a relief to have the three of them all on the same team. Greta waved to Iris as the two families settled into the children's area.

When she turned back toward the library entrance, she had to bite back a curse. Cindy Fields wandered in, and Greta rearranged her mouth into what she hoped was a professional smile. "Good morning, Cindy."

The middle-aged woman seemed to be perpetually looking down her nose at Greta. "Indeed."

"Is there anything I can help you with today?" Greta kept her tone light even as she wailed inside. She didn't want to get roped into assisting Cindy. She wanted to give her full attention to Josie.

"I don't need any assistance from you, thank you very much. In fact, I'm sure I could run circles around you in this library. Lord knows I've been around for far longer and have far more experience with matters of both life and literature. I dare say you're quite useless to me."

Greta's smile faltered, but she was proud of herself for not physically flinching. Maybe it was because her nerves were shot, or maybe she was just tired of the woman's constant insinuation that Greta was somehow beneath her and not equipped to do her job, but Greta couldn't stop the snark that snuck into her voice, even as she shot Cindy an innocent smile. "No one would argue that you're more advanced in age than me, Cindy. But do let me know if you change your mind and would like my help."

Greta spun around, leaving Cindy slack-jawed and sputtering. She'd pay for that later, but she could hardly bring herself to care at the moment as a voice Greta didn't recognize came through her earpiece and stole her attention. Cindy huffed off behind her with a, "While I never!" and Greta covertly tried to push the earbud more firmly into place.

"Ms. Vale? I'm Miranda Cash. I have five minutes if you'd like to come this way."

Josie had done it. She was actually going to speak to Miranda Cash.

Greta was about to dodge back into the office so she could focus when Detective McHenry and Chief Sorenson ambled into the library. Greta suppressed a groan. First Cindy, and now these two?

"Good morning, Chief. Detective. Was there something you needed?"

"I was just telling Mark the library has a great collection of jigsaw puzzles. He's a big fan. Thought I'd show him where you kept them in case he wanted to check them out."

"You're a puzzle guy?" Greta's voice dripped with disbelief. Doing jigsaw puzzles was such a normal hobby. If she had to wager a guess, she would have assumed he kept busy by stealing foul balls from little kids at minor league baseball games. Or going to bingo night at the area nursing home just so he could win and rub it in. Or giving trick-or-treaters boxes of raisins. Or perfecting his frown in the mirror. Something like that.

"Is my appreciation for puzzles a problem, Miss Plank?"

She daubed on a smile and, using the first excuse that popped into her head, skirted past them. "Not at all! Help yourself. I'm going to run to the ladies' room. Excuse me."

Greta made a mad dash for the restrooms in the hallway, trying not to dwell on how strange her behavior must've appeared or on the fact that if Cindy noticed she'd left the desk unattended, she'd definitely bring up Greta's negligence with the mayor.

In her ear, Josie was doing her best to charm Miranda Cash. "I appreciate you seeing me on such short notice. Well, on no notice." Josie laughed.

Greta barely recognized the cheer in her friend's usually austere tone. If Greta didn't know any better, she'd say Josie was channeling her.

"Anyway," Josie was saying. "I was hoping you could shed some light on the Kennedy Development we're hearing all sorts of buzz about."

"What sort of buzz?" Miranda's voice sounded smooth and powerful.

Greta conjured an image of the woman in the photograph. The voice matched the picture. She paced the linoleum bathroom floor, waiting to see what Josie would come up with.

"That's what I wanted to talk to you about." Josie kept her tone breezy and confident.

"Oh?"

"You see, no one can nail anything down. Ed Kennedy—" Josie paused. "You'll have to pardon me if you two are close?" When Miranda didn't confirm or deny it, Josie prattled on, undeterred. "Well, he's being sort of tight-lipped about it. Almost shifty. It's got me wondering if there's something he's afraid to share."

Miranda's laugh rang over the line. "Funny. I'm afraid my impression of Ed has been about the same as you've described. There's not much of a story here, Ms. Vale. I have family who spent time at his cabins. They told me what a charming place it was and how the owner had mentioned expansion. So, I researched him and his holdings. He's sitting on a literal gold mine, in my opinion, and he has the capacity to take his business to the next level. But he needs more land and a solid business plan. I've told him so...countless times. He continues to say it's all in the works, and he's merely waiting for pieces to fall into place. He doesn't want to lose my financial backing, but I've told him in no uncertain terms that unless he gets himself together and can move forward, I'm out."

"Any idea what he's got in the works to pull this all off?" Josie asked.

Greta was impressed. Josie was keeping her chill like she regularly impersonated a journalist to glean incriminating information.

"Honestly, I'm not sure other than he said he had a lead on a property he assumed was going to be up for sale soon. He talked about wanting to open a luxury bed and breakfast. I'm guessing he has a location in mind, and he's waiting to move on it."

"Hmm. When did he tell you about this?"

"Gosh, it must have been three or four weeks ago."

Greta gasped as her brain tried to sort through the implications of everything Miranda was saying.

"You have been exceedingly helpful, Ms. Cash. Would you mind if I used this information to try to press Mr. Kennedy to come clean on his dealings?"

"By all means. Quite frankly, I'm ready to walk out on him. However, I was in Larkspur recently, and I admit I have a soft spot in my heart for northern Wisconsin. It's charming. I'd love to be involved in a project there, but like I said, if Ed's not the man to spearhead it, I'll go at it from a different direction."

"A woman's got to have options."

"Amen," Miranda responded.

Greta listened to rustling, which she assumed was the two women exchanging a handshake. The elevator ding rang through the phone, and Josie bid the receptionist goodbye.

Greta glanced at her watch. She'd been in the bathroom for several minutes. Hopefully, nothing was going awry in the library. She needed to talk to Josie before she hurried back to work.

More static rustling sounded through her earpiece. "Greta, are you still there?"

"Josie! You were incredible! Oh my gosh."

"That couldn't have gone better." Josie laughed, and the car door slammed on the other end of the line.

"I can't believe it."

"Me either. Did you hear everything?"

"Pretty much. I'm in the bathroom. I had to make an excuse to get out from under the watchful eyes of Chief Sorenson and Detective McHenry. Now they probably assume I have some serious intestinal issues."

Josie snorted. "Worth it. Do you realize Miranda gave us a timeline?"

"I know. If the property Ed told her about that would be coming on the market soon was Franklin's, he was either sure Franklin would sell to him, or he had plans in place to make sure the property was vacated."

"Exactly." Josie was quiet for a beat. "It does seem like faulty logic, though. How could Ed know Franklin wouldn't leave his property to someone else? What is happening with the house, anyway?"

"I don't know. I should try to talk to Liam Shark about what's in Franklin's will. I haven't heard anything about it, but it was pretty widely known Franklin didn't have family, so Ed might have assumed it would go on the open market, and he'd be able to scoop it up."

"Could be. Alright. We'll talk more when I get back. ETA on my GPS has me in Larkspur by twelve."

"Okay. Drive safely. You're a natural investigative reporter." Greta stepped out into the hallway.

"I know. I missed my calling."

"Wish I could have been there with you. Stupid detective."

123

Josie laughed again. "I'm sure there will be more adventures in our future. Bye, G."

"Bye."

Greta clicked the off button on her earpiece and turned toward the library only to run into the chest of Detective McHenry.

Chapter Twenty-Three

Greta teetered, and the detective snaked his arm out and caught her.

"Did you just call me stupid?" Detective McHenry's gaze was like a heat-tracking missile, and Greta was a blazing fire.

"I-I-No. I mean, I didn't try to." Greta winced, not sure where to look. She was a terrible liar, and as always, the detective's expression remained unbothered, which really ground her gears. "Anyway." Greta recovered, meeting his stare and ignoring the way her cheeks burned. "I guess I was returning the compliment. I'm pretty sure you called *me* stupid on Saturday."

Detective McHenry looked her up and down without a word.

Greta decided to ignore him and took a step toward the library.

"Where was I keeping you from going?" His voice echoed in the deserted hallway.

Greta tossed a grin over her shoulder. "Wouldn't you like to know?"

He opened his mouth, closed it, and clenched his jaw.

Greta turned, smirking to herself. She couldn't help but notice how the click-clack of her heels on the floor sounded especially triumphant as she left him staring after her.

Sidney glanced up from the center table where she'd set up shop as Greta approached. "Chief told me you'd gone to the bathroom. I was about to send out a search party."

Greta chuckled, taking a quick inventory of the library. "I actually had an important phone call come in. How is everything in here?"

The storytime crowd was still milling about before Iris began her program.

Shrieks of glee came from the toy train table. Greta felt the look of pure disdain Cindy shot her from where she was browsing the new releases, but she ignored it. Cindy was of the mind that libraries should remain silent sanctuaries with strict rules and minimal fun. Greta agreed with her in part—libraries *were* sanctuaries, and they'd continue to be that. But they were also the last true third space—a place where life happened. As such, life had to happen in the library. And life, in some cases, was loud. Greta's goal as director of the Larkspur branch was to ensure the library was a community hub—a resource for the town's people and a place where they could gather and feel at home. Greta was willing to die on that hill—metaphorically speaking—if Cindy continued to fight her on it.

"Hey!" Iris took a few quick steps ahead of Dean as the two approached from the children's area, effectively cutting off Greta's musings. "Any news?"

"I just hung up with Josie."

"And?" Iris grabbed for Greta's arm, slightly breathless with nervous anticipation.

"She talked to Miranda, and we've got a couple more leads to run with." Iris squealed. "Incredible!"

"Wait. What are you guys talking about?" Sidney asked.

Dean came and draped an arm over Iris's shoulder. "I'd like to know, too."

Greta gave the library another once-over before leaning in and explaining Josie's errand to Sidney and Dean.

Sidney rubbed her hands together. "Wow. So what's next?"

"I'm not sure yet. But I can't sit here and do nothing while Detective McHenry is constantly hovering over my shoulder, trying to prove my guilt." Greta absently wrapped a curl of hair around her finger. "Anyway, I'd call this morning progress. At least we have something to go on."

"Do you know what Detective McHenry is pursuing?" Dean asked.

"No." Greta frowned. "He's keeping everything about his investigation under wraps."

"Except for the fact he's accusing you. It's awful." Iris pouted.

Greta offered Iris a small smile. "I know, but it won't last forever. We'll figure this out. My mom is friends with Lori, Detective McHenry's receptionist, so I might have to tap into her for some more information on where the police are at in the investigation. We'll see. There're a couple other angles I need to work." Greta would start with the text message from Liam Shark that was waiting for her response.

Sidney chuckled. "You sound like a full-blown sleuth!"

Greta shrugged. "A girl's got to do what a girl's got to do." She caught sight of Dolores coming their way, and she waved to the older woman.

"We should get to work." Dean pointed to the computer open in front of Sidney.

"Keep us posted. I'm glad this morning was a success." Sidney gave her a thumbs-up before she and Dean busied themselves at the research station.

Iris angled her head, bobbing it toward the children's area. "I'm going to get started over there."

"You're the best. Thanks." Greta smiled at Iris, who hurried off, before turning to greet Dolores. "Dolores. How are you?"

"I'm doing alright, dear. Yourself?"

"Better now." Greta motioned Dolores closer until they were standing off to the side of the research area. "I've been working to try to piece together the puzzle of Franklin's death, and we had a breakthrough this morning."

Dolores gave her an appraising look. "I didn't realize you were investigating Franklin's murder by yourself."

"Not exactly by myself. Josie is helping me. Iris, too. We're trying to figure out a way to clear my name." Greta paused. "And yours. And determine who is actually behind this."

Dolores looked thoughtful. "We should put our heads together and see if we can come up with something you haven't thought about before. I never did tell you everything Franklin and I discussed during our first and final meeting." Dolores swallowed hard. "I'd love to help in any way I can." She straightened and took a resolute breath. "Now, I need to pick up a title off the hold shelf, and I'll be going. I've got some work to do around the house."

"I can swing by on my way home from work today and give you more details on what we've learned so far, if you want," Greta said, her voice low.

"Sounds lovely. I'll have tea ready. You know, I wouldn't want anyone else on my side of this whole mess, Greta dear. It sure is nice having you in town. Thanks for what you're doing."

Greta's spirits soared at Dolores's kind words. As the older woman headed over to the shelves in the middle of the library where patrons' holds were alphabetized and waiting to be picked up, Greta renewed her resolve to figure this out. Fortunately, between Josie's morning interview, a promising meeting to schedule with Liam, and a conversation to have with Dolores, she found herself overflowing with avenues to follow. Now if only one would lead somewhere so she could bring to book a killer.

Chapter Twenty-Four

After work, Greta made the brief drive down Larkspur Lane to Dolores's house. She'd fired off a text to Liam before she left the library, and she was anxious to see if he'd respond, but for now, all her focus was on getting to Dolores and rehashing the time she'd spent with Franklin before his death.

Greta pulled into the driveway leading to the small, one-car detached garage. The garage door was open, and Greta recognized Dolores's Mazda parked inside. On either side of Dolores's car, the garage walls were organized to perfection, with mounted peg boards serving as the home for an array of garden tools, each hanging in its particular place. A scarlet and gold Marine Corps flag was tacked neatly to one side.

Greta stepped out of her own car and straightened her pencil skirt before heading to the front door. She knocked and stepped back. A minute passed, and Dolores didn't come to let her in. Greta knocked again and held her ear up to the door, listening for noises inside. Was Dolores vacuuming? Greta paused. No. A car hummed by on the street, but otherwise, all was quiet.

"Dolores?" Greta knocked for a third time. "It's Greta."

Still no response. Greta stood up on her toes, but she couldn't see through the window on the top of the door.

She climbed back down the steps and off the front porch. She'd check the backyard, and if there was no sign of Dolores, she'd give up and go home for the night.

Greta cut through the space between the garage and the house that opened into a neat, postcard-sized backyard. Dolores had quite the green thumb.

Her backyard might be small, but its foliage was lush. Golden mums lined the side of the garage, and flowering kale and cabbage provided some color along the back lot line. Greta admired Dolores's handiwork, but she didn't see Dolores herself. Perhaps she'd gone out for a walk. Still, it was peculiar. Her garage was wide open, and she wouldn't leave her prized gardening possessions unlocked if she left the premises, even in Larkspur. The sound of dripping water met Greta's ear, and she scanned the yard to find its source, figuring Dolores must not be far if water was running.

Greta spotted a puddle along the side of the house and traced it to the exterior spigot. She jogged across the yard as much as she was able in her slim skirt. The ground was soggy, but she propped herself up against the house with one arm and bent over the muddy puddle until she could reach down and twist the handle to the right. It squeaked and groaned as the trickle of water stopped. Greta grimaced. Her shoes were now sunk into the mud. She pushed off the house and stood upright, casting an eye over the yard again. She didn't like this one bit. Where was Dolores?

Greta took a step toward the driveway and stilled. An abnormal sound came from inside the storm cellar. Greta crept closer to the old wooden doors, which were shut up tight—not unusual, since spaces like it were only used during severe storms. Greta paused in front of the cellar and listened. There it was again, a deep, guttural sound. It sounded to Greta like some sort of wounded animal.

Greta stood frozen, unsure what to do. This wasn't technically her property, and she didn't really want to see what creature had lodged itself in Dolores's storm cellar. Or, she thought with a wry grin, have Detective McHenry write her up for trespassing. Then again, how could she abandon the poor animal when it was obviously injured?

"Help!" A feeble voice rose up from the cellar.

Scratch that. Animals couldn't talk.

Greta leapt to the cellar door and wrenched it open, staring down into the darkness. As the sunlight seeped in from behind her, she saw a crumpled figure at the bottom of the earthen steps.

"Help!" The figure wept.

Greta hiked up her skirt and flew down the steps. Dolores was lying in a ball on the damp ground.

"Dolores!" Greta dropped to her knees. "Dolores. Oh no. What happened?"

Dolores moaned, her eyes clamped shut. Her face was covered in dust and dirt, and lines of agony creased her forehead. Her leg was sticking out in a funny direction, perpendicular to the rest of her body. Greta took a sharp breath in an effort to keep at bay the lightheaded haze threatening to tunnel her vision. She didn't dare try to move Dolores. Instead, Greta pulled her phone from the outside pocket of her purse and called for help. She spoke to the 911 dispatcher and gave directions to Dolores's house.

"Help is coming, Dolores. I'm right here." Greta wasn't sure if Dolores could hear her, but she forced her voice to remain steady anyway. Every time she looked at Dolores's leg, bile rose in her throat, and she had to swallow it back down. Greta did the only thing she could do in the moment—she started praying. Less than two minutes later, sirens from the ambulance rang out in the distance, and a cool wave of relief washed over her. An emergency vehicle must have been close by. "We're going to take care of you, Dolores. You're going to feel better in no time."

Dolores groaned in response as EMTs clomped down the muddy stairs and into the small cellar. As soon as they reached Dolores's side and Greta gave them a rundown of everything she knew—or rather, didn't know—she climbed back up and into the daylight. She squinted against the harsh rays of the sun, filling her lungs with fresh air and trying to get her brain to focus long enough to piece together what happened.

Had Dolores fallen? The cellar steps were pretty steep, and Greta had seen an overturned watering can lying by Dolores. But why would Dolores have been in the cellar with a watering can? If she tripped on the stairs on her own, why were the doors to the cellar shut?

Greta shuddered, afraid she'd stumbled upon something more sinister. Again.

The hairs on the back of Greta's neck stood up. She planted her feet, her gaze roving over the backyard. Greta took a steadying breath and gave herself a mental shake. What did she think? The perpetrator was going to jump out and attack her? She was being ridiculous.

"Miss Plank."

Greta started at the sound of her name and swung around to see Detective McHenry striding across the lawn toward her. Greta tensed and wrapped her arms around herself.

The detective came to a stop in front of her. "What happened?"

"I don't know. I came to see Dolores after work and found her in and out of consciousness in the cellar." Greta paused as the EMTs emerged with Dolores in a neck brace on a stretcher. She hurried over, but one of the techs stepped in front of her.

"I'm sorry, Miss, but we need to keep her stable."

Detective McHenry flashed his badge. "What's her status?"

"Signs of a concussion and what looks like a pretty badly broken leg. My guess is she'll be in surgery soon to try to set it."

The detective gave a curt nod, and the EMTs began to load Dolores into the ambulance.

"I should go with her." Greta couldn't bear the thought of Dolores heading to the hospital all alone, whether or not she was conscious. She climbed up into the ambulance before anyone could argue and was thankful when Detective McHenry didn't try to stop her. She glanced at him over her shoulder.

He ran a hand through his dark hair. "I'll follow and meet you there. I need to ask you some questions."

The back doors of the ambulance closed on Greta's reluctant nod. She slid into a seat by Dolores's head and reached for her hand. "Who did this to you, Dolores?"

The only answer came in the steady rise and fall of Dolores's chest—cold comfort under the circumstances. The ambulance lurched forward, and Greta let her head fall back against the padded wall. Nothing about any of this made sense, and her belief in a happy ending was slipping away.

Chapter Twenty-Five

By the time Greta gave Dolores's name and address to the nurses and got her friend checked into the hospital, Detective McHenry stood off to the side of the ER waiting room. Greta pursed her lips and walked in his direction, figuring she may as well deal with him right away. *Like ripping off a Band-Aid...a Band-Aid in need of an attitude adjustment.* She couldn't help the sardonic afterthought.

"I tracked down her daughter's phone number." Detective McHenry pushed off the wall as she approached.

Greta stopped short. She hadn't yet considered contacting Dolores's family, but she was grateful Detective McHenry had. Knowing Dolores would have Stacey by her side soon was a relief. "Thanks for doing that."

Detective McHenry gave a decisive nod. "How is Mrs. Jenkins?"

Greta sunk into a blue plastic chair. "They didn't tell me much. They can't, since I'm not family. But it's like the EMTs thought. A broken leg. They were going to take her to surgery."

Detective McHenry stood in front of her, his wide stance blocking the view of the rest of the waiting room. "I need to take your statement."

His tone was as unyielding as ever. Would this man always hold her in suspicion?

"What exactly do you want to know?"

The detective sat next to her and pulled out his notebook. "I need you to take me through everything."

Greta sighed and described the events of the evening, everything from leaving the library until finding Dolores.

"You mentioned you saw Dolores earlier today? How did she seem?" Detective McHenry looked up from his notes and shot her a side-eyed glance.

Greta raised both palms in a shrug. "She was fine. She came in to pick up a book she had on hold. We talked briefly about Franklin. She got borderline emotional, but pulled herself together. We made plans for me to visit after work." Greta decided against telling the detective what they planned to discuss. He wouldn't like to hear they were hoping to put their heads together to try and figure out what happened to their friend, what with expressly forbidding her to carry out an amateur investigation and all. She cleared her throat. "That's why I looked around for her when she didn't answer my knock. It isn't like her to commit to something and not follow through."

"I see." The detective jotted down a line in his notebook. "And can anyone confirm your whereabouts this afternoon?"

Greta winced and readjusted her position in the chair. She'd been expecting this question, but it still stung. "You actually think I had something to do with this?"

Detective McHenry stared at his notebook for a beat longer before raising his head, angling his upper body in her direction, and bringing his gaze to hers. "Answer the question, Miss Plank."

Greta crossed her arms over her chest. "Yes, both Josie and Iris and half a dozen library patrons can vouch for where I was this afternoon. I worked through lunch, and we all left the building together at five o'clock."

Detective McHenry made another inscription, and his nonchalance wormed its way under her skin. She leaned back in her chair. She hated this.

"Is there anyone in Larkspur who might have a grudge against Dolores? Anyone who might have it in for her?"

"Absolutely not. She's one of the town's matriarchs. She's known and loved by everyone."

Detective McHenry flipped his notebook shut, his mouth flattening into a thin line. "That's what I was afraid of."

Dread pulsed in her ears. "What, exactly, are you afraid of?"

"This is likely somehow connected with Mr. Halloway's murder."

Greta pulled in a shuddering breath. Yep. She hated this. "At least Dolores is no longer a suspect, then, right?" As far as silver linings went, it was a stretch, but Greta was grasping at straws at this point.

Detective McHenry quirked his brow but didn't say anything.

"Oh, come on. The poor woman will be glad to know she's off the hook when she comes to. And you have to know there is no way she would stage a fall and break her own leg. No way." Greta repeated herself in an effort to get it through the detective's thick skull.

Detective McHenry just leaned back and extended his long legs in front of him. "I need to get Dolores's statement."

"Unbelievable," Greta huffed, slumping into her own seat. If Detective McHenry would give an inch—just an inch—maybe they wouldn't have to be so at odds. They all wanted the same thing, didn't they? Franklin's—and now Dolores's—attacker brought to justice. Why couldn't he understand that and work with her a little?

Out of the corner of her eye, Greta took in Detective McHenry's appearance. His face was set as he stared straight ahead. She could practically see him turning over the case in his mind, examining it from different angles. Judging from the stress lines at the corners of his eyes and the way he kept clenching his jaw, the detective was stumped. Something tugged at her chest. He was trying his best. She had to believe that. His hypotheses were all wrong, but he was trying.

"You'll figure it out," she said.

Detective McHenry slowly swiveled his head. His gaze rested on her for the briefest moment before he looked out over the waiting room. "I know."

Okay, then.

A part of her wanted to tell him what she'd found out about Miranda Cash, but she hesitated. She had to get her ducks in a row before looping him in. It might be nothing, and then she'd make a fool of herself. Plus, she didn't need to give him any other reason to hawk on her and her comings and goings.

Before Greta could think more about it, the emergency room doors blew open, and Stacey ran in. She headed straight for the nurses' station, but when Greta stood, recognition dawned on Stacey's face.

"You." Stacey changed courses and met Greta halfway into the waiting room.

"Greta." Greta reminded Stacey. "Your mom is in surgery. They're setting the bone in her broken leg. They gave her some drugs to help with the pain, but they made her drowsy, so I couldn't talk to her before they took her to the OR. We haven't heard an update."

Stacey's chin trembled. "Thank you. Can you tell me what happened?"

Greta told the story again, and Stacey's eyes widened in horror. "Someone intentionally tried to harm Mom? Why? That doesn't make any sense."

Detective McHenry stepped forward. "That's what I'm working to find out."

Stacey ignored him and hurried toward the nurses' station. A minute later, she took a seat next to Greta, looking shaky. "Nothing to report."

Greta reached over and gave the woman a hug. "It'll be okay." She whispered the words as much to Stacey as she did in another prayer.

The three of them settled back to wait.

Stacey crossed and uncrossed her legs for the better part of an hour until a nurse in scrubs came out asking for the family of Dolores Jenkins. Stacey scrambled to her feet, and Greta stood in support.

"Ms. Jenkins came through surgery fine. She's still waking up from the anesthesia, but we'll take you back to see her now. I'm sure seeing a familiar face will go a long way."

Stacey exhaled and rushed to join the nurse.

Detective McHenry moved to follow, but Greta grabbed his arm, holding him in place. "Give them some time together. Your investigation can wait."

The detective opened his mouth, and Greta prepared for him to argue with her, but he must have thought better of it and only called out to Stacey. "When your mom is ready, can you page the ER? I need to ask her some questions to try to figure out what happened."

Stacey's mouth twisted, but she gave a single nod, and then she was gone.

Detective McHenry settled into one of the uncomfortable molded plastic chairs. "You don't have to wait here with me."

Greta sniffed. "I'm not waiting here *with you*. I'm here for Dolores. My friend."

"Fine then. I see how it is. Here I thought you were trying to be nice."

Greta gaped at Detective McHenry. "Did you just attempt a joke?"

The detective didn't meet her gaze.

"Huh." Greta sat back, a swell of surprised satisfaction hitting her. She might be a haphazard heroine in this story, but she hadn't been bested by him yet.

Chapter Twenty-Six

While they waited to hear from Stacey and Dolores, Greta pulled out her phone and started scrolling through missed texts and social media alerts. She tapped out a quick message to Josie and Iris explaining what happened, and she managed to cover a gasp when she saw a text response from Liam.

Liam: How does tomorrow night sound? I have to work late, but I could meet you somewhere.

Greta hardly remembered texting him before leaving the library—so much had happened since. Her fingers shook as she responded, agreeing to meet him at Mugs & Hugs at seven the following evening. Greta palmed the thin phone after sending the message, and uncertainty ate at her from every direction. What would Detective McHenry say about her meddling? Was it fair to Liam to be using him to try to get insider information on Franklin's will? Was it fair to be meeting him at all when she didn't feel ready to date again after Nathan?

The page from Stacey drew Greta out of her thoughts. Dolores wanted to see them.

Detective McHenry held the door open and let Greta enter Dolores's room first. Greta rushed to the bedside, where Dolores was pale but awake.

Greta reached for her hand. "Dolores, how are you? I am so sorry this happened."

"It's alright, child." Dolores's fingers were chilled, and traces of dirt still clung to her nails. "You found me. How can I ever thank you? Heaven knows how long I'd have been down in the cellar." Dolores shuddered, and Stacey reached out and tucked the hospital bed blankets more firmly around her shivering mother.

"You're safe now, Mom. We won't let anything happen to you, will we?" She glared at Detective McHenry, her words coming out as more of a demand than a question.

The detective stepped up to the foot of the bed. "Mrs. Jenkins, I'm glad you're okay. Can I ask you a couple questions?"

Dolores's grip on Greta's hand tightened. "I suppose."

"What can you tell me about what happened before you ended up in the cellar? Anything out of the ordinary?"

"Nothing at all. I was working in the backyard, watering my flowers, when someone came up behind me and gave me a shove. It was probably a little after noon."

Greta pursed her lips as the timeline of the afternoon's events set in. If Dolores had been shoved into the cellar at lunchtime, she lay there for nearly five hours before Greta came on the scene.

"Did you have the storm cellar doors open?" Detective McHenry asked.

"I had been up and down a couple times. I store canned goods in there, and I was fetching some. I didn't shut the doors after coming up with my final load." Dolores' gaze was unfocused.

The detective jotted down this detail. "Did you see anything about your attacker? Did he or she say anything?"

"No, nothing. Other than a grunt. I had bent down to pull up some weeds around the cellar door, and the next thing I knew, I was shoved down. I didn't hear him or her close the door above me, but I must've lost consciousness. I came to here and there, but I was disoriented. Everything hurt, and it was dark, so I called for help when I could muster the strength." Dolores squeezed Greta's hand. "I remember your soothing voice, dear."

Greta squeezed back, her throat clogging with an upsurge of tears. She couldn't stand the thought of what would have happened if no one would have found Dolores.

The detective closed his notebook. "Thank you, Mrs. Jenkins. We should let you rest. Let's go, Miss Plank."

For once, Greta didn't argue with Detective McHenry. She reached down to hug Dolores, careful not to disturb her injured leg. "I'm so thankful you're okay."

"After she's discharged, I'm planning to take Mom home with me while she recovers. I took a family medical leave of absence. I trust her leaving town won't be a problem with you, Detective?" Stacey dipped her forehead in the detective's direction, and her expression dared him to object. Greta could picture her using that look on a group of squirrely students, and she made a mental note to have Stacey teach her how she did that.

Detective McHenry glanced between the three women before answering. "That's likely best for Mrs. Jenkins's health and safety."

Dolores's face paled even further.

"Detective McHenry will catch whoever did this to you," Greta said, trying to be reassuring. Dolores offered her a weak smile, and Greta held up her cell. "I'll be in touch soon. You have my number in your phone. Don't be a stranger, and holler if there's anything I can do."

The mother-daughter pair agreed, and they both thanked Greta again as she left the room.

Greta shadowed Detective McHenry back to the waiting room, and it dawned on her she'd ridden in the ambulance, and her car was at Dolores's house.

"You can ride with me." Detective McHenry didn't break his stride.

That he read her mind was a bit disconcerting, but what else could she do? She trotted behind the detective, trying to keep up with his pace. "You're not going to make me ride in the back, are you?"

"Not unless I have to."

Greta bit back a retort and got into the front seat. The car smelled earthy and slightly sweet, a mixture of sandalwood cologne and leather. A worn holy card with an image of St. Michael the Archangel was wedged under the dash, off to the side of the speedometer. Greta felt like she was invading the detective's private world. She wanted to take in every little detail, dying to sort out what made this enigma of a man tick. At the same time, she wished she could close her eyes and pretend she wasn't sitting next to a police detective, driving away from a hospital where her friend lay injured following an attack.

Twenty minutes later, Detective McHenry pulled up to Dolores's house. He put the car in park. "I've got to hand it to you, Miss Plank."

Greta's ears perked up.

"You're either exceptionally good at staging crimes and evading the authorities, or you're rock solid in a crisis."

"Was that supposed to be a compliment?"

Instead of responding, Detective McHenry coughed a *this-conversation-is-over* cough and turned his attention to the computer beside his seat. "Like I keep telling you, don't leave town."

Greta narrowed her eyes. "If I was behind this, I would have already left. Isn't me staying in Larkspur proof of anything to you?"

The detective flicked his gaze to meet hers again. "You have no idea how criminals think."

"Because I'm not a criminal." Greta smirked, angling out of the car. She grabbed the cold metal lip of the car door to steady herself and leaned down enough to meet the detective's gaze. "Good night, Detective. You know where to find me if you need me. Remember, if you're going to make any substantiated claims, I'm going to need to ask you to contact my attorney. She'd be more than glad to speak to you."

Greta slammed the door without waiting for a response. She crossed the driveway and dropped into the front seat of her car, hitting the auto-lock button on the door at the same time. She waited for Detective McHenry to back out of the driveway before she put her car in reverse and made the quick drive to the safety of her cabin.

Speaking of her attorney, Greta owed her mom an update.

Chapter Twenty-Seven

Greta didn't have to read between the lines to figure out her mom wasn't pleased with the latest developments.

"I do not want you to talk to Detective McHenry anymore unless I'm in your presence. You hear me?"

Greta held her phone away from her ear. "Yeah, Mom. I do. You're being screechy."

Ignoring her, Louisa plowed ahead at maximum volume. "This has gone on much longer than I anticipated, and it seems like he's no closer to finding any other suspects. I don't like it one bit."

"You all should have listened to me in the first place and stayed out of it." Her dad's voice coming through the speaker held a hint of pride alongside the censure.

"Oh hush, Dale."

Greta chuckled and was suddenly reminded of when she and Kelly had crouched around the corner of the living room wall at the house they grew up in and watched as their mom scolded their dad over something—Greta couldn't even remember what anymore. Their dad had just cranked up the volume on the TV. Greta and Kelly had clamped their hands over their mouths to contain their giggles as their mom planted herself, hands on her hips, right in front of the television, matching its noise level with her voice. Their dad had tried to coax her to move, but eventually, he gave up, pulled her into his lap, and silenced her with a kiss.

Greta couldn't help but grin at the thought of the gagging sounds she and Kelly had made, alerting their parents to their presence. Her smile faded as the memory of Kelly often made it do. How she wished she could have another day to laugh and joke with her.

She shook her head. No use dwelling on her dead sister right now, especially since her parents were extra concerned with her safety because of Kelly.

"Okay, you two. I'll let you go. I promise I'll steer clear of the detective, and I'll be careful."

The next morning, Greta sat in the office tapping her pencil against the small desk and trying to focus on the budget, which she was set to present at the end of the month for final approval.

She'd slept horribly and felt like a bear. To make matters worse, her date—or whatever she was calling it—with Liam was later that day, and every time Greta thought about it, her stomach tumbled with unease. She was not in any sort of headspace to be considering a relationship right now, and her guilt at using him hadn't gone away.

Greta had worked herself into a funk, going around and around about it. Thankfully, it was a quiet morning at work. No story time meant their crowd was much smaller than on Monday, and there was no sign of Dean or Sidney, or any of their other regulars. Mercifully, Cindy Fields was also absent.

Iris popped her head into the office. "You look miserable."

Greta twisted her face into a half smile, half grimace. A physical pinch of stress tugged at her shoulder blades. It was amazing how yesterday morning she'd been so enthused, so sure they were making progress when Josie got all that information from Miranda. But then Dolores was attacked, and now everything seemed bleak. Greta sighed, her gaze flicking from Iris to Josie, who popped her head up and over Iris's shoulder.

"No more moping," Josie announced. "The books are put up for now. The budget looks better than it's looked in years. Leave it. Let's do some research on the mystery book collector."

Iris clapped her hands. "Yes. Let's. I want to help. You two have been pulling all the weight of the investigation."

Greta sat up straighter, buoyed by Josie's determination and Iris's desire to help. "You're right." Greta pulled up her list of book collectors and sent it to the printer. She followed Josie and Iris out into the library proper and retrieved copies of her list. She drew two lines on the page, splitting the collectors into three even groups. "Here's what I've got. It's a lot of names, but between the three of us, we can make a dent today."

The three librarians settled at the computers behind the desk and got to work. Greta began searching the names one by one, looking for any red flags or anomalies, but it was impossible to know what information was relevant.

Ten minutes in, an older gentleman stopped by the drop-off receptacle and deposited a whole stack of sci-fi books.

"Books, books, and more books." Iris collected the titles and began scanning them back into the system.

"Wait a minute." Greta froze mid-keystroke and swiveled around to face Josie and Iris.

Josie's forehead wrinkled. "What is it?"

"Iris, you gave me an idea. I can't believe I didn't think of this before. We've been going about it wrong."

"How so?" Josie leaned an elbow on the counter and rested her chin in the palm of her hand.

"We've been trying to find a person. Someone whom we know absolutely nothing about. What we should be looking at is the book...something we know a whole lot about!"

Greta let her fingers fly over the keys on her computer as she typed a search into the database. In no time, Greta was up to her neck in articles and book collecting societies' web pages. She worked backwards and looked for any and all hints about a person who may be interested in James Bond first edition collectibles. She found a smaller contingency of collectors this way, and they seemed to congregate on the internet and discuss their love for Ian Fleming and his super-spy creation. She narrowed her search to those from around the Midwest. Now she needed to cross-check them with the list of Wisconsin-based collectors.

Greta clicked print and retrieved three copies of the list from the printing station. She handed one each to Josie and Iris. "Let's go through these names."

"Much more doable." Iris slumped in relief, and they all set to work.

Greta clicked on the social media page of the James Bond Book Collecting Society, JBBCS for short, and leaned forward again when an album of photos appeared. Greta enlarged them and started scrolling through the pictures—fifteen images in total—but didn't find anything of note. The members of the JBBCS must've had a gathering because there was a group photo along with a picture of a cake bearing a strong resemblance to Sean Connery, and a couple of images of first-edition rare books. Greta checked the titles to do her due diligence. These photos were taken well before Franklin died, which was long before she and Josie stumbled upon the intruder, who she was pretty convinced stole the book. As such, there was no way any of the books pictured could have been the *Live and Let Die* title in question, but she made sure.

Greta swallowed a groan at another dead end as she clicked over to the last picture. She was about to exit the digital album when she did a double take. "Oh my gosh."

Chapter Twenty-Eight

"What is it?" Iris asked as she and Josie made a beeline for Greta's side.

"What are we looking at?" Josie squinted at the photo.

It was another group picture, but there were a few more people included.

Greta pointed to the corner of the screen. "The man in the back row. I almost skimmed over him in the photo, but his tweed jacket stood out. I'm ninety-nine percent sure I recognize him from Franklin's memorial service. This has to mean something, right?"

"Nothing is a coincidence. That's crime fiction 101. I'd say it applies here, too." Josie tapped the screen with her pointer finger. "So, who is Mr. Tweed-coat?"

Greta scrolled over the image. "He's tagged as Richard Bennings." She clicked on his name to see what information she could glean from his profile. It was a private account, so she couldn't see anything but the avatar he used for a profile picture and a blank heading image. "There's nothing much on here other than his name."

"On it." Iris flitted to her computer. "I'll run a records search and see if we can find out where he's from." She typed quickly, the clicking of the keys mimicking the pattering of Greta's heart.

Greta held her breath, praying this was the break in the case she needed, but she was hesitant to get her hopes up. Dolores's injury, Detective McHenry's insinuations, and her mom's warning to be safe weighed heavily on her.

"Yahtzee." Iris's exclamation had Greta rushing to her side.

Iris pointed to the screen. "Richard Bennings is in the state DMV database. He drives a car registered to an address in Karrington." Iris clicked around. "I'll print you a hard copy of this info."

Greta slipped from behind the desk as the printer purred to life, a nervous energy bubbling up in her chest. This had to be the guy. He was a James Bond enthusiast, he lived nearby, and he was at Franklin's funeral. It was a triple whammy. "I've got to go talk to him."

"Whoa, whoa, whoa."

"Now, wait a minute."

Josie and Iris spoke at the same time.

"Are you sure that's the best idea?" Josie asked.

Greta looked between her two friends after she retrieved the printout. "Well, I'm not going to go right now, if that's what you're worried about, but I can't sit on this information. The entire point of finding this guy was to figure out what happened between him and Franklin. The only way to do so is to have a conversation with him."

"Yeah, but what's your angle?" Josie asked. "You can't just knock on his door and be all, 'Hello sir, you don't know me, but I'm wondering if you murdered a man. My proof? Oh, well, a couple of internet leads is all.'" She halted the mimicking tone of her voice. "Going in pointing fingers won't go over well."

Greta rolled her eyes. "I'll go in with a little more tact, thank you very much."

"You're not going to go see him alone." Iris covered her face, peeking out between her fingers. "He could be dangerous."

"I'll go with you. I'm much more intimidating than you, and I have a great right hook, thanks to my kickboxing classes." Josie gave the air in front of her a one-two punch.

"Impressive, but no. I simply want to talk to him. You can come if you want, but there'll be no need to attack anyone."

Josie dropped her arms to her sides and shrugged, but Iris looked unconvinced.

Greta glanced at the clock. "I wish I could go today, but I've got a stupid date with Liam tonight."

The way her friends' faces instantly changed from worried about her safety to worried about her love life would have been humorous if Greta was in any mood to be humored. Josie and Iris shot each other sly grins before looking back at Greta.

Iris's eyes twinkled. "You should start thinking of this date in better terms. Not stupid, but serendipitous."

"Yeah, G. Wouldn't you like to find a partner in crime?"

Greta scowled. "You guys are my partners in crime."

How could her friends be talking about romance? Especially when they'd stumbled upon their most solid lead yet.

Josie huffed. "You know what I mean. A relationship. A partner. Liam seems to be a good option. People have met under stranger circumstances."

Greta wasn't sure about that. "This is a work meeting, anyway. I shouldn't have called it a date."

"Again, I say, there have been other instances in the history of relationships where what began as mere business partnerships blossomed into something more. Also, I doubt Liam is looking at this as a work meeting. Just be open to it." Josie pressed her hands together in the Namaste position and retreated into the office.

Greta stuck out her tongue at her friend's back before swinging around to find Iris smiling at her. "It's going to be great. You'll see."

"If you say so."

At home after work, Greta forced herself to eat dinner, even though her appetite was peanuts. She spent her time getting ready to meet Liam, trying to recall every movement she'd seen Richard Bennings make at Franklin's memorial service—every expression, every person he talked to. Unfortunately, her memory was fuzzy, mostly because she could only remember seeing him twice, and in both moments, it had been at a distance. Of course, she hadn't known she should be looking for something incriminating or helpful to solving the case. It was infuriating. She'd been so close to him, but she'd missed a chance to learn more because she didn't know he held the key. Well, maybe he did, anyway. Her thoughts shifted to Ed Kennedy and what they'd learned from Miranda Cash—what she was going to try to find out from Liam about Franklin's will.

"I don't know about any of this, Biff." She reached up to try to pull apart some of her tangled curls and sighed, facing the pair of sea-green eyes staring back at her as she stood in front of the mirror. Franklin's cat had become Greta's sounding board. It turned out she quite liked coming home to the tabby each day. Biff couldn't have been a more agreeable companion. He was a great listener, and he kept Greta laughing with his playful antics. "If only you could talk. You saw what happened to Franklin, didn't you, buddy? I'm sorry about that, but I wish you could tell me about it so we could put it all to bed."

Biff ran off, leaving Greta to tame her curls and her thoughts alone.

Chapter Twenty-Nine

When it was time for her non-date, Greta opened the glass door of the café and took in her surroundings. It wasn't exactly a busy night, but it wasn't quiet either. Maybe telling Liam to meet her at Mugs & Hugs wasn't such a good idea. It was her home turf, which was especially helpful for first dates—or business meetings. But glancing around and spotting no fewer than seven library patrons, Greta was kicking herself for her lack of foresight. Now, she'd be under the microscope in town with everyone asking about her unidentified man. Greta loved Larkspur, she did, but like most small towns, she'd quickly discovered it was a hotbed for gossip.

Greta tugged at her neckline with one hand and scooted into a booth. Her eyes scanned the café again, and she had to cross her legs to keep from bouncing her knee up and down.

Allison joined her. "Hey, girl. Can I get you anything?"

"Actually, I'm waiting on someone." Greta attempted to keep her expression neutral, but her ears burned when Allison's mouth formed a perfect "o."

"It's not like that. It's just—"

"Greta, hi." Liam stepped over to her table, looking dapper in slacks and a button-up shirt, as if he came straight from the office but ditched the suit coat, tie, and top button on the drive over.

Greta banged her knee on the table as she stood. "Liam. It's good to see you again."

They gave each other an awkward side hug while Allison looked on and

150

behind Liam's back mouthed, "Nice."

Greta widened her eyes at her before she cleared her throat and smiled at Liam. "Where are my manners? Liam Shark, this is Allison, the owner of this fine establishment. Allison, this is Liam Shark. He, um, also knew Franklin."

Allison's eyes lost a little of their mischievous spark. "I'm sorry for your loss, then."

Liam gave a good-natured shrug. "Thank you. Though ours was purely a professional relationship. Still, I never thought I'd be dealing with Franklin's assets so soon. A rough around the edges guy like him, well, I figured he'd be a client for years to come."

Greta gave Liam a half smile. "Should we order?"

"Please. I'll follow your lead. I gather you're a regular here?"

Greta and Liam made small talk in between selecting an array of pastry desserts from Allison's glass display case. Greta was pleased with how easy it was to hold a conversation with Liam. They covered their days at work (Greta left out her discovery of Richard Bennings); the weather (a universally safe topic of conversation); and the best chain ice cream establishments (Greta had argued for Culver's, but Liam maintained he was a Dairy Queen kind of guy).

Liam made Greta relax, which was…unexpected. She forgot how nice it was to have a pleasant evening out with a man, and she was relieved she hadn't completely forgotten how to be amiable. Admittedly, there weren't any fireworks where he was concerned, but, of course, she hadn't expected them. Her game plan coming into tonight was to try to steer the conversation to Franklin and somehow bring up his will. From there, she was going to wing it.

"So, what's your favorite book?" Liam asked her around a bite of his double chocolate brownie.

Greta swallowed the last of her cookie. "You're basically asking a mother to pick her favorite child. I've never met a book I didn't like."

"Seriously? Tell me more."

"I admit, I don't always love the content of the books I read. Or the writer's style. But I can always learn something from them. I maintain there is at least one decent line, one takeaway, if you will, in every book. That's why I like them all. There's something good somewhere in every book."

Liam looked thoughtful. "Do you have a book collection, then?"

"No. Not by definition. I have a large home library for sure, but I don't collect around a particular topic or author."

"Do you aspire to collect?" Liam licked his fork and set it on his plate before leaning against the back of his side of the booth.

"Someday. I did always admire Franklin's book collection. He had the most interesting titles."

Liam stared at her long enough that Greta self-consciously touched her face to make sure she hadn't left a trail of cookie crumbs around her mouth.

"Good for you," he said after a minute, flashing her a smile.

Greta wondered if she'd imagined his odd reaction to her desire to collect, but she quickly realized he'd given her a segue to the topic of conversation she was most interested in. "Speaking of collections, how's everything going with Franklin's things from your end?"

Liam sat up straighter and tossed a quick glance over his shoulder before leaning toward her. "Honestly, it's nothing short of a nightmare."

"Really? Why?"

Liam gripped his hands in front of him, flexing his thumbs out in a shrug. "Like I told you at the memorial, I was in possession of the will, but I didn't study it in detail until Franklin was laid to rest. I wasn't expecting his financials to be so convoluted. He had assets spread all over the place. It's going to be a lot more complicated to sort out than I was expecting."

"Huh." Greta didn't have much background about wills and will readings other than what she read in books, and even that knowledge was primarily based on Jane Austen's England, so Greta was pretty certain it wasn't up-to-date information.

"Yeah." Liam seemed to be lost in his own thoughts. "I have to submit it to probate court. Soon." He sighed. "Which is going to open up a whole other can of worms."

"How so?" Greta sat on her hands to stop from fidgeting.

"After probate, beneficiaries will be notified, and people can contest the will, and I'm going to have to figure out how to tie up the loose ends of the estate, which'll probably be easier said than done," he added with a rueful shake of his head. "I didn't draft Franklin's will. He had another lawyer do so, an old family friend, if I'm remembering correctly. He passed away, and Franklin hired me. He only had me make a handful of changes in the past few months...." Liam trailed off, as if he'd said too much. Before Greta could press him about what he'd changed, he recovered himself. "Anyway, I didn't realize the magnitude of the estate or the questions I'd have until I dug into it this week."

Greta chose her next words carefully, sensing this was her chance to get information about Franklin's property, but not wanting to be obvious about it. "What's going to happen to Franklin's house, anyway? Are we going to be overrun with foot traffic from all the real estate showings?"

"Actually, Franklin designated exactly who he wanted to have his property. That part's easy. It's the financial allocations that'll give me gray hair."

"I see." Greta digested the news, equal parts relieved and frustrated. If Franklin's house wasn't going to go on the open market, Ed wouldn't stand to gain anything from killing Franklin.

Unless he didn't know Franklin had bequeathed his property to someone else. In which case, he killed a man based merely on an assumption. That didn't seem right. Ed wasn't stupid.

Otherwise, what if Ed knew he was in Franklin's will to inherit the house? But that didn't add up with what Franklin told her about not wanting to sell to Ed. Why would he deny the man's advances with such vehemence if he was going to leave it all to Ed in the end anyway? Wouldn't Franklin have mentioned that to her?

Greta wanted to pound her head against the table. Instead, she forced herself to act casual. "So, do I know my new neighbor?"

"Sorry, I-I'm not at liberty to say. I mean, I would, but I've found it's easier to get all the beneficiaries together at one time and tell it to them at once. Otherwise, I risk information spreading like wildfire. And sometimes people get burned. It's not that I don't trust you, but—"

"No, it's fine." Greta rushed to cut him off. "No need to apologize. I didn't mean to pry. I was curious."

Liam had an unreadable expression on his face, and Greta wasn't exactly sure what to make of him—or of the trajectory of this conversation. Did he know she was trying to gather information from him? Did he resent her? She got the distinct sense there was something he was hiding about Franklin and his will. She couldn't put her finger on why she felt that way, but it made her unsettled.

After a few more minutes of small talk, she decided she was ready to escape to the comfort of her cabin and the uncomplicated company of Biff. "I should get going. I've got a busy day of work ahead."

Liam motioned for her to lead the way out of the café.

Greta waved to Allison before turning and walking out into the chilly night.

She paused just outside the door, and Liam faced her. "Listen, this was nice."

"It was. Thanks for coming."

"It was my pleasure. Can I see you again?"

Greta readjusted the strap of her bag. "I've got to be honest with you, Liam. I'm not really looking for a relationship at the moment, but I'd like to be friends for now."

Liam studied her for a beat before his face cracked into an easy smile. "Me too. Can I walk you to your car?"

"Sure. I'm right over there." They wove through a smattering of vehicles, and Greta looked across the street to the library. The building was dark, but a lone figure strode across the parking lot. It was Detective McHenry.

Their gazes snapped to each other as if magnets. He stopped en route to his squad car and stared at her, but Greta quickly glanced away, annoyed that she was self-conscious about being seen with Liam. She clicked the unlock button on her key fob and came to a stop by the driver's side door. "This is me."

"Okay. Thanks again for a lovely evening. Drive safely, Greta. I'll talk to you soon." He held open her door for her, and Greta sunk into her car.

She pulled out of the café's parking lot and drove toward the lake, making an active effort not to glance in the direction of the library parking lot. When she finally let herself look in her rearview mirror, Detective McHenry was gone.

Chapter Thirty

The next morning, Greta got to the library early. She was going stir crazy at home, and being productive would help ease her frayed nerves. She flicked on the overhead lights, dropped her bag in the office, and prepared to do battle with the computers. If she was lucky, she could pull all the hold titles and get a jump on planning the library's monthly newsletter before Josie and Iris arrived for the day. When they got there, they could help her dissect last night's conversation with Liam.

After a couple minutes, she had the click list generated. She strode out into the library, but paused and retraced her steps, double checking that the glass doors to the library were locked behind her. Even though the lights were on early, she didn't need anyone trying to enter and taking her by surprise.

Especially not a certain detective.

Greta cleared her throat. Like she told herself countless times last night, there was no use dwelling on what Detective McHenry thought of her, or what his next moves were. She could only control what she could control, and she hadn't done anything wrong. She needed to remember she was innocent when the detective started to get under her skin. Besides, she had a game plan for moving forward: if he tried to talk to her, she'd call her mom.

Greta rolled her eyes at herself, grimacing as the cart bowled over her toe. "Focus," she muttered.

Greta set about with renewed vigor, methodically working her way through authors' last names and retrieving the titles she needed. When she rounded the corner from the children's area back to the circulation desk,

Iris was unlocking the glass doors with Dean and Sidney standing behind her.

Greta waved. "Good morning, everyone!"

"Greta, wait until you see this!" Iris's voice was more breathless than usual, and her cheeks glowed pink.

Greta's heartrate kicked up. "What is it? What did you find?" Greta abandoned the cart next to the desk and stepped toward them.

"Find?" Iris gave her a blank stare, and, after a second, she widened her eyes. "Oh! No. This has nothing to do with the case."

Greta's stomach sunk back into place, and she had half a mind to slap herself for being so self-centered. The whole world didn't revolve around her and her ability to figure out what happened to Franklin. Even though her life had been overtaken by it, other people's lives hadn't been. She would do well to remember that.

Josie hurried into the library. "Hey."

Greta waved again, and Iris clapped her hands. "Oh, good! Jos! You're just in time. I was about to tell Greta. Dean has pictures of some properties he wants to show me for our new house. Potentially." Iris looked up at Dean, her blush intensifying.

Dean winked at her before spreading some printed images out on the counter. Sidney, Josie, Greta, and Iris crowded around.

"Wow. These are incredible." Greta admired the images. It was hard not to. Some were lakefront properties; some were on wooded acreage. Each site was more spectacular than the last, with the sun-kissed greens, yellows, oranges, and reds of the trees' autumn leaves.

"I'm sure Iris told you I'm trying to convince her to move in with me," Dean said.

"She did." Greta caught Josie's eye and gave her a pointed look. In response, Josie managed what Greta could only describe as a compulsory smile.

"Good. You can help me convince her it's for the best." Dean grinned and pulled Iris to his side.

Greta looked between them. "This is a big step for you two."

"Yeah, but the timing is right, and we've never been happier, right, Iris?"

Iris nodded, her cheeks dusted a pretty pink, and Dean grinned down at her. "I figured I should jump on it."

"Wow. This is stunning!" Iris held up an image with a view of a lake.

"Where is that?" Josie asked.

Dean took the photo from Iris and flipped it over, reading a small notation on the back. "This one is on Shadow Lake."

Josie frowned. "Isn't that an hour farther north?"

"It is."

"Iris, would you commute?" The corners of Josie's mouth drooped even more.

Before Iris could respond, Dean held up a hand. "Nothing is finalized. I was hoping to steal Iris away for lunch so we could talk about options and make a decision."

Iris glanced between Josie and Greta. "Do you guys mind if I take an extended lunch?"

Greta waved her hand in front of her. "By all means. We can cover things here."

"Yeah. As long as you're okay to close up so Greta and I can go run the, *ahem*, errand we discussed?" Josie added.

A fizzle of anticipation bubbled in Greta's stomach. She had a book collector to meet.

"Deal." Iris squealed and launched herself at Dean. "I can't wait!"

Chapter Thirty-One

That evening, Greta stepped out of her car in front of an apartment complex on the outskirts of Karrington. She and Josie spent the drive rehashing her time with Liam, but now Greta's mind was locked in on Richard Bennings.

Josie slammed the door and stared up at the brown, nondescript building. "You think he's here?"

"We're about to find out."

They crossed the parking lot and entered the exterior door, walking into a small, dimly lit lobby. Straight ahead was another door.

Josie marched up to it and tried to open it. "Locked."

Greta spotted an intercom system. "What's his apartment number again?"

Josie pulled out the paper Iris printed for them. "He's in apartment four-oh-four."

Greta pressed the button on the intercom. It buzzed, and they waited.

"Who's there?" A voice crackled through the speaker.

"Richard Bennings? My name is Greta Plank. I'm a friend of Franklin Halloway. I'd like to talk to you if you have a moment." She kept her voice firm but cordial—just like they taught her in library school—and stared at the intercom, waiting to see what Richard would say.

Eventually, the intercom sputtered to life again. "Uh, sure. Come on up."

Greta looked to Josie, who cocked her head to the side in a shrug. The door clicked open, and Greta took the lead.

"Fourth floor." Josie directed her from behind.

Greta's heeled booties echoed in the stairwell as they climbed the steps.

By the time they reached Richard's hall, her heart was pounding. "I feel like I'm in a movie," she whispered.

Josie snorted behind her. "Totally. It's like the dimly lit corridor of doom."

"Right?" Greta let go a nervous laugh. She was grateful Josie was with her. "We might need your right hook yet. Here we are."

Greta knocked on Richard's door. Shuffling sounded through the paper-thin walls before the door swung open.

"Richard Bennings?" Greta flashed her cheeriest smile. "I'm Greta Plank, and this is my friend, Josie. May we come in?"

Richard locked gazes with Greta, and the hairs on her neck stood up.

"What's this about?" he asked.

Greta froze, unable to formulate a sentence. Something about Richard's expression was familiar to her. Something she couldn't place.

Josie took a small step forward. "We have a couple questions for you about Franklin. We're visiting everyone local who knew him."

Richard unlatched his gaze from Greta and glanced in Josie's direction. He studied her, as if trying to make out the validity of her claim. After a second, he opened the door wider. "Okay. Come in."

Josie cut between Greta and Richard, and Greta took the opportunity to collect herself before following Josie inside.

"Take a seat. Oh, sorry." He hurried across the cramped living room and moved some hard-covered books off one of the chairs.

Josie sat there, and Greta perched herself on the edge of the threadbare couch. While the books seemed to lend themselves to her theory that Richard was indeed their mystery book collector, his living situation had her second guessing herself. Wouldn't someone who had a passion for collecting expensive, rare books have a more affluent home?

"Why are you here? *How* are you here?" Richard eyed Greta and Josie with skepticism.

Greta folded her hands in her lap. "We got your name from the memorial service coordinator." Greta delivered the lie with as much aplomb as she could muster and hoped Richard wouldn't call her bluff.

Josie leaned forward, picking up the conversation. "Like I said, we're paying visits to Franklin Halloway's friends and acquaintances. Research shows it can help the grieving process for all involved to converse about the deceased and share good memories about time spent together. We were hoping you'd be willing to talk to us about Franklin." Josie sat back and crossed her legs.

"I don't have much to say. Franklin and I had a business relationship."

"What kind of business?" Greta attempted to draw him into conversation. There was something shifty about the man, and she was afraid they wouldn't be able to pin him down.

"Rare books. We both collect. Or we both did."

"You're a book collector. Fascinating." Josie shot Greta a look. "So, you ran in the same collecting circles as Franklin, then?"

"I wouldn't say we were in the same company often." Richard rubbed his thumbnail against the pad of his pointer finger. "Franklin didn't get out much, from what I could tell."

"How did you two meet, then?" Greta quirked her brow.

Richard paused. Greta could practically see him trying to figure out how much he wanted to reveal. "We go way back."

Greta kept her features smooth, fighting off a frown at Richard's vague response. Determined to get some information out of him, she plowed ahead with a different line of questioning. "Had you seen him recently? Before his death, I mean."

"Actually, I saw him for the first time in a long time the week he died. I was at Franklin's house on that Wednesday. We were meeting about a book I hoped to buy from him."

"How nice you got to see him one last time." Josie offered Richard a consolatory smile while Greta fought the urge to point at him and yell *ah ha!* They had officially found the rare book collector in question.

As much as she wanted to cheer, she was quick to realize they could be sitting in the same room as Franklin's killer. With that thought, she had to swallow down a pang of unease before she spoke up. "We love books. We're librarians. What book did he sell to you?"

Richard glanced away from them. "As a matter of fact, uh, Franklin decided he didn't want to sell at the time."

"Oh." Josie looked crestfallen, and if this were a movie, Greta would give her friend an Academy Award for best actress. "What book was it?"

"*Live and Let Die.*"

"Ian Fleming. Nice. I'm a James Bond fan myself." Greta was talking quickly in an attempt to keep Richard from noticing how much information he was sharing. "How was Franklin when you saw him? He usually loves chatting about books. He and I always talked about what we were reading, too."

Richard sighed. "Honestly, he seemed a little preoccupied. Like he couldn't wait to finish our meeting. I must say, I expected...I don't know...a little more of his attention, given our, er, history. We did make plans to meet again the following week, though. So, I guess that was something."

"I wonder why he was distracted during your meeting," Greta said. If only she had the answer to that question.

Josie flashed her a warning look before blinking back at Richard. "I'm sure he still appreciated getting to see you, though."

"Right. Of course. He invited you back after all." Greta brushed some lint from her orange corduroy pants, trying to be less obvious. "When did you hear about his death? It must have been quite a shock for you, especially since you'd just seen him."

"Greta is the one who found Franklin's body," Josie explained.

Unbidden, tears sprung into Greta's eyes. She tried to gulp them down, but they hit her hard and fast. "Sorry." She flapped her hand back and forth in front of her face.

Richard produced a handkerchief from his pocket.

"Oh gosh. Thank you." Greta took it. "This is so nice." She dabbed her eye with the cream-colored fabric.

Richard smiled and seemed to relax. "Mumsy always made sure I carried one as a boy. Said I'd never know when it would come in handy. The habit stuck."

Greta's breath hitched, but she forced a smile. "Your mother sounds like my kind of woman."

"She was the very best. Actually, I was visiting her gravesite when Franklin passed. I was staying with friends, and I didn't learn the news until I returned here and saw the obituary."

Greta bobbed her head up and down. "Would you mind if I used your restroom to freshen up? I'm afraid I'm a bit of a mess."

"Sure. Down the hall, past the study, and on your left." He gestured to a narrow passageway, and Greta headed in that direction. She cast a quick glance over her shoulder and her gaze connected with Josie's. Greta hoped her eye contact relayed that she needed her friend to stall.

Josie—bless her—struck up a conversation with Richard about his hometown as Greta hurried down the hallway.

Greta peered into the study before opening the bathroom door and shutting it again without entering. Then, she ducked into the study and figured she had three minutes, tops, to find what she was looking for.

The "mumsy" moniker, coupled with Greta's instinct that Richard's mannerisms reminded her of something, had her inquisitive mind trying to piece things together. Could Richard and Franklin be related? Franklin never mentioned a sibling to her, but he might still have had one. Richard had told them he and Franklin went way back. Was he talking about family lineage?

Greta chewed the inside of her cheek, letting her gaze sweep over the room as she tried to figure out what she could look for to prove her theory, as harebrained as it might be.

She silently trod across the floor to the large table that served as a desk, flinching when Richard's voice sounded from the front room. She didn't dare make too much noise, and as she approached the desk, she could only hope she didn't have to open any drawers.

She scanned the surface, but there wasn't a picture frame in sight. Greta spun around and skimmed the bookshelves lining the entire wall. There was nothing very personal there, either.

Greta's time was running out. She'd have to give up her search here and see what she could come up with researching online. Or at Franklin's house.

She gave the bookshelves a last once-over before turning to leave when her knee connected with the leg of Richard's desk, sending a file scattering onto the floor.

"No, no, no." Greta bent to scoop it up and shoved the contents back inside. When she replaced it on the desk, she gasped.

Sitting there in a clear plastic bag was a first-edition copy of *Live and Let Die*. Greta was certain it was Franklin's book. She didn't have the time or gloves she needed to touch it, open it, and get specifics. Instead, she pulled her phone from her back pocket and snapped a quick picture.

"I'll go check and make sure she's alright." Josie's voice sounded from the front of the apartment.

Greta set the file back on top of the book. Taking three large strides, she made it across the room. Greta peered into the hallway, stepped in front of the bathroom door, and opened it as Josie appeared, her eyes flared wide.

"What are you doing?" she mouthed to Greta.

"Not now. Let's go," Greta whispered and pointed back to the living room.

Josie glanced over her shoulder and returned to her full voice. "Hey, there you are. I wanted to make sure you were okay." She winked at Greta.

Greta gave her a thumbs-up. "I know. I'm sorry." She spoke louder than usual, hoping her voice would carry. "I needed a minute." She closed the door to the bathroom with a snap as if she was just coming out and followed Josie back to the living room.

"Richard, I apologize for falling apart. We've kept you long enough, but I appreciate you talking with us about Franklin. It helps me to process the sudden loss."

Richard rose from his seat, and Greta met his gaze, praying her eyes didn't give her away. Why would Richard lie about the book? Unless he was the one who stole it. And if he was related to Franklin, why keep it a secret? He must have a good reason. A chill shot down Greta's spine at the thought of how he'd react to someone finding him out. She fixed what she hoped was a guileless expression on her face and moved to the door.

With a fleetness of foot Greta hadn't anticipated, Richard crossed the room and blocked the exit. Richard's forehead creased as he stared her down.

Greta gulped, schooling her features. "Thank you again for having us."

Finally, he turned the knob slowly, opening the door for them. "This has been...unexpected. But if it was useful for you in any way, I'm glad."

"It was. It definitely was." Josie shoved Greta along.

Her friend had no idea.

Greta forced a smile and walked into the hallway. "Bye now, Richard."

The two librarians made their way down the stairs in silence. When they reached the lobby, Josie opened her mouth to speak, but Greta cut her off. "Let's get out of here first."

They rushed to Greta's car. The second they were both seated inside, Greta hit the auto-lock button.

"Are you going to tell me what the heck you were doing in the bathroom for five full minutes?" Josie threw up her hands. "I hate small talk."

"I know. I'm sorry, but it was worth it. I was checking out Richard's study." Greta held up the image of *Live and Let Die* for Josie to see.

Josie gaped at it. "This was just sitting out in Richard's office? Talk about being careless. Or way overconfident."

"In his defense, it was buried. I accidentally discovered it."

Josie snorted. "Accidentally while looking for it, you mean."

"I actually wasn't looking for this." She explained her hunch based on the mumsy moniker. "We need to go to Franklin's house to look for a connection between the two men. What if Franklin and Richard are brothers?" Greta was strumming with energy. This could be the break in the case she'd been waiting for.

Josie held up a hand for a high five, and Greta slapped it. "Let's do it."

Greta put the key in the ignition when her attention was taken by a familiar sedan pulling into the parking lot. "Oh no. Duck!"

Chapter Thirty-Two

"Why?" Josie stared at her funny.

Greta reached up and yanked her friend down in her seat. "Because Detective McHenry just pulled in, and I don't want him to see us here."

Greta and Josie crouched down, staring at each other with eyes like dueling pairs of headlights.

"Is he inside yet?" Greta whispered after a couple of seconds.

"I don't know, but you do realize he can't hear you, right?" Josie chuckled.

"Ugh. Yes, but he puts me on edge. Trust me, if he ever pins a murder on you, you'll understand." She poked her head up and chanced a glance between the steering wheel and the dash. "He's walking toward the building now. Okay." Greta nibbled her lip. "And he's inside."

"Good. Let's get out of here." Josie scooted up and buckled her seat belt.

Greta didn't need to be told twice. "This is good timing, actually."

"Why?"

"Because, since he's here, he won't catch us breaking and entering at Franklin's."

"Is it breaking and entering if you have a key?" Josie asked.

"Detective McMeany-face would find a way to say I committed a crime." Greta scowled, but then she sighed. "I know he's just doing his job, but I wish he'd realize I had nothing to do with Franklin's death."

"Maybe he does. He's here, isn't he? Talking to Richard, I mean." Josie hooked her thumb behind her.

Greta thought about that. "Lori must have been able to track down the

166

book collector."

"And if Detective McHenry is following up, he clearly knows he doesn't have enough to convict you with."

"I'll take it."

In fifteen minutes, Greta pulled into Franklin's driveway.

She unlocked the door to his house and opened it. The scent of lemon, which Greta always associated with Franklin, wafted out. She pushed down her lingering sadness.

"Why don't you check the picture frames in Franklin's office? I doubt there's anything there, because the police would have found it. But let's be sure. Feel free to poke through his desk, too, but use your sleeve, so you don't leave fingerprints."

"Alright." Josie peeled off toward the office, calling over her shoulder, "Where are you going to look?"

Greta was replaying her last visit with Franklin. He'd mentioned sharing his secrets, and he'd motioned toward the bookshelves on either side of the fireplace. It could be nothing. Or nothing related, but...

"I'm going to start in the living room." Greta took off toward the back of the cabin, and when Josie joined her a couple minutes later, she pointed up—way up. "Do those look like photo albums to you?"

Josie followed her gaze. "There's only one way to find out."

Greta looked around. "How are we going to grab them, though?" The shelves flanking Franklin's fireplace were as tall as the twelve-foot ceilings. What appeared to be old photo albums were on the second to the top shelf, and she didn't have the gift of agility like Biff did. If Greta tried to scale the shelves, she'd end up in a heap on the floor, likely with a broken bone or two.

Before she had too much time to worry about it, Josie stepped onto the stone fireplace hearth and, holding on to the mantle, used the shelves like a rock-climbing wall. She was up and back down with three albums in less than a minute.

"Here you go." Josie shot Greta a grin.

Greta took the albums gratefully. "What would I do without you?"

She brought them over to the couch and placed two albums on the coffee table, and took the third into her lap, flipping it open. It was caked with dust, and the pages were yellowed. Josie took a seat next to her.

"Oh wow, this is more like a scrapbook than it is a photo album." Someone had taken the time to paste souvenirs and clippings, as well as photos from throughout the years. "I'm not exactly sure what we're looking for." A seed of doubt sprouted like a thorn jabbing at her foot, but Greta ignored it. "I'm hoping it'll jump out at me."

"Let's divide and conquer." Josie grabbed one of the remaining two albums off the coffee table. "You take that one, and I'll go through this one."

Greta was already engrossed in the history pasted all over the worn pages. From the age and quality of the photos, the scrapbook she was looking through was from deep in Franklin's family tree. A newspaper clipping from the 1940s about a general store owner confirmed her suspicions. The store owner was pictured with a gaggle of children. "John Davidson and Friends" the caption read. According to the article, most of the kids pictured were John Davidson's children. Greta studied the faces closely. If any of them were Franklin's relations, she wasn't going to be able to tell from a grainy, old photo.

Greta sighed as she flipped to the final page of the album. "Not a lot here." She set it back down on the table, no closer to determining if Franklin and Richard were related.

Josie was silent for a moment as she looked intently at the page in front of her.

Greta waited, and finally, she looked up.

"From what I can tell, Franklin's mother was named Carly Davidson. And here's a picture of her going to her high school prom dance with a guy named George Halloway."

Greta peered over at the picture. The shy, closed-lip smile on Carly's face reminded her a bit of Franklin, and George Halloway looked every bit the gentlemen in his suit and tie. "Yeah. I remember the names Carly and George from Franklin's obituary, I think."

Josie grabbed for the final album. "Let's hope this gives us some more recent information." She placed the newer-looking book between the two of them and pulled open the first page. Sure enough, it was a wedding photo, and the couple pictured was definitely the same one from the prom photograph.

"So, Carly Davidson married George Halloway," Greta stated as Josie flipped the page. "And they had a son."

There in front of them was a baby picture. Beneath the image was scribed the name *Franklin Daniel*. The next few pages showed happy family photos. One from Franklin's first birthday, an image of the three of them around a Christmas tree when Franklin appeared to be about three years old, a picture of them on a dock overlooking a body of water.

"Is that Larkspur Lake?" Greta squinted to get a better look.

Josie peered at the image. "Tough to say, but it could be."

She peeled back the next page and found a newspaper article. The headline read, "Local Businessman among Those Dead in Vietnam."

"Oh no." Tears pricked at the corners of Greta's eyes as she and Josie read silently the article detailing Captain George Halloway's heroics in the face of insurmountable odds before succumbing to death on the battlefield. The last line of the article spoke of the wife and child he left behind.

"You know what this means?" Josie said.

Greta exhaled. "If Franklin's dad died, his mother could have remarried, which would account for Franklin and Richard having different last names but the same pet name for their mother."

Josie turned the page. The next set of photos looked newer, as if time had passed since the article from the early seventies. The images on this page showed Franklin's mother, looking older, with a different man, and an infant.

"Baby Ricky." Greta read the caption. "1980."

She looked up at Josie, who stared back at her, her mouth hanging open.

"I was right?" Greta asked.

"It appears so. Check out this caption."

Sure enough, there was Richard's name listed along with his father, Lewis

Bennings.

"No wedding photo of Lewis and Carly, though." Greta chewed her lip. "Maybe they never actually married?"

"Could be.

"It's weird Franklin isn't in any of these pictures." Greta kept her eyes peeled for him as Josie flipped quickly through the remaining pages. A more recent color photo of a baby slipped out.

Greta picked it up off the floor. "I'm guessing this isn't Franklin," she quipped. "Actually, I can't even tell if it's a boy or a girl infant." She peered at the image of a newborn swaddled in a plain white blanket. The baby wasn't wearing a colored hat on his or her head to tip her off one way or the other, either. She turned the photo over, but there was no label and no glue marks on the back. It was as if someone had stuck the free-floating photo into the album for safekeeping, but hadn't gotten around to placing it. She handed it over to Josie with a shrug. "Anyway, back to Franklin. Why isn't he pictured on any of the pages here?"

"They might have had a falling out. Or maybe they were never close in the first place. If Franklin's mom had Richard nine years after Franklin's dad passed away and Franklin was around ten years old when his dad died, he would have been eighteen or nineteen when his mom was having a new baby. Nearly two decades between siblings is a pretty big spread. He was probably out of the house, living at college when Richard was born."

Greta sighed. "I wish Franklin were here to fill in the gaps."

Josie closed the album. "What are you going to do now?"

"I'll verify everything with a records search. I'm guessing no one looked much into Franklin's family because, as far as anyone knew, he didn't have any. Even Liam said as much at his memorial service. Anyone looking for Franklin's next of kin probably stopped when they saw both his mother and father were listed as deceased. Especially if they looked at the date of his dad's death."

"But there's a half-brother in the picture." Josie stood to replace the albums on the shelf.

"That changes things." Greta gazed around Franklin's cabin. "We should get out of here before we get caught snooping, though."

Josie hopped down from the fireplace and dusted her hands. "Agreed."

They walked outside, and Greta locked the door to Franklin's cabin before they made the quick drive back to her place, where Josie had parked.

"Thanks for coming with me." Greta slammed the door and gripped her keys, meeting Josie in front of the car.

"I wasn't going to let you go alone. And hey, speaking of the danger you're putting yourself in..." Josie leveled her with a look.

"No one was speaking about that."

"Come on, Greta. This is becoming more and more of a tangled web, and you know it. You need to go to the police with what you've learned."

"And have Detective McHenry turn on me?"

"I'm the first to admit he's not the easiest to work with, but what other option do you have? You're not a professional, and while no one can say we haven't held our own, more could be accomplished, and faster, if we shared what we've found out. You said it yourself—he's just doing his job. This will help him, and in return, it'll help you get out from under suspicion."

Josie was right, even if Greta didn't like it. She was getting in over her head. "I'll talk to my mom and see what she wants me to do."

"Good." Josie reached out for a hug and squeezed Greta tight. "See you in the morning."

Chapter Thirty-Three

Greta's mom agreed with Josie and insisted they set up a meeting with Detective McHenry as soon as possible. Since Louisa was in court all day, she'd tasked Greta with making the call to schedule the appointment.

Now, Greta was doing what any millennial did when faced with an uncomfortable task: procrastinating. When she'd arrived at work, she'd gone straight to the office to work on the monthly library newsletter. That complete, she'd taken up a stack of books marked "Damaged: In Need of Repair" and began going through them with great care. She'd been taping pages, contacting patrons and asking about stains, and indexing issues for the better part of the morning.

She told herself she was taking the necessary time to get in the right frame of mind to call Detective McHenry. Truth be told, her mom's words from the previous night's phone call rang in her ears, and she was having a hard time dislodging them. Even now, they played on loop:

> *"Greta. Are you crazy? Snooping around at Richard's house? Do you know how much danger you put yourself in? You had no idea what kind of mental state Richard was in when you visited him. What if he'd found you going through his things? And I'm not even going to mention the lack of forethought in entering Franklin's house. Were you trying to borrow trouble? What if the police had found you there?"*

Greta squirmed with discomfort as she straightened a stack of newly mended books. Even though Richard hadn't found her out and she *had* been careful taking Josie with her, she understood where her mom was coming from. She was lucky things yesterday didn't end differently.

Greta glanced up at the old clock hanging on the wall. It was after noon, and her mom would be even more unhappy with her if she failed to make an appointment with the detective for the next day. So she slid her rolling chair across the floor to where she'd set her canvas tote and started digging around to retrieve her phone.

She jumped when her bag started vibrating and her cell chimed, alerting her to an incoming call. Greta wedged the phone out and checked the caller ID. She scrunched up her nose as Josie joined her in the small office.

"What's that face for?"

"It's Liam." Her skin pricked as she remembered the odd feeling that he was keeping something from her.

"Ooh-la-la." Josie's eyes danced.

Greta's cheeks heated. She held the phone out in front of her as if getting too close to it would give her cooties. "It's not like that. Why is he calling me? I told him I only wanted to be friends, and he seemed okay with it. He didn't come across as one of those guys who'd be all clingy."

Josie chuckled as she made her way to the filing cabinet on the opposite wall. "Answer it and see what he wants!"

Greta blew out a breath. Josie was right. She was being ridiculous. Besides, if nothing else, Liam's call gave her a last-ditch excuse to avoid phoning the detective. That tipped the scales and had her clicking "accept."

"Hello."

"Greta, hi. Liam Shark here. Is this an okay time? I'm sure you're at work."

"Yeah. Totally fine. What's up?"

Josie was staring at her now, and Greta made a shooing motion. She didn't need an audience. Josie crossed her arms, smirking. Greta scowled at her, returning her attention to Liam.

"I admitted Franklin's will to probate, so it's public record now. This is sort of last minute, but I was hoping to gather all the relevant parties to go over a couple items from it this evening. I can clear up any questions or concerns in person."

"Uh…okay." She wasn't sure why Liam was telling her this. He said he'd keep her posted, but this seemed like a pretty standard detail. Did it merit a phone call?

"Greta. You're in Franklin's will."

"What? Oh!" Greta leaned against the wooden desk the librarians shared. "Seriously?" She held up a finger to Josie, signaling her to wait in the office for a second.

"Yeah. Sorry I didn't come right out and tell you the other night. Like I said, I wanted to get everything organized first. So, can you meet to discuss things?" Liam asked.

"Sure." A surge of relief filled her chest. *That's* what Liam had been keeping from her. She was in the will. It was nothing sinister, which was a relief. She may not want a relationship with him, but he seemed like he'd be a good friend. She grabbed for a pen and, in less than a minute, she had details from Liam about the time and whereabouts of the will reading. "Hey, will Detective McHenry be there tonight?"

Liam huffed. "Considering he's been breathing down my neck to get access to the will, he was my first call."

Good. She'd pull the detective aside and set up a meeting when she saw him tonight. No need to make an awkward phone call ahead of time.

She said goodbye to Liam and hung up.

Josie was staring at her expectantly. "Well?"

"I'm in Franklin's will." Greta was stunned. Sure, she considered Franklin a friend, and she knew she'd wormed her way into his heart—mostly because she wouldn't leave him alone. Franklin once likened her doggedness to that of Jo March, and Greta had never received a higher compliment. A surge of fondness for her former neighbor welled up in her chest, intermingling with her grief as she filled Josie in on what Liam told her.

They walked into the library, and Greta told Iris the latest.

Iris pulled her phone from beneath the circulation desk. "Dean texted me. He has a client meeting, so he's sending Sidney to represent their office. Liam wanted someone on hand in case anyone had questions about Franklin's financials."

Greta breathed a sigh of relief. At least she'd have a friend there.

After an afternoon meeting with Mayor Collins to discuss the plan for the upcoming fall festival, Greta left the library and drove to the address Liam had given her. Her GPS took her to a strip mall between Larkspur and Karrington. A sign reading *Shark Law* hung over the unit in the middle of the complex. Greta parked nearby, and the car to her left was none other than Detective McHenry's sedan. She gritted her teeth. She could do hard things, and she'd get the meeting scheduled with him if it was the last thing she did. Still, for the sake of everyone involved, she offered up a silent prayer Richard Bennings hadn't told the detective about her and Josie's visit. She didn't want to answer questions without her mom by her side.

Greta collected her things and walked toward the law office.

The moment she entered the frosted glass front door, a wave of sadness at facing Franklin's loss crashed into her, followed quickly by another ripple of confusion as to what she was doing here. Not to mention her swelling anxiety over another meeting with Detective McHenry.

Liam strode across the room. He reached out his hand to her, squeezing her fingers warmly. "You made it."

Greta drew in a haggard breath. Her emotions were all over the place. She offered Liam a wry smile. "Barely."

Liam's expression softened. "These are moments I consider celebrations of my clients. I get to carry out their wishes, and there's something beautiful in doing so, don't you think?"

The question was rhetorical, but Greta had never thought of it that way, and it bolstered her spirits a little. Franklin wanted her here. For now, that was all that mattered.

The detective appeared in the doorway Liam had come from. Greta's gaze snagged on him, but he had turned his attention to Liam. "Mr. Shark, are we waiting on anyone else?"

"This should be everyone." Liam applied subtle pressure to the small of Greta's back as he guided her forward. She tried to relax her shoulders, remembering his words. But when she entered the conference room, Greta stiffened again. Across the large oval table sat Richard Bennings.

Sidney, who was seated a chair away from Richard, waved to Greta before calling Liam over. The two put their heads together in conversation, leaving Greta on her own. A rush of heat spread through her entire body, followed by a cool tingly sensation in her extremities. She ran her hand through her curls, shoving her hair behind her ear and casting what she hoped was a casual glance at Detective McHenry. Did he know about her visit to Richard's apartment? She couldn't tell.

Greta feigned a shocked but pleased smile as she stepped around the table. "Richard. What a surprise! It's good to see you." She dropped into the chair next to him, her mind churning. It made sense he was here since he was related to Franklin, but had Detective McHenry figured out as much?

"You too." Richard's voice was barely audible, and beads of sweat dotted his upper lip. Judging from his appearance and the way his gaze ricocheted around the room, never landing directly on her, he wouldn't respond well to small talk, so Greta kept her mouth shut.

Sidney and Liam parted, and Sidney took the seat next to Greta. She struck up a conversation, and Greta made noises when appropriate, but her thoughts were on Richard. Why was he nervous? Was he banking on getting something from Franklin's will? Or was he anxious to be in the presence of a cop again because he was guilty of something?

Liam and Detective McHenry took spots across the table from them. Sidney finally stopped talking, and an awkward silence filled the room before Liam launched into a description of how things were to go down.

"This is rather unnecessary." Liam shot Greta's side of the table a sheepish look. "Anybody can read the will for themselves at the county courthouse since it's now available to the public. But I wanted to talk to you all in person and thought this would be easiest. So, I'm going to go through this." He shuffled some papers in front of him. "Dean Sprangers was Franklin's financial advisor, and Sidney is here from his office to answer any questions I can't."

Sidney sat up straighter next to Greta, and Greta took advantage of Liam's pause and peeked at the detective. His chiseled jaw was set at a right angle, and his granite gaze moved between Greta and Richard.

Greta didn't have time to dwell on Detective McHenry's ominous expression as Liam started reading from a list of items. She was about to find out why she was here.

Chapter Thirty-Four

After reading through a bunch of legalese, Liam glanced up. "Franklin Halloway has left his cabin to Mr. Richard Bennings." Greta snapped her head in Richard's direction.

Richard leaned back, a small smile playing on his lips, almost as if he was pleased to have his expectation realized.

Detective McHenry crossed his arms and stared at Richard. Greta got the distinct impression he was trying to figure out why Franklin would leave his house to a virtual stranger. That answered one of her earlier questions. He must not know about the relation.

Liam plugged along. "Greta, this will be important for you to hear."

Greta knocked her knee on the underside of the table as she turned her attention to Liam.

"It says here, 'I, Franklin Halloway, give my cat, Biff, or any other animal I may own at the time of my death, to Greta Plank,' and it lists your address."

A grin spread over Greta's face, and she nodded her understanding. She hadn't let herself think about what would happen if she would have been forced to give Biff to someone else, and now she didn't have to. She pressed her hands to her cheeks, grateful to Franklin for a gift she didn't even know she needed. This must have been one of the changes Franklin had asked Liam to make to the will after Greta moved in next door. She vowed then and there to become the best cat owner this side of the Mississippi.

"The other item of note is as follows." Liam dropped his gaze and read directly from the will. "'To my neighbor and friend, Greta Plank, I leave my entire rare book collection.'"

Greta, whose mind was still on Biff, didn't register Liam's words. But when Richard let out a strangled gasp next to her, she replayed them in her head.

Wait. What?

The air pressure in the room seemed to drop, and Greta's limbs prickled, as if she'd just emerged from an ice bath. Franklin left her his collection, too? His books were worth thousands and thousands of dollars.

She forced herself to pick her teeth up off the floor, swallowing a couple times to regain control of her mouth. "For real?"

"It says so right here." Liam tapped the paper in front of him, and Greta closed her eyes and pressed her pointer fingers to her lips. Big, sappy tears of gratitude, mingled with disbelief, pooled behind her eyelids as she considered Franklin's generosity. She blinked away her emotions, figuring it was no use making a scene in public, and opened her eyes again. Detective McHenry was staring directly at her. The displeasure in his gaze made Greta want to cry for another reason.

Liam was talking again. Greta gladly turned her attention to him as he detailed how assets and Franklin's savings would be distributed, based on his wishes. Liam read off several names, explaining these recipients would be notified by letter and on and on and on. "Most of Franklin's money will be donated to charities of his choice."

Sidney raised her hand. "We're happy to help coordinate."

Liam dipped his head. "Thank you, but Franklin was clear I handle it, and I intend to follow his wishes. I will certainly reach out if I have any questions. Speaking of questions, Richard or Greta, do you have any for Sidney or myself?"

Greta shook her head slowly.

"Alright." Liam fidgeted with the papers in front of him before glancing up again. "I have a question for both of you, then, and I'm afraid it might be a shocking one."

Greta braced herself. She wasn't sure how much more unexpected news she could handle in this meeting without dissolving into a puddle.

Liam cleared his throat. "Since you two appear to have been Franklin's closest friends and confidants, I'm curious if he ever mentioned anything to you about his estranged daughter."

Next to her, Sidney sucked in a breath. Across the table, Detective McHenry dropped the pen he'd been holding. It rattled on the tabletop. Greta sat stock still. Richard, too, seemed to have frozen in place in his seat. Had they heard Liam correctly? Franklin had a *daughter*?

Liam glanced between Greta and Richard. "Judging from your reactions, I'm guessing you were as startled by this revelation as I was."

"I had no idea Franklin was a dad," Greta said on an exhale.

"Me either," Richard said.

"I figured, but I thought I'd check anyway."

"Can I ask why it matters?" Sidney piped up, and Greta found herself nodding. She wanted to know, too.

"Franklin's will stipulates that if his biological daughter is found, she is to receive an inheritance from him. I had no idea this was a part of the will until I looked at it more closely this week. Unfortunately, Franklin didn't provide any clues or hints as to who this woman is. I don't believe he knew himself. I'll continue the search, but unless Franklin's mystery daughter is found, those funds will be transferred to his charities of choice."

Greta's jaw had gone completely slack as her brain tried to catch up and catalog this new information. Franklin had a daughter, but he didn't know who she was? How? When? *Who?*

"Okay, then. Thanks anyway. That's everything from me for now." Liam stood up.

Sidney rose and walked around the table toward him. Greta barely registered their hushed conversation about Franklin's assets, and something Dean had asked Sidney to run by Liam. She was still too stunned to think straight.

The only thing that forced Greta out of her fog of astonishment was Detective McHenry's severe tone as he came around the table.

"Any idea why Franklin would leave his cabin to you, Mr. Bennings? If, as you told me, you and Franklin were merely acquaintances?"

Richard didn't meet the detective's gaze.

Talk about being wedged between a rock and a hard place. Greta could hardly withhold Richard's familial ties from the detective now only to meet with him tomorrow and spill it all. That would come across as fishy. And if she did that, wouldn't the detective also assume she knew something about Franklin's daughter that she wasn't saying?

Greta looked between Richard and Detective McHenry, who were engaged in a staring contest to end all staring contests. Finally, she threw up her hands. "Franklin and Richard are brothers."

Richard let out a shocked cry, turning wide eyes in her direction. Greta shot him an uneasy glance before staring straight ahead.

With painstaking deliberateness, the detective swiveled his head to face her. "Excuse me?"

"They're related. I'm sure that's why Franklin left Richard his house."

Detective McHenry jammed a menacing glare down Richard's throat. "Is this true?"

Richard lifted his chin. "I didn't lie."

"A lie of omission is still a lie." The detective placed his hands on his hips, and Greta gulped.

To his credit, Richard didn't flinch. "Is there anything else you needed, Detective?"

"Not at the moment," the detective bit out. "Stay available, though."

With that veiled threat made against him, Richard hurried from the room.

"Miss Plank." Detective McHenry spun his attention from a departing Richard to her.

Oh dear.

"Yes?"

"I have some questions for you."

Greta stepped back. "I-I'd like my lawyer to be present for any interrogation. We have some information to share with you, too."

Detective McHenry scanned her face. "Very well. First thing tomorrow morning, then." Without giving her the chance to agree, the detective strode around the table and, after saying a word to Liam, left the building. The rattling of the glass door reached Greta's ears, and she sagged against the table.

Liam and Sidney rushed to her side. "Greta." Liam squinted at her with concerned lines bracketing his eyes. "Are you alright?"

Greta pinched the bridge of her nose. "Yep. I'll be fine."

"Come on. I'll walk you out." Sidney touched Greta's elbow.

Greta offered her a faint smile before turning to say goodbye to Liam.

He held up his cell phone. "I'll be in touch about the books. Be sure to let me know if you have any questions."

"Thank you. This has been…a lot. But I'll reach out soon to figure out the logistics of acquiring the collection. Are the books still in Franklin's house?" Greta knew full well the answer was yes, but she didn't like the idea of Richard having access to the books if he took ownership of the cabin immediately.

"For now," Liam said. "We figured we'd leave them be until you have the adequate space available, and we could get a professional in to handle and transport them."

"What about Mr. Bennings? Won't he want the house cleared out?" Greta asked.

"Mr. Halloway's will stipulates the estate should get the house in order before Mr. Bennings takes ownership, so he won't receive keys or the deed to the land until I sign off on everything that needs to be done."

Sidney chuckled. "Franklin always was a stickler for order. I'm not surprised he had this all thought out."

Greta remembered Franklin's orderliness with fondness and agreed with Sidney. "Thanks, Liam."

She and Sidney left the law office together. Once outside, Sidney tugged at Greta's arm. "Are you sure you're okay? You don't seem well."

Greta wasn't sure how to respond. All she wanted to do was get to her car, drive home, and spoil Biff. She also needed to talk things through with her mom and figure out what she should do to prepare herself for tomorrow morning's meeting with Detective McHenry.

She flashed Sidney a forced smile. "Sorry. My brain is so scattered. I never even thought about Franklin leaving me anything."

CHAPTER THIRTY-FOUR

"You meant a lot to him."

"I guess so." She tucked her chin. "Honestly, the only way I feel like I can repay him is to discover what happened the day he died. I'm getting close to figuring something out, but I'm not sure what yet."

Sidney studied her, worrying her lip. "Just be careful, okay? None of us want to see anything happen to you."

"I know, and I will be. Thanks, Sid."

They hugged goodbye, and Greta got into her car and dialed her mom.

Chapter Thirty-Five

L ouisa picked up on the first ring, and Greta unloaded the entire story to her.

When she finished, her mom was silent, and when she finally spoke, she sounded dead serious. "I'm afraid Detective McHenry now believes you have motive for murder."

Greta froze in place where she had been climbing the steps to her cabin. She groaned. "The books?"

"Ding. Ding. Ding." Greta could picture her mom pacing as she laid out all the facts. "I need you to think very hard. Did Franklin ever hint he was planning to leave you anything when he passed?"

"No!" Greta unlocked her door, walked inside, and slammed it shut, eliciting a low, drawn-out purr from her cat. "I was blindsided by this. I had no idea. We didn't talk about who he would leave his collection to, and I certainly never assumed it would be me. I also never assumed he'd wind up dead or that he had a daughter somewhere, so I guess my assumptions mean absolutely nothing." Greta laughed nervously. Everything seemed so out of her control—like a horrible story, but, in this case, she couldn't set the book down and walk away. This was real life. "So, what do I do?"

"We'll go to the meeting with the detective tomorrow. You won't say a word. I'll do all the talking. We'll present the information about Richard having the book."

Greta let her bag fall off her shoulder. It landed with a thud on the floor in her front hall. Discovering the missing collectible in Richard's possession seemed like a lifetime ago. Had it only been yesterday? Biff coiled his way between her legs as she walked into the living room. "The detective will try to use the rare book discovery against me somehow. Like he keeps doing."

"Not if I have anything to say about it. But you have to promise me you'll be careful. Now that we know what we know about Richard, and he knows what he knows about you acquiring Franklin's book collection, there's no telling what he'll do."

"What are you saying?" A sudden fear crept over Greta. She flopped down on her couch, letting the suede fabric hug her.

"I'm saying if it's like you thought and books were at the root of Franklin's murder, you now have a big target on your back."

Greta held in a gasp. "When you put it like that, I sort of want to hide under the covers and never come out."

Her mom's voice softened. "Honey, I'm not trying to freak you out. I'm just trying to make you see the seriousness of the situation. You got home okay, right?"

"Yeah. I'm at my house." She scanned her cabin. It was a cozy, warm space, and she felt safe within the wood-plank walls. No boogeymen or rabid rare book collectors could touch her here. Speaking of rare books... Greta glanced around again. Where was she going to put Franklin's collection?

"Do you need anything tonight? Otherwise, why don't I meet you at the library first thing in the morning, and we'll go see the detective. It's about time I give him a piece of my mind."

Greta chuckled. "You're the best, Mom. I'll see you in the morning."

"Good night, dear. Love you."

"Love you, too." Greta hung up the phone and stared straight ahead until the photos lining her wall blurred. She closed her eyes and thought over the events of the past two days. Like she'd told Sidney, she was close to a breakthrough. She had to be. But it was like whatever it was seemed just out of her sight. Just beyond her grasp. She had the key, but she needed to figure out what it was and what it unlocked.

"Come here, Biff." She made kissing noises, and the tabby happily joined her on the couch, scampering along the backrest before circling and settling onto a nearby cushion.

Greta reached over and scratched the markings between Biff's eyes. "How'd you like to stay here with me?"

Biff raised his head, and his whiskers twitched.

Greta smiled. "Good. I'd like it, too." She sat with the cat for a moment but soon started pacing. Her conversation with her mom left her feeling on edge. Greta double-checked the lock on the front door before crossing the living room and opening the back door out to the deck. Biff had disappeared into the kitchen, and Greta walked outside. She let the sounds and smells of the autumn night wash over her. The lake water was still, but the breeze rustled the leaves in the trees, and the scent of the damp sand wafted up to her.

Greta slid her phone out of her pocket and sunk down into an Adirondack chair. She typed a quick text to Josie and Iris. She waffled but eventually decided she'd tell them about the rare books acquisition in person tomorrow. Greta grinned at how shocked the two would be. If anyone would understand the magnitude of such a gift, it was her librarian friends.

Greta placed her phone on the arm of the chair. She leaned back, letting her mind drift to the titles in Franklin's collection. She couldn't wait to get her hands on the books. It was sort of thrilling, all the treasures she'd discover when she could go through them. What a way to remember Franklin. A buzz of anticipation zipped through her, but Greta tempered it. She didn't want the detective to have any ammunition to use against her. She needed to table her excitement about the collection until after their conversation in the morning.

The thought of the upcoming interrogation and sitting across from Detective McHenry, while he accused her of murder, sent a ball of tension rolling across her back. She stood up and paced the deck before walking down the steps and out onto the dock that jutted into the lake. The structure creaked and dipped under her weight until she stopped at the dock's edge.

The lake was a black sheet of glass stretching out before her. Greta gazed at it for a long time and then looked up at the star-splattered sky.

Kelly would have loved her little cabin on the water, and her sister would have appreciated a chilly night like this one on the lake. Kelly and Franklin would have hit it off, too. Her big sister could charm anyone. Everyone knew Greta to be cheerful and friendly, but she had nothing on Kelly. Kelly's mantra had always been, *a joyful heart is the body's best medicine.* Her sister had truly believed she could handle anything life threw at her as long as she smiled through it. And that's how Greta remembered Kelly—smiling. Always smiling.

Greta wanted more than anything to carry that same torch, but life sure had tried to snuff it out of her a time or two in the past few years. She wrapped her arms around herself, cradling her aching heart. "I miss you, Kelly," she whispered, her voice lost in the sudden gust of wind. Shivering, Greta shoved thoughts of her sister aside.

Across the lake, she could see the lights of Kennedy's Cozy Cottages, and to the left, Franklin's cabin stood dark. Pretty soon, she'd have to call it Richard's cabin. Unless he was, in fact, behind Franklin's death. In that case, Greta wasn't sure what would happen to the property. Ed might get his way after all. Maybe that had been his goal all along.

Greta added a moan of frustration to the groan of the tree branches swaying in the wind along the shoreline. She stared out over the water, going through different scenarios and outcomes, until the chill in the night air snapped her out of her thoughts. She could no longer feel her nose.

She was about to return to her cabin when abnormal movement to her left caught her eye. Greta leaned forward as far as she dared over the edge of her dock. A figure, slinking through the shadows, appeared at the base of Franklin's deck on the far side of the cabin.

Greta strained her eyes across the water to try to get a better look as the wind whistled around her, tossing her curls into her face. She couldn't be sure, but it looked like the person in the shadows was Richard. Liam had said he wasn't to take ownership of the cabin yet, so what was he doing there?

Greta weighed her options, cursing herself for leaving her phone on her deck. She rarely brought it down by the water, because, with her luck, she'd drop it into the lake, but her well-intentioned rule was backfiring. Granted, she wouldn't have been able to get a decent picture of the intruder in the dark at this distance, and a lit-up phone screen may have tipped him off. Still, she hated to leave her position on the dock while there was a chance to see what Richard was up to. But then her mom's warning to be careful flashed across her mind, and Greta knew she should abandon her station as lookout and contact the authorities.

Her decision made, Greta turned around to sneak up to the deck and grab her phone when, out of nowhere, a large branch came arching through the air, straight for her.

Before Greta could register what was happening, see who was swinging, or scream, the branch connected with her head.

Chapter Thirty-Six

Greta regained consciousness underwater. Years of being a swimmer and the associated muscle memory had her kicking before she even registered what was going on or remembered what had happened.

Had she tripped and fallen into the water? That was so like her and her clumsy self. Greta struggled against the inky liquid. Her arms were as heavy as lead, but she used all the strength she had in her legs to break through the water's surface. She took a wheezing breath before she floundered and went under again. She was fully clothed, and every article of clothing weighed on her like a bag full of books as she struggled to keep kicking and get her mouth above the surface. Her head pounded, and a hazy picture of how she'd ended up like this developed in her mind as she forced herself to kick.

She'd seen Richard at Franklin's house. Someone hit her with a branch. She lost consciousness. She must have been thrown into the lake.

It was then she registered the cold. She maneuvered herself so she was on her back and could exert the least amount of energy possible, but, with her failing strength, how was she going to get herself out of the lake? The dock was too high to hoist herself up onto. She'd stored the ladder for the winter after she and Josie had their last paddleboard adventure of the season. She'd floated well away from the shore, and to swim the distance back seemed impossible in her current state.

Greta's chest tightened, and her next panicky breath came with a mouthful of lake water.

"Greta?"

The voice pierced through the night air and penetrated her foggy brain. Someone was coming for her. Greta kicked hard, ignoring the burning in her lungs.

"Greta, can you hear me?"

The closest Greta could come to a response was a sputtering cough as she tried to clear the water from her windpipe.

"Hang on!"

Greta couldn't identify who the male voice belonged to, but a flashlight beamed across the lake and over her before feet pounded on the dock and something splashed into the water. In no time, a strong arm wound around her, and, in spite of her aching muscles, she tried to keep kicking as her rescuer started swimming them to shore. She closed her eyes against the pain.

"Hey, Greta. Listen to me. I need you to keep your eyes open. I know it's hard, but I need you to try."

Greta groaned and tried to do as she was instructed, but her eyelids were like crisp, new paperback bindings—continuously snapping shut.

"Hang on. We're almost there." The water became shallower, and soon her rescuer was walking. He heaved Greta into his arms.

"It's okay. I've got you."

"Richard?" Greta mumbled.

He didn't respond. Instead, he tightened his grip under her knees and around her back and started the trek up the steps and toward her cabin.

The indoor light was harsh on Greta's eyes. She moaned and tried to use her arms to shield her face as Richard brought her inside.

"Take it easy." He set her down on the couch and reached for the quilt she kept hanging over the recliner chair. She sat like a child and let him wrap her in it. She closed her eyes again as he rushed into her kitchen. Something clanged, and she grimaced.

Biff catapulted himself onto the couch, rubbing against her shoulder and licking at the water dripping from her hair before dropping to the floor and scampering around in a circle, meowing. The poor cat had seen her at her worst twice in as many weeks.

Richard reappeared and thrust a mug of hot tea into her hands. "Drink this. It'll warm you. We're going to the ER."

"No. I don't need to see a doctor." As Greta tried to protest, Richard pressed a towel he must've grabbed from the kitchen onto the side of her head, and she cried out, pulling away from him. "What are you doing?" The pain of the pressure he was applying, coupled with the lake water she'd consumed, made her stomach revolt.

"You're bleeding." He continued pushing the towel to her temple, ignoring her objections. "I'm sorry this hurts, but you don't want to mess around with a head wound. Try to take some deep breaths to help with the nausea."

Greta didn't have enough energy to argue. She willed herself to stop shaking even as a water drip fell from her nose.

After a minute, Richard adjusted his grip on the towel. "Can you apply pressure?"

Greta's head still thundered, but she released the blanket with one hand and took the towel from Richard.

"I'm going to run next door and get my car. Is there anyone I should call for you?"

Greta grimaced. Her parents were going to freak, and she didn't want to deal with them right now. "Call Josie. My phone is out on the deck."

"I'll grab it." Richard jogged through the door and returned with her cell. "Here, can you unlock it? I can talk to her if you want." Greta dismissed the lock screen via facial recognition. "Okay. I'll call her on my way to get my car. I don't want to waste any more time. Don't try to move until I come back."

Greta whimpered her assent as Richard hustled from the room, phone to his ear. How was he here? Thank God he was. Greta shivered again, but not from the cold. If Richard hadn't come, she might be at the bottom of the lake right now.

Chapter Thirty-Seven

When they arrived at the hospital, Josie was waiting. Richard stepped to the side as nurses whisked Greta into an open room.

"Make sure she stays warmed up," Richard called out.

"We have warming blankets ready." The nurse, whose name was Tracy, gestured to a giant mound of Pill Fleece Fabric at the end of the bed.

"Get Richard a change of clothes," Greta muttered to Josie, who was with her in the exam room as she de-robed and donned the hospital gown as instructed.

"Huh?"

"He jumped in the lake after me. He must be freezing." Greta climbed cautiously onto the hospital bed and pulled the heated blanket up to her mouth.

"Dang. He didn't say. Are you okay in here for a second? I'll go make sure he gets some scrubs or something."

"I'm fine." Greta's eyelids drooped. She was finally warming up, and all she wanted to do was go to sleep and pretend this whole night was a bad dream. Greta pinched her eyes shut, but she wasn't dreaming. Someone had tried to kill her. If she had any solace left in the goodness of people and in the safety of her little town after Franklin's death, it was now completely ripped away. Larkspur was supposed to be an oasis for her. A new beginning. A place where no harm would dare come. Now it was marred with the stain of death and attempted murder.

The door to her room creaked open, and Greta clamped the covers to her chin, but it was only Josie with Tracy, who was back to do her initial exam.

Greta willed herself to release the tension that had her holding her entire body rigid, as if she was poised on the precipice of fight or flight and getting ready to flee.

"Richard said he's fine." Josie pulled a chair next to Greta's bed and sat down. "He's running out to his car to get a change of clothes. I told him he didn't have to stay, that I'd bring you home. But he insisted. He wants to talk to you in a little bit."

Greta sighed. A man not an hour ago she was convinced had probably murdered her friend had saved her life. Talk about a plot twist. What was she supposed to make of that?

Josie sat quietly by as Tracy examined Greta. "You've got a bruise forming here on your hip." Tracy stepped over to a cabinet drawer and retrieved a small ruler. Holding it up to the abrasion, Tracy snapped a quick picture. "Where else does it hurt?"

"Mostly my head."

Tracy started peeling back layers of Greta's tangle of curls. She was trying to be gentle, but every time she came close to the spot on the left side of her head where she'd taken the blow, Greta saw stars, and the room spun.

"You've got quite a laceration here." Tracy used one gloved hand to keep Greta's hair back and the other to take a picture. "It's good you got pressure on it when you did. We're going to have to stitch you up. Fortunately, you won't even be able to tell because it's under your hair."

The next hour passed in a blur of nurses, lab techs, and exam rooms. The doctor who was tending to her bustled into her room after all was said and done. "You have a concussion, but your CT scan confirmed there's no bleeding on your brain. The effects of this night will linger for a couple days, but you'll make a full recovery, and your stitches will dissolve on their own, so I don't need to see you again unless you have any issues."

"That's good news. Thank you."

"Of course." He smiled kindly. "Do you have someone who can stay with you tonight? Protocol has changed, and now it's not necessary to wake concussion patients every few hours to check on them, but I'd be relieved if you weren't going home to an empty house."

"I'm staying over tonight." Josie stepped forward. She grabbed Greta's hand in both of hers. "Iris said she will come too if you want, but I told her to get a good night's rest so she can open the library for us first thing tomorrow."

"Sounds like you have a plan in place," the doctor said. "I'll get Tracy in with your discharge papers, then. Please don't hesitate to call us if you need anything. Oh." He stopped and faced her again from the doorway. "We'll turn over all evidence to the Larkspur police detective who has been waiting outside, per his request."

"What detective?" Greta pressed a gentle finger to her temple and looked to Josie.

Josie pulled a face. "Yeah, Detective McHenry is here. Richard called him."

"Richard? Is he still here, too?" Greta asked, and when Josie nodded, Greta looked heavenward but then grimaced at the pressure it put on her head. "Ow. Okay. Let's get this over with."

After Tracy ran through her discharge instructions, Josie helped Greta stand, and they made their way into the ER waiting room.

Detective McHenry and Richard rose from where they were sitting three seats apart in the uncomfortable blue plastic chairs. Greta was glad to see Richard was in a pair of black joggers and a sweatshirt.

"Miss—" The detective's voice came out warbled, and he cleared his throat before trying again. "Miss Plank. How are you feeling?"

"Concussed." Greta shrugged. "And tired."

"I want to get some questions answered from you right away. If you're up for it. I won't keep you too long." Detective McHenry shifted his weight in a way that made Greta think he was almost reluctant to have to put her through this. Then again, she'd just suffered a head trauma, so maybe she was reading too much into his body language.

Greta leaned against Josie. "I'm not sure what I can say that you don't already know, but I'll try."

"Good." Detective McHenry motioned to the chairs behind him. "Let's sit."

When they were situated, Detective McHenry pulled out his notebook. "Okay, Miss Plank. Start at the beginning." He clicked his pen and sat at the ready.

Greta spoke to the floor tiles. "I went down to the dock after I got home from the will reading. I was trying to clear my head, and being near the water always helps. At least it used to." Greta pressed her eyes closed for a minute before looking up and starting again. "I couldn't have stood there for more than five minutes when I-I turned to head back inside." She paused and gave Richard a doleful look. "I thought I saw you over by Franklin's property."

"Mr. Bennings informed me of his whereabouts." Detective McHenry swooshed his pen, waving off her concern. "Please, continue."

"I saw movement. I recognized it as a branch swinging through the air. I must have blacked out the moment it hit me because I don't remember impact."

The detective jotted down a quick note. "Did you see who swung at you?"

"No. It was so dark by the lake, and it was windy. That must have masked the sound of the person approaching me from behind. I don't know. Everything happened so fast. I didn't even register what was going on, let alone have the wherewithal to try to get an ID."

"Understandable." The detective scribbled another note without sparing her a glance.

Greta sat back, her mouth gaping with her shock. This might have been the first time Detective McHenry had understood *anything* she said. She was staring at him when he matched her gaze.

"What?" he asked.

Suddenly, she was dizzy again, but Greta shot him a small grin. "I'm just wondering if I should look for pigs flying or something, because you don't seem to be holding this little swim against me. At least in relation to Franklin's case. It's a miracle."

Detective McHenry blinked a drawn-out blink before shaking his head once. He returned to scribbling notes. She'd rendered him speechless. Too bad her head hurt like the dickens—she couldn't even enjoy the moment.

Instead, Greta turned her attention to Richard. "Did you see anything when you got there? Thank you, by the way. For rescuing me."

Richard acknowledged her gratitude with a slight dip of his head. "Like you said, it was really dark and shadowy down there. I was walking the outskirts of Franklin's property. Yeah, I haven't taken ownership yet, but after I ate dinner near Mr. Shark's office, I decided I wanted to see Franklin's house before I drove back to Karrington. I was on the far side of the cabin, so I didn't notice you or hear anything until the splash. I took off through the woods, and all I saw was a figure fleeing up the ravine on the opposite side of your house before I turned my attention to the lake and tried to help you."

Greta started shaking, and Josie reached her arm around her shoulders.

"Thank goodness you were there." Josie smiled at Richard.

Greta was more grateful than she could say, but anxiety gripped her like a mechanical claw around a stuffed toy. This was tied up with Franklin's murder. She was sure of it, and she no longer wanted any part of this case. She'd leave everything to the professionals. As for her, well, the person who attacked her was somewhere in Larkspur. Greta shut her eyes against the black spots clouding her vision.

"Why did this happen?" Josie asked.

Detective McHenry spun his notebook shut. "I can't say for sure. It seems highly suspicious to me this comes right on the heels of Franklin's will reading."

Greta remembered what her mom said about her having a target on her back.

Josie's face twisted in confusion. "What does the will reading have to do with it?"

"You didn't tell her?" Detective McHenry asked Greta.

"I was going to tell her in person tomorrow." Greta turned to Josie. "Franklin left his entire rare books collection to me."

Josie's mouth dropped open. "Holy sh—"

"I know," Greta cut her off. "It's a huge deal."

Detective McHenry interjected. "Did you tell anyone else about the will reading?"

"I called my mom, but that's it." Greta sighed. She still had to call her parents and tell them what happened to her. They were going to flip, and not in a good way.

The detective pressed his mouth into a firm line. "The will is public record, so anyone could have found out about your inheritance, but it seems more likely the only people who know are you, me, Richard, and the other people who were present."

Greta leaned forward and rested her head in her hands. "Liam and Sidney."

"What's your relationship with Mr. Shark?"

Greta's elbow slipped off her knee, and pain shot through her head. She groaned.

"Easy there." Josie reached over and patted Greta's arm.

Greta winced and looked at Detective McHenry. "He's my friend. He didn't have anything to do with this, if that's what you're implying."

The detective flipped his notebook back open. "And Sidney?"

"Also, a friend." Greta stood and blew out a breath. "This is ridiculous. And I'm tired. Can I go home now?" She swayed, exhaustion shoving at her from all directions. Josie stood and placed a steadying arm around her waist.

Detective McHenry rose and pocketed his notebook. "I'll walk you both to your car, and I'm going to follow you back to your place. Miss Plank, I'd like to make sure your house is secure before I leave for the night."

Greta agreed and said goodbye to Richard. She wanted to hug him, but their relationship hadn't reached hugging level. It was only yesterday she'd been nosing around his apartment. And there was the fact he'd been snooping around Franklin's house...

Nope. Greta wasn't going to try to figure it out. She was done.

When they pulled up to her cabin, Greta could almost hear her bed calling to her, but her stomach barreled a hard left at the thought of going inside. She was glad Josie was staying the night.

Someone tapped on Josie's window, and Greta screamed before covering her mouth.

"It's only the detective." Josie used one hand to roll down the window and the other to give Greta's knee a comforting squeeze.

"Sorry." Greta's body thrummed with adrenaline.

Detective McHenry poked his head in. "Miss Plank, do you leave a spare key anywhere?"

"No, but here. I have my set in my purse." Greta rummaged around in the bag Richard had brought to the hospital for her and retrieved her key ring. She reached across Josie to hand it to the detective, her fingers brushing his and sending a shock snapping between them. Greta shook out her hand as Detective McHenry strode to her front door and inserted the key. Her pulse reached every corner of her body, pounding out a painful rhythm in time with the throbbing in her head. "He better not find anyone inside."

"This is just a precaution." Even Josie's voice trailed off as they watched the detective pull a gun from underneath his jacket.

Time slowed to less than a trickle—a hanging drip of water clinging to the lip of a faucet, refusing to fall. Greta's head started to spin, but she didn't tear her gaze from her front door. Finally, Detective McHenry appeared and waved them inside. When they stepped out of the car, he spoke. "All clear. The cat's in the living room perched on your bookshelf."

"Thank you for checking." Greta's voice sounded robotic. She was so tired. Now that she could rest assured no one would jump out of her closet and try to murder her or Biff in the middle of the night, she didn't think she'd have any problems sleeping.

Detective McHenry stepped out of the way so they could enter the house. He'd flipped the lights on for them. "Here's my card. It has my cell phone number on it, too. Reach out if you need anything." He handed a business card to Josie, who passed it to Greta. "Miss Plank, we planned on meeting tomorrow morning, but let's postpone for the time being. I'll need you to sign your formal statement, as well, but that can wait."

All Greta could do was nod. Josie and the detective whispered to each other as she walked into her bedroom, but she had no desire to know what they were conferring about. She got out a spare blanket and pillow from her closet and set them on the couch for Josie as her friend shut and locked the front door.

"Greta," Josie called as she headed to her room.

Greta stopped, waiting for her to say more. When she didn't, Greta couldn't decide if the sadness and pity in Josie's expression made her want to cry or run.

"It'll be okay," Greta said. But the words tasted all wrong on her tongue. Lies usually did.

Greta completed her nightly routine on autopilot. She took a shower to wash away the grime of lake water. She was careful so as not to aggravate her head, and by the time she stepped out and was donning her warmest pair of flannel pajamas, Greta was relieved to find the pounding had stopped. In its place was a dull ache—likely as much from the mental blow as the physical one. Because the truth she'd been shoving to the back of the shelf since Franklin's death and Dolores's accident was made perfectly clear to her tonight: Larkspur, her safe haven, was no longer safe.

Chapter Thirty-Eight

Greta wasn't sure how long she slept, but all of a sudden, she was awake. It was still dark in her bedroom, and for a while, she listened to the beating of her own heart in her ears, willing her body to relax and rest, but it was no use. Greta groaned and untangled her feet from under the covers. She twisted on the lamp and jumped at the shadows suddenly dancing on the far wall. Greta gripped her bedsheets with one hand and grabbed her phone with the other. 3:45 am.

She'd only slept for a few hours. Now what? She could hardly go into the living room and wake Josie. She was putting her friend out enough as it was. She sat on the edge of her bed and scrolled mindlessly through her phone. Not finding anything worthy of her attention, Greta stood and paced the floor in her bedroom, cracking her knuckles and wringing her hands. On her fifth trip to the front wall, she pulled the curtain back.

A small light was visible in the otherwise black night. It illuminated the face of Detective McHenry, sitting in his car, still parked on the road outside her cabin. He appeared to be looking at his phone, too.

Greta let the curtain fall back in to place and stood still. A sensation she couldn't quite put her finger on swirled in her gut and made her chest tighten. Greta leaned forward and stole another look out the window to be sure she wasn't imagining it.

Detective McHenry was still there—in all his hard-angled, brooding glory.

Greta looked around her darkened room, wincing at the tug on her scalp from her stitches. Moving carefully, she grabbed her bathrobe and slid on her rubber-bottomed slippers. She opened the door to her room, trying not to make any noise. Biff was curled up in his cat bed, asleep, and Josie's breathing was rhythmic as Greta crept across the living room floor and down the hall to the front door. She unlocked it, and when the deadbolt clicked, Greta waited and listened, letting out a puff of relief when Josie's breathing remained undisturbed. She opened the front door enough to squeeze outside and shut it behind her without a sound, walking into the night. Greta wasn't sure what she was doing or what she wanted to say to Detective McHenry, but she was like a caged animal in her room, so if nothing else, the fresh air would do her well.

The detective's head snapped up from his phone, and his hand went to the holster at his hip, but when Greta waved, he relaxed into his seat. He reached to the side and pressed the unlock button. Greta opened the passenger door and got inside, grateful to be out of the chilly night air.

"Couldn't sleep?" Detective McHenry spoke as if he had some experience in the insomniac department.

Even with her muddled head, Greta wondered again at his past life in Chicago. What kept him up at night?

Greta cleared her throat. "Yeah. No. What are you doing here?"

"Watching your house. I had a cruiser stationed here until about three, but we're short-staffed, so I told them I'd take a turn."

Greta stared into her lap, her eyes prickling. "Aren't you exhausted?"

"I'll get enough sleep here and there. I'm not worried."

Greta didn't understand how a couple winks here and there constituted enough sleep. She dreaded how boorish she was going to be in the morning, based on the measly amount of shut-eye she'd gotten. She'd be a regular Ebenezer Scrooge. She functioned best on a full eight hours of rest. She could manage with seven and a large cup of coffee, but anything less and it was bound to be a rough day. Greta sighed. It had been a rough couple of days already. As if to make sure she hadn't forgotten about the entire ordeal, Greta's head thumped with renewed intensity, so she closed her eyes.

"Anything you want to talk about?" Detective McHenry's voice punctured the darkness. Greta glanced at him out of the corner of her eye. He wasn't looking at her. He had his head back on the headrest, his dark black hair melding in with the black leather, the scent of which was providing Greta with a peculiar sort of comfort.

She mirrored his position, closing her eyes again and letting her head rest. "I don't know. Not really." She clenched her fingers together. "I give up."

"What?" The tone of the detective's voice was urgent.

She rolled her head to the left and met his concerned gaze. "Don't worry. Not, like, give up on life. Just on people and on this place. I don't know what to do or how to be anymore."

Detective McHenry sat back. The lines around his eyes eased, but his face still held a slight frown.

When he didn't say anything, Greta continued. "It's always been my default to find the best in everyone and to trust in happy endings, but my faith in people—in everything working out—keeps being shattered. I've bounced back in the past, but I don't know anymore. Now I'm not safe in my house, in this town...a place I love. I don't know if I can stay here. It's all a mess."

They sat in silence. Thoughts about different aspects of the case were attempting to steal her attention, but Greta was tired of thinking about it all—worrying about it all—so she focused on counting all the lights along the detective's dashboard until he reached out and placed his hand over hers. She tensed under his touch, and a streak of warmth spread from her arm to her heart.

"I'm going to figure out who did this. To you and Dolores and Franklin." Detective McHenry's words were softly spoken, but they reverberated around the cop car with the force of an oath.

Greta's throat was thick. She didn't try to say anything. She wasn't sure she could. She wasn't sure she believed him.

Chapter Thirty-Nine

Greta awoke to the sun shining through the windshield. She was slumped in the passenger seat of the detective's sedan, with a trail of dried drool running from her mouth to her neck. She tried to inconspicuously wipe it away and save face, but when she looked to the driver's seat, the detective wasn't there. Greta sat upright. According to her phone, it was only six thirty.

Detective McHenry and Josie were standing on her porch.

Greta pushed the car door open and unfolded her cramped body. Her head barely hurt anymore, which was a pleasant surprise, but she was stiff all over, and she imagined if she pulled up her shirt, she'd see a pretty nasty bruise from where she had fallen after being struck.

"Morning, sunshine." Josie led the detective down the porch steps, and they walked toward Greta.

Greta stifled a yawn. "Morning."

"I'm going to get going." Detective McHenry ran a hand through his hair. "I'll give you a call later to check in, Miss Plank. You have my number if you need anything in the meantime."

The fog of sleep hadn't fully lifted, but if she didn't know better, she'd say Detective McHenry was being—dare she say it?—nice.

Greta thanked him, and Detective McHenry climbed into his car. She took a step back, and Josie slung her arm around Greta. "I called your parents. I didn't want your mom to drive all the way over here for your meeting with the detective only to find out what happened last night."

"Oh gosh. Thank you." Greta closed her eyes, bracing for the worst. "How were they?"

"I started by telling them you're okay."

Greta chuckled. "Smart."

Josie nudged her side. "It's good to see a smile on that pretty face of yours."

"It's been harder than usual to smile these days."

"I get that." Josie inclined her head. "We're not going to focus on the bad, though. Your mom and dad are going to be here in a couple hours. For now, I'm going to make you a breakfast fit for a queen, and we're both going to go to work."

"I don't want to see anyone," Greta protested. She'd planned on calling in sick.

"You can sit in the office then, but I'm not leaving you alone until your parents get here. And besides, what would you do all day if you weren't at work? Sit around and dwell on the what-ifs? That's not healthy or productive. Come." Josie pivoted toward the cabin and waved her hand over her shoulder. "First, we eat. Then we work."

Josie was right. Being at the library was good for Greta. After greeting Iris, who gripped her in a bone-crushing hug, and saying hello to a worried-looking Dean and Sidney, Greta holed up in the office and got to work patching the rest of the books in the "in need of repair" pile. The mindless work calmed Greta. She pulled up an instrumental playlist of pop hits on her phone and let her mind go blank as she bandaged ripped pages and glued separated spines.

Greta was so engrossed in thinking about nothing she jumped and dropped a book when Josie popped her head into the office two hours later. "Your parents are here."

Greta was in her mom's arms in no time, the familiar scent of rose and honey from her mom's shampoo an elixir for her weary heart and mind. Tears threatened against the back of Greta's eyes, but she pinched them away. She didn't want to break down—not at the library.

"Thank you for coming." She finally pulled back, but one look at the worry lines creasing her mom's brow, and Greta buried her head back into her mom's chest.

Her dad stroked her hair like he used to do when she was a child. "Of course. And we'll stay for as long as you need."

"It sounds like Josie took good care of you." Her mom eased Greta upright and reached out her hand to Josie.

Josie squeezed Louisa's hand. "Nothing Greta wouldn't have done for me. I'm just glad she's okay."

"We all are." Iris approached with Dean and Sidney. "Greta, why don't you take the rest of the day for yourself. Josie and I can handle things here, right Jos?"

"Of course. I was going to suggest the same thing."

Greta pressed her lips together. She had the best friends.

Greta retreated to the office for her purse and jacket before leading her parents out of the library. They paused in the vestibule.

"What do you want to do for the day, honey?" her dad asked.

"Something that doesn't remind me of Franklin, or the case, or the fact a person tried to seriously hurt me last night," Greta said without hesitation.

"About that." Her mom was twiddling with the beaded necklace she wore. "Since I'm here, I think it makes sense to have a word with this detective. You do still have information on a possible suspect. We need to share it with the police."

Greta groaned. Her mom was right, but something had shifted between herself and Detective McHenry last night. They had established a rickety sort of truce, and she didn't want to ruin it. She also didn't like the idea of throwing shade at Richard, the man who saved her life, but she didn't have another option—not with her mom staring at her, determination etched across her face.

Greta sighed and pointed down the hallway. "The police office is this way."

Chapter Forty

They walked down the corridor, and Greta pulled open the back door to the police station.

"You let me do the talking, G." Greta's mom patted her arm and walked inside. "Lori! Hi! How good to see you."

"Louisa Plank! As I live and breathe." Lori skirted her desk to embrace her friend. "When I heard the news about your daughter, I figured you'd show up in Larkspur." Lori reached over to hug Greta next. "And Greta, I'm so glad you're okay. When Detective McHenry told me what happened last night, I was convinced he was fibbing. It's awful."

Greta dipped her chin but didn't have a chance to say anything before her mom started talking again. "Speaking of Detective McHenry, I'd like to have a word with him. As Greta's legal counsel."

"He's in his office. Let me get him for you." Lori put her desk phone to her ear and tapped a button on the base. "Detective McHenry? Yes. Greta Plank is here to see you. No, she has her lawyer here, too." Lori's gaze snagged on Louisa, and the two friends shared a smile. "Okay. Yes. I'll tell them. Thanks." Lori hung up the phone. "He'll be out in a couple minutes."

Louisa began examining the old street maps and vintage safety posters lining the walls of the police department.

Greta's dad took a seat in one of the chairs to the side of Lori's desk. "I'll stay out here and let you two take care of your business. Then I vote we go out for lunch."

Greta smiled at her dad before shifting on her feet. Where did she stand in Detective McHenry's estimation? Before last night, she would have assumed she was still at the top of his suspect list. But it seemed all she needed to do to prove her innocence was get knocked over the head and shoved in the lake. Greta tugged her coat more tightly around herself.

In the detective's defense, though, he'd proved himself committed to her. Or her safety, at least. It said something about his character that he stayed outside her house all night long.

Greta's head jerked up at the sound of a door opening down the hallway. A second later, Detective McHenry strode in her direction. His jaw was lined with day-old scruff, and her heart flew into her throat. He probably hadn't been home to shave since standing guard at her house. The knowledge that he cared about her enough to forfeit a night's sleep seeped its way through her pores and settled into her skin like the words of her favorite comfort reads.

Detective McHenry's face was marked with tired lines, but his eyes were still sharp as he looked her over before turning to her mom.

Louisa straightened her tortoiseshell glasses before holding out her hand. "Detective McHenry, I presume?"

"Yes." He shook her proffered hand. "And you must be Miss Plank's lawyer."

"I am. Louisa Plank. Lawyer and mother."

Detective McHenry looked between Greta and her mom before he narrowed his gaze at Lori, who was doing an excellent job of not making eye contact. He cleared his throat. "I see. What can I do for you both today? Is everything okay, Miss Plank?"

Greta opened her mouth to speak, but her mom held up her palm, silencing her. "We have some information we'd like to share with the Larkspur Police Department regarding the Franklin Halloway case. I've instructed my client not to say another word until you've fully cleared her from suspicion. Is there someplace we can sit down and talk?"

Detective McHenry directed them to the conference room, and Greta sat next to her mom, listening as she efficiently and succinctly laid out the evidence of the stolen book Greta had found in Richard's apartment.

"And I understand it's also been brought to your attention Richard

Bennings is Franklin Halloway's half-brother." Her mom stared down the detective and rolled her eyes when he neither confirmed nor denied it. "There's no need to act so stern. Greta told you about the relation, and I'm certain you've done your due diligence and checked it out on your end. But just in case you haven't had a chance to do so, here's the proof." Her mom presented the detective with relevant articles and a family tree with the genealogy cited.

Detective McHenry took the documents and studied them before turning to Greta. She squirmed under the intensity of his stare. "You've been investigating, then?" he asked.

Greta sucked in a defensive breath, but her mom put her hand on Greta's knee, stopping her response. "What my client has been doing is neither here nor there. She's merely been researching in an attempt to clear her name. Nothing against the law about it, if you're implying otherwise."

Greta had nearly forgotten her mom cut her teeth as a defense attorney in Chicago before leaving big-city life behind in favor of small-town law. She hadn't lost her edge.

"Perhaps the better question is what sort of investigating have *you* been doing, Detective? Because not only is Mr. Halloway dead, but I understand Mrs. Jenkins was attacked and injured, and Greta could have been killed." Her mom shot daggers across the table at Detective McHenry, who pressed his lips together, so firmly his mouth became a pale white line.

"As I told Miss Plank"—Detective McHenry raked a hand through his hair and glanced in her direction before meeting Louisa's glare—"I will figure out who did this. To Franklin, Dolores, and her."

Greta's mom paused, staring down the detective as if sizing up his sincerity. Greta couldn't tell if she was still functioning in her role as attorney or if she'd slipped into mom-mode. Finally, Louisa shot the detective a dazzling smile before standing up. "That's all I needed to hear. Thank you, Detective. Please keep us posted if we can be of any further assistance. I'll leave my card with Lori." Her mom swept out of the room with all the panache of royalty. Out of the corner of Greta's eye, she caught a small smile on Detective McHenry's lips, but when he saw her looking at him, he schooled his features and gave her a single nod.

Greta hurried after her mom.

"So, where should we get lunch?" Her dad rubbed his hands together as soon as they rejoined him in the office lobby.

"Somewhere good. I worked up an appetite. Sparring with the police is quite fun." Her mom's eyes sparkled with good humor as they said goodbye to Lori.

Greta laughed despite the circumstances. "Mom, you were great."

She hooked her arm through Greta's. "It's easy when my client is innocent."

Chapter Forty-One

Greta spent the weekend playing board games, watching movies, and acclimating Biff to her parents. By Sunday night at dinnertime, she almost felt normal—at least until she caught a glimpse of the squad car creeping past her cabin. Over the past two days, it had become a common occurrence. Every time she was in her kitchen, she had the sensation she was being watched...because she was. Greta had no doubt Detective McHenry had ordered the patrolling officer to keep a close eye on her. At least now he was doing it for her safety and not because he suspected her of committing a crime.

Greta tore her gaze from the window and cut the water to the sink, shaking out a colander of freshly washed grapes. She tossed them into the bowl of fruit salad and joined her parents at the dinner table. After saying a meal prayer, they dug in.

"We are so thankful you're okay, Greta." Her mom spoke around a mouthful.

Greta sighed. She'd dodged this conversation all weekend, but they wouldn't have been her parents if they hadn't made her talk about it eventually. "Me too."

"I can't even imagine what we would have done if something would have happened to you." Her dad looked at her with a mixture of pain and adoration flickering in his eyes, and it wasn't difficult for Greta to tell he was remembering Kelly.

Greta bit down on her lip and refused to meet her parents' gazes. She didn't want to think about it, and she didn't want to cry. She was afraid once she started, she wouldn't stop.

"How are you holding up, G?" Her mom's voice was gentle but firm. She was going to make Greta face the reality of it all.

Greta's throat felt tight. "I don't feel like myself anymore. This whole thing with Franklin…it's messed with me. I'm skeptical of everyone, and it's like I've completely lost my optimism."

Her dad scratched the stubble on his jaw. "That's understandable, given what you've been through."

"But what if I never go back to normal?" Greta's voice cracked. "It's like the part of my brain that trusted everyone was innocent and kind and believed everything would always work out has been replaced with the conviction that everyone is bad. Ever since I started looking into Franklin's case, I've become suspicious of everyone. I don't like being cynical, and I don't like not trusting people. Is this how it's going to be in Larkspur for me now? I don't know if I can do it. I might need to move."

Her parents exchanged glances.

"What?" Greta asked, ready to defend her decision. She'd been turning it over in her head all weekend. "It's not like I can stay here. This place was ruined for me last week."

"Ruined how?" her mom pressed.

"My entire sense of security was shattered. I can't stay here knowing there are people out there who want to hurt other people."

Her dad squinted one of his eyes shut. "You'll find people who act badly everywhere."

"You're missing the point. Larkspur was supposed to be a storybook town for me to build my life in. The whole reason I came here in the first place was because it was quaint and adorable and happy."

Her parents stared at her before her mom spoke slowly. "Didn't you come here to start over after that scum bag Nathan had his way with you?"

"Well, yeah. But I picked Larkspur because this is such an idyllic little community. Nothing bad was supposed to happen here."

"I hate to break it to you, G. But I'm sensing a pattern here. You left Churchill for college after Kelly died, right? And you didn't want to move back."

Greta hesitated. "I needed a fresh start."

"Sure. But then you got settled in Green Bay, started dating Nathan, and everything blew up with that. Then what?"

"I moved here. Again, because I needed a fresh start."

"And in both cases, did it work? Did you escape the memories of Kelly and of Nate?" her mom asked softly.

"Yes and no. I'm never going to forget Kelly, and I don't know if I'll ever live down what happened with Nathan. But at least I found my happy place here...until all this."

"That's my point, G. You've got to realize running from this place isn't going to make it any easier to forget what happened here. Just like Kelly, and to a lesser extent, Nathan, it's going to stay with you forever. If you leave, you're leaving behind the life you've built. Which you love." Her mom paused, waiting for Greta to meet her gaze before continuing. "And the friends you've made. Do you really want to start all over? Again?"

Greta's mind filled with images of her life in Larkspur, and her eyes filled with tears. Of course, she didn't want to leave here. She didn't want any of this. But...

"How can I stay with everything that's happened?"

The same feeling she'd felt in the marrow of her bones after she found out Kelly was dead—and then almost a decade later, when she found out Nathan, the man she was happily dating, turned out to be married, *married!*—had leached into her consciousness again here. Every fiber of her being was screaming at her to flee the scene. To get out and put the pain behind her.

Greta's mom sat back in her chair. "Do you think the next place you go won't have anything bad attached to it, and nothing bad will happen there?"

"I should hope I'm not first on the crime scene of a murder nor the victim of an attempted murder the next place I settle," Greta said flatly.

Her mom balled up a napkin and threw it across the table in her direction. "Don't sass, young lady."

Greta couldn't help but smile. She was thankful her parents hadn't pressed her up until this point. She needed the weekend to digest what she'd been through. Now, though, talking it over with them was easing some of the strain on her heart and settling her overactive mind.

Her mom turned serious again. "What I mean is there will always be bad things that happen, to greater or lesser degrees. You can't run from the bad in the world, Greta. You'll spend your whole life running. In my experience, it's better to put roots down and surround yourself with people who'll support you and lift you up when you get trampled down by some of the bad. Look at us." She paused, motioning between herself and her husband. "When Kelly died, our friends in Churchill were our lifeboat. They fed us for months, made sure we got out of the house, and prayed for us through the hardest moment in our life. And it sure seems like you have that sort of a community here. Josie and Iris are true friends, and you've got a lot of people looking out for you here. Even the detective is doing his part, sending officers by to check on you."

Greta's dad cut in. "Moving would mean you let the circumstances of this month get the best of you. You let whoever is behind this win. Like your mother said, there's no guarantee you'll find more happiness elsewhere."

"That's depressing." Greta's monotone delivery earned a laugh from her parents.

"You know what I'm saying." Her dad lowered his head and drew her gaze. "You, Greta Plank, can turn any situation into a happy ending with the right people by your side. Combine your kind heart with that clever brain of yours, and my money is on you."

Greta sat up, suddenly feeling like she was on the cusp of figuring out the proper combination of one of those sliding tile puzzles, and the full image was about to be revealed to her. "Wait. Say that again."

Chapter Forty-Two

Her dad looked bewildered. "What? That my money's on you?"

Greta stared between her parents. "Could this all be about money?"

Her mom scratched her cheek. "I'm not following."

"The money. Franklin's money."

"Walk us through it, G." Her dad leaned forward in his chair.

"We've been focusing on Franklin's book collection, right? Mom, you said it yourself. If word got out I acquired his collection, I'd have a target on my back."

"Right. So, whoever pushed you into the lake probably wanted the collection."

Greta held up her pointer fingers. "That's what has been gnawing at me. The collection as motive for my attack doesn't make any sense. The books aren't even in my possession for the attacker to steal. Even if they'd killed me, they wouldn't have gotten the collection unless they were in my will. You two are the only people in my will, and I'm pretty sure you didn't shove me in the lake."

Her mom crossed her arms. "Of course not."

"Exactly. They would have been better off just trying to steal the books before they came into my possession. I must have been targeted for another reason. Maybe because someone thought I was getting too close to figuring out what happened to Franklin. And that's where the money comes in. It's the only other variable."

Her parents looked a little dazed. "Sorry, G. We're not much help," her dad said.

Greta bounced her knees and held her eyes closed, thinking. "When I was at Franklin's house the week of his death, there were financial documents on his coffee table. I accidentally bumped them, and they fell on the ground. I collected them for Franklin and didn't think any more of them. But now I wonder what he was working on to have had the paperwork out of his office and on his coffee table." Greta opened her eyes. "And Liam Shark told me Franklin's finances were going to be more of a headache than he expected."

Greta pressed her hands against the table, her body vibrating with energy. "Mom, can we go talk to Detective McHenry again tomorrow? I never told him about those papers because I didn't think they were anything important. I'm not sure he ever saw them or collected them."

"We can try, though he doesn't have to share anything about his investigation with us."

A steely mix of determination and desire to see this through coursed through Greta's veins. "It's worth a shot."

The next morning, the Plank family stood outside the police department, waiting for someone to show up and let them in. It wasn't quite seven o'clock. Greta had two hours before she had to be at the library.

When Lori arrived, she gave their faces a quick scan and chuckled. "I'll get Detective McHenry for you right away."

They followed her into the lobby and waited while she paged the detective. Greta's heart drummed an anxious beat, but she forced herself to stand still.

A moment after Lori hung up the phone, Detective McHenry appeared from down the hall, eying them all with uncertainty. "What can I help you with?"

"Greta, er, my client has a theory to run by you."

The detective looked heavenward before turning on his heel. "Follow me."

They piled into the small conference room. Greta and her mom took their seats at the large wooden table with her dad standing behind them like a guardian angel.

"Alright. I'm listening." Detective McHenry flipped open his notebook.

Greta glanced to her mom for permission to speak, and when she motioned it was okay, Greta explained herself. She rested her elbows on the table and clasped her hands after she finished sharing her thoughts. "So, what if this all has to do with Franklin's money? Not his book collection, but his actual finances?"

Detective McHenry tapped his pen against his notebook. "You realize you're throwing suspicion on two people."

Greta clenched her teeth together, leaning away. This was the part of her hypothesis she didn't love. "Dean, as Franklin's financial rep, and Liam Shark, as his estate manager."

"I did interview them both already." Detective McHenry ran a hand along the back of his neck. "And what you're saying is purely circumstantial at this point. But, can you describe the documents you saw for me?"

Greta glanced at her mom, who signaled for her to go ahead.

Greta closed her eyes, trying to recall exactly what she'd seen. "One was a bank or investment statement of some sort. It had a formal-looking company letterhead printed on it.

"Another was some type of list in Franklin's handwriting. I didn't want to pry, so I didn't look too closely. I asked him where I should set the papers, and he said he'd take care of them."

Detective McHenry frowned.

"What?" Greta asked.

"We don't have anything like you've described filed in evidence."

Greta sat back, and her dad let out a low whistle.

"At first, I found it odd we didn't come across any type of current financial documentation on the property when we did our initial forensic canvas and general investigation. But when I learned Franklin employed Liam and Dean, I figured he let them both handle his finances, so I didn't question it. To this point, I've gotten all my fiscal information on Franklin from the two of them," Detective McHenry explained.

"So, unless Franklin passed the paperwork to Dean when he saw him on Thursday before he was killed—?" Greta paused for confirmation one way or another.

The detective shook his head. "Dean provided copies of everything he and Franklin discussed at their last meeting. He didn't have a handwritten list or anything else like you've described."

"Then Franklin either disposed of it somehow, or it's still in the house. What if he hid it? Like Nancy Drew!"

"Nancy Drew hid things?" Detective McHenry sounded skeptical.

Greta threw up her hands. "Haven't you read any of her books? She doesn't hide things, but she often found hidden things. Like a notebook in an old family clock. Or a mysterious staircase." Detective McHenry squinted at her, and Greta flashed him a smile. "It might be nothing, but it could be something. We should go find the papers I saw."

Detective McHenry frowned. "We?"

"Dale and I are glad to be extra sets of hands, and Greta is the only one who has seen the papers. I'm no expert, but she'd probably be good to have around." Her mom winked at her.

Greta's smile broadened. "Excellent point."

Detective McHenry looked pained. "I do have Richard Bennings coming in to discuss the book."

"What time is that appointment?" her dad asked nonchalantly.

Detective McHenry gritted his teeth. "Nine o'clock."

Her mom beamed. "Plenty of time for a little search, then, isn't there?"

Greta cupped her hand so it was covering her mouth, leaned over to her mom, and dropped her voice. "Or we could go on our own."

"What's that?" Detective McHenry pinned her in place with his glower.

"Oh, nothing." Greta twirled a strand of her hair and gave him a closed-lip smile. She never had let him know Franklin left her a spare key.

Detective McHenry relented. "Fine. I'll meet you at the Halloway house."

When the Planks pulled up at Franklin's cabin, everything was quiet and still. The detective appeared behind them and parked in the driveway. He got out of his car and strode to the front door. Greta and her parents waited for him to find the right key. Eventually, he did, and the door opened. He flipped the interior hall light on and motioned for them to come inside.

Greta was anxious to get started. She hurried ahead to where Detective McHenry stood waiting for them before turning back to her mom and dad. "Now, don't touch anything unless you're wearing gloves."

Detective McHenry snickered as he held the door for them.

"Something funny?" Greta wrinkled her nose. "I don't need you accusing my parents of tampering with evidence."

"Wouldn't dream of it."

Greta screwed up her mouth at him but let loose a grin. She was lighter somehow. The pep talk from her mom and dad last night had worked. She could do this. She had people in her corner, and she could face the bad in the world without losing sight of the good. She wasn't going to run. She owed it to Franklin. And to Kelly. And she'd prove herself to Nathan and all the people who were more than happy to gossip about her, telling horrid, untruthful tales of how she'd been the one to lure Nathan into a relationship. Mostly, she wanted to prove herself to herself.

She marched toward the living room where her parents already stood, surveying the space.

"This is remarkably similar to your place, Greta." Her dad drew his head back, taking in the high ceilings.

"Did Franklin have an office?" Her mom asked. "That would seem like a good place to start looking for financial documents."

"Not a formal one, but he kept his desk in the spare bedroom." Greta pointed to a door slightly behind her and off to the right side of the hallway.

"We can begin in there." Her mom shooed her dad into the spare bedroom.

"Here. Your daughter is right." The detective shoved gloves at them. "You should wear these if you want to touch anything."

As her parents donned the latex gloves, Greta stared into the living room.

Detective McHenry stood silently alongside her until she looked in his direction. "Here's a pair for you."

"Thanks." Greta took the gloves and pulled the skin-tight latex over her fingers, frowning slightly. "Do you want to take the fireplace or the floorboards?"

"For real?"

CHAPTER FORTY-TWO

"Yep. You can have the fireplace because you're taller. Let's get to work."

Chapter Forty-Three

"Found something!"

At her dad's exclamation, Greta, on hands and knees, jerked and slammed her head on the underside of Franklin's end table. She had spent the last fifteen minutes going along the wood floorboards, looking for some sort of spring mechanism. It was probably foolish of her, as Franklin's paralysis would have made hiding anything underground a distinct challenge, but she was going to leave no page left unturned.

After all, this whole mission might just be the definition of foolish, and yet, here they were. Sure, she'd talked a big game at the police office, but all she was going off of was a hunch, so she had been battling back the feeling that maybe she had this all wrong since they started their search. But she wasn't going to give up. And maybe—just maybe—her dad had found something worthwhile.

"You okay?" Detective McHenry looked half-concerned, half-amused at her clumsiness.

"Fine." Greta huffed and got to her feet. "After this is all over, my head is going to need a rest for a while. Figuratively and literally."

The detective snorted but covered it with a cough.

Greta smiled to herself.

"You two, come quick!" Her mom's excited voice rang out, and Greta hurried from the living room into Franklin's office with Detective McHenry trailing her.

"What do you got?" The detective joined Greta's dad behind Franklin's desk.

Greta stepped up next to her mom.

"Lookie here." Her dad had a desk drawer pulled open.

The detective leaned in, and his mouth parted. "Your Nancy Drew hypothesis wasn't far off. There's a false back in this drawer."

"Are you serious?" Greta hurried around the desk. Her dad stepped back so she could take a closer look. "How did you find it?" Greta dipped her head, peering into the opened drawer. Sure enough, the back panel of the drawer jutted out enough for someone to slip their finger behind and remove it. From the looks of it, her father hadn't done so yet.

"We started on the far side of the room, so I just got to the desk now. There wasn't much of note on the surface, so I moved on to the drawer. I took everything out." Her dad pointed to the pile of office supplies on top of the desk. "And I started tracing my hand along the base of the drawer. When I got to the back side, or what I thought was the back side, one of the panels pressed in, and the whole false back sprung out. Greta, you should do the honors." He nudged her forward.

Greta held up her hands in protest. "No, Dad, you found it. And Detective McHenry, this is your job."

"Stop it, honey, and see if there's anything worthwhile back there," her mom demanded.

Greta flicked her gaze to Detective McHenry. He stared at her with his intense gaze and gave her a subtle nod.

"Okay then. Here goes nothing." Greta snuck a finger along the lip of the drawer back and gently pulled it forward. She handed the false panel to her dad and bent again to see what she would find. "There's definitely something back here." Her pulse kicked up. Greta reached to the real back of the drawer and dragged out several sheets of paper.

Greta skimmed the top sheet. "I can't be sure, but these remind me of the papers I knocked on the floor the week of Franklin's death. It's an investment statement." Greta paged to the next sheet of paper. "Look, it's a list of names—people from town." She handed the handwritten sheet of loose leaf to Detective McHenry.

"Dolores Jenkins is at the top." The detective scanned the sheet before looking at Greta again. "What else is there?"

"It's a printed email from Franklin's bank. This is interesting." She handed a second paper over for Detective McHenry to see.

"Read it out loud." Her mom craned her neck to try to get a better angle over Greta's shoulder.

"It looks like a back-and-forth correspondence between Franklin and a financial services representative."

"Why would he be working with another financial rep when he used Dean?" Greta asked Detective McHenry, her stomach sinking. "The first email is dated the week he died. He asked to see a copy of his account statement from his bank. That must be this printout."

She handed the first sheet to the detective. He studied it before glancing up to her. "What else?"

"In his next email, he asked if they'd be willing to take him on as a client with one of their in-house financial reps. The bank said they'd be glad to work with him at his earliest convenience. Franklin's last message says he'll get back to them as soon as possible."

Her dad widened his eyes. "These documents are a bit more than circumstantial, I'd say."

Greta hated to agree, but she couldn't deny the facts. "This sure makes it sound like Franklin was going to be pulling his business from Dean. Now the question is, was Dean aware of this, and if so, was it motive for murder?"

Greta's statement hung in the air as the four stared at each other, no one daring to venture a guess.

Detective McHenry eventually broke the silence with his no-nonsense tone. "I need to get back to the station for my interview with Richard. I'm taking all these documents into police custody. I'll have to bag them as evidence. I'll start bringing in the folks on this list to establish a common denominator."

Greta handed the rest of the papers over. "We know Franklin reached out to Dolores, so he might have spoken to some of the others, as well."

"I agree. We were assuming his association with Dolores was personal, but there could have been another motive."

"That sounds malicious." Greta was horrified at the thought that Franklin would have used Dolores for something sinister. "Besides, Franklin asked me for her phone number, and he blushed when he did." She vividly remembered their final conversation, and she'd bet her life Franklin's interest in Dolores was not financial.

The detective moved his head from side to side. "I'm not arguing with you. I'm just saying if she's on this list, maybe he was able to kill two birds with one stone by talking to her."

"I guess we'll find out."

"*I* will find out." Detective McHenry held Greta's gaze before looking at her parents. "While I appreciate your assistance, I need you to let me do my job. Everything found and discussed here must remain strictly confidential. I trust you all understand the magnitude of the situation?"

Greta sucked in a breath. She didn't have to read between the lines to understand what the detective was not so subtly reminding them of—her attack. As if she needed a reminder.

Swallowing hard as the phantom taste of the musky water scraped at her throat, Greta readily agreed. She was more than happy to leave the apprehension of Franklin's killer to the professionals.

At the library, Greta ushered Josie into the cramped office behind the circulation desk to fill her in on her conversation with her parents and what had transpired at Franklin's house. Confidentiality did not apply to her best friend and partner in crime—er, solving crime.

"You were going to move away and leave me?" Josie exclaimed when Greta finally took a breath.

Greta rolled her eyes. "Out of everything I told you, you're most focused on me leaving town?"

"You even thinking about abandoning me is clearly the most important piece of information you shared." Josie grabbed for Greta's hand. "Now that it's settled, you're here for good, we can move on to the other details. Didn't I say there was something off with Dean?"

Greta held up a finger. "Wait a minute. We can't make a full-blown accusation without proof. Where's Iris?"

"She isn't here yet. She texted and asked me to cover for her. She was grabbing a late breakfast with Dean." Josie glanced at the door. "Should we be worried?"

"Not yet. I'm deferring to Detective McHenry and waiting to hear next steps."

"How's he going to get proof?"

"For starters, he's going to interview the people on the list Franklin was keeping hidden in his desk. Hopefully, something or someone will jump out at him." Greta nibbled her lip. She wanted answers, and she wanted them now. Actually, she would have liked them yesterday, but at this point, she'd settle for as soon as possible.

The bell on the circulation desk dinged. Greta yelped, and Josie jumped.

"Don't do that." Josie swatted at her. "You're making me all panicky."

"Sorry." Greta snuck a quick look out the open the door to see who needed help. "It's Ed." She tucked a wayward curl behind her ear before walking with Josie out of the office.

"Morning, Greta." He might have greeted her, but Ed's gaze shot directly to Josie.

Greta turned to see if her friend had noticed the attention, but Josie was busying herself with something on the computer. Greta cocked her head. That couldn't be, since they hadn't booted up the computers yet. Why was Josie pretending to be engrossed in a screen that was black? Greta turned to Ed. "What can we do for you?"

"I'm not sure." Ed fished into the open zipper pocket of his messenger bag. He rustled around before producing a document. "I have something I think belongs to you, or someone. I don't know."

"What is it?"

He held it out for her to take. "See for yourself."

Greta scanned the document.

"What is it?" Josie repeated Greta's question, effectively giving up on her computer shenanigans and joining Ed and Greta at the end of the counter.

"It's an investment statement." Greta annunciated her words, the full weight of the thin sheet of paper she held hitting her like a toppling stack of books. "Franklin Halloway's investment statement."

Chapter Forty-Four

"What?" Josie snatched the paper from her hand and looked it over. "Ed, why do you have this?"

"I found it at the bottom of the pile of library flyers I've had on hand at the cabins. I've been giving them to my guests so they have the information about the library programming." He pointed between himself and Greta. "Like we discussed."

"Right. I printed copies of the flyer for you and grabbed them from the printer here." Greta motioned to where the laser printer sat. "This must have been left in the tray by someone else." Closing her eyes, Greta dug back into her memory. Her mind picked up pace as she rehashed the events of the day. Ed had come in asking for flyers to hand out. She'd printed a bunch. Iris and Josie wanted her to help with planning the next round of events.

Greta's eyes popped open. Ed and Josie were staring at her.

"What?" Josie asked.

Instead of responding, Greta hurried behind the desk and grabbed her purse, sifting through it for the detective's business card. "I need to call the detective." Greta glanced at the clock. It was a little before nine. She hoped to catch him before his meeting with Richard.

Finally, Greta put her hands on Detective McHenry's card and dialed his number, her fingers trembling.

"McHenry." His deep, gruff voice sounded after two rings.

Greta breathed a sigh of relief. "Detective. Yes, hi. This is Greta Plank. Can you come to the library? We found something."

"I'm walking in the main doors of our building now." The line went dead.

Greta pulled her phone back and hung up, not even offended by his abruptness. She stashed her phone in her bag, and a minute later, when the detective joined them at the circulation desk, she held up the document Ed had brought in.

Detective McHenry took it from her and glanced over it. His jaw pulsed, and he narrowed his eyes. "Where did this come from?"

Greta looked to Ed, who held up his hands in defense. "I found it this morning at the bottom of a stack of brochures Greta printed for me. I returned it to her first thing," he said.

Greta stepped forward, drawing the detective's attention. "It must have been left on our printer tray, and when I printed brochures for Ed, I scooped it up, unbeknownst to anyone."

Detective McHenry ran his hand over his clean-shaven chin. "Okay, but this still doesn't explain why one of Franklin Halloway's financial statements was floating around the library."

Greta cringed. "I think I can answer that, too. I was replaying the day Ed came in." She detailed the morning for them, and when Greta mentioned being called into the office for event planning, Josie cut in.

"I remember. I asked for Iris's help first, and then for Greta's."

"Right." Greta transferred her weight between her legs. "But before you asked for Iris's help, Iris had been with Dean. That was the day Dean told us he and Sidney would be using the library as their office while their space was being rewired. They were using the library's printer."

Greta waited for the words to register.

Detective McHenry looked at the document and then at her. "You're sure?"

"Positive." Greta held his gaze.

The detective stared back. "You know what this means?"

Greta nodded once. "Dean was printing account statements. Which isn't a crime in and of itself. But the total amount listed there…." Greta's voice trailed off. All the blood seemed to rush from Greta's extremities, and her heart pounded a heavy beat. The amount on this statement was higher than the one she'd pulled out of the drawer in Franklin's desk earlier. She was sure of it.

Ed cleared his throat. "Someone want to tell me what's going on?"

Greta blinked and turned to him. "Ed, why were you trying to buy Franklin's property? You spoke to him about it before he died."

Ed's mouth opened on a slight gasp before he closed it, a sheepish shade of red coloring his cheeks. "I didn't realize he told anyone. He shut me down so fast, it was a non-starter." He sighed. "I didn't mean anything by it. I just wanted to feel him out. It's prime real estate, and if he was at all considering selling, I wanted to jump on it. I'm looking into diversifying my assets. I actually have plans to open a bed and breakfast in Karrington. I'm hiring more staff to help with development and marketing and am planning to expand. I've got to move some capital around to make it all work, but I'm excited about the prospects."

That explained his work with Miranda, and it made sense. Greta hadn't considered that the property Ed was trying to acquire could have been somewhere other than Larkspur, but as she thought about it, she realized Miranda had never specified where the new development was set to take place.

"Now, can someone please fill me in? I promise I had nothing to do with Franklin's death," Ed added.

With a raise of her chin, Greta waited on Detective McHenry's lead, and he gave her a slight nod.

"Actually, Ed." Josie's gaze bounced between Greta and the detective. "Why don't we run across the street and grab a coffee? I can clear some things up. Do you have time?"

Ed's facial expression turned from confused to elated. "Sure. I mean, if you can get away from work."

"Of course she can. I'll handle things here." Greta walked to the door and held it open for Josie and Ed to leave, mouthing "thank you" to Josie. Greta was going to drill her about Ed in the near future. But first things first.

As soon as they were out of earshot, Greta swung back to Detective McHenry. "What do we do? Should I be worried about Iris? I'm worried about Iris."

"Miss Plank, take a breath."

CHAPTER FORTY-FOUR

At Detective McHenry's directive, Greta filled her lungs, and her mind cleared.

"Good. Now, there's nothing to be concerned about yet. Dean has no idea we know what we know. I want you to go about business as usual. Text Iris to ask when she's getting to work, but otherwise, don't mention any of this. Let me handle things from my end. I need to double-check this statement against the one Dean gave me, the one from this morning, and the one the bank is faxing over. I'll decide on next steps then. If anything happens, or if anything feels off, you call me, got it? Otherwise, play it cool."

Greta let out a frazzled puff of air. "You don't know me at all, do you? By definition, I'm the opposite of cool, but I'll do my best."

The detective stared at her. "Don't sell yourself short." He said it with a completely straight face before turning and striding away.

Greta gawked after him, a nervous laugh bubbling up and escaping from her lips. She closed her eyes for a second. *Soon,* she thought to herself. *Soon this will all be over.*

Chapter Forty-Five

When Iris walked through the library door five minutes later, Greta gave her a big hug before she realized she was definitely not playing it cool.

"Wow, at least someone is in a good mood today." Iris giggled.

"Just happy to be alive and happy to see one of my besties." Greta was so busy trying to cover for her uncoolness she almost missed what Iris implied. "Wait, who isn't in a good mood today?"

"Ugh. Dean." Iris's cheery face clouded over.

"What happened?" Greta kept her voice even and, taking a cue from Josie's act this morning, pretended to busy herself with computer work.

"I don't know. He wanted to grab breakfast. I was excited to spend some more time together, but he was all snippy. We sat through our meal in basic silence, and when I tried to draw him into conversation, he shut me down, saying he didn't want to talk and had a lot on his mind. When I asked if there was anything I could help with, he laughed a bitter laugh and told me it was his situation to deal with. I'm not sure what's going on, but I'm worried about him."

Greta's heart wilted. She knew all too well what it felt like to be in a relationship with someone you thought you knew, only to have the rug cruelly pulled out from beneath you. She wished she could spare her friend the pain, but it seemed inevitable at this point. If Dean had committed the crime—and all signs were pointing to him—Iris was going to be crushed.

"I'm sure it'll all be okay." She was clicking around on the computer in an attempt at normalcy. "What's going on with the houses and properties he

230

was looking at? Are you guys still planning to move in together?" When Iris didn't answer her, Greta glanced in her direction. Her friend's eyes were filled with tears. "Oh, Iris!" Greta abandoned the computer and rushed to wrap Iris in a hug. "I'm sorry. I didn't mean to bring up a touchy subject."

"No, it's fine." Iris waved her hand in front of her face like a windshield wiper. "It's just...I don't know! Dean went from being so gung-ho about getting a place with me to so preoccupied. I'm beginning to think he's having second thoughts."

Greta wasn't sure how to offer any sort of consolation when the idea of Iris moving in with Dean now made her nauseous. Fortunately, she was saved from having to respond when several families entered the library. The parents had questions, and the kids needed help exploring the children's section, so Greta and Iris split up and got to work. Soon, Josie returned and gave Greta a quick nod, communicating she'd handled Ed.

The rest of the morning ran like clockwork. Josie led story time. Iris manned the counter. Greta did some work on the budget and added to her upcoming book order.

At lunchtime, Greta shooed Josie and Iris across the street. "I'll grab something when you get back," she assured them.

"Okay. Let's go, Jos. I'm starving." When Iris fetched her coat, Greta and Josie exchanged a glance behind her back, having a silent conversation with the one look. Greta was thankful for Josie's poker face. Her friend was much more equipped to talk with Iris over lunch and not spill the beans about their suspicions about Dean than Greta was.

When they left the library, Greta used the lull in patronage to send a quick text to Dolores. She'd been checking in on the older woman whose leg was healing well. Greta hadn't told Dolores about her plunge into the lake because she hadn't wanted to upset her. With everything that had happened, Stacey had been right to take her mom out of town. Detective McHenry had been smart to let her go.

As if his ears were ringing, the detective appeared, striding down the hallway toward the library.

Greta waved him inside. Most of the morning patrons had gone home for lunch, and so far, the afternoon rush hadn't picked up. She hoped Detective McHenry was making progress sorting things out because she wanted everything resolved and her people safe before the end of the day. She didn't like the thought of Iris going home to have dinner with Dean.

She dropped her voice, even though the library was empty. "What have you found out?"

Detective McHenry looked around for himself, and Greta fought the urge to tap her pencil in impatience. Once he seemed satisfied they were alone, he rested his elbows on her desk. Greta leaned in so she didn't miss a word.

"I've spent the morning calling everyone on Franklin's list."

"And?"

"And, without giving away too much information about the investigation to them, I've been able to ascertain they all have one other thing in common beyond their residence in Larkspur."

Greta stood upright and crossed her arms as if to physically shield herself from what she was afraid was going to be unsettling news. "What's that?"

"They all use Dean as their financial representative."

Greta cringed. "What do you make of it?"

"That's not all I confirmed."

"There's more?" Greta's shoulders slumped.

The detective nodded. "I compared the document Ed brought in this morning to the information I had from Dean himself. It's Franklin's latest bank statement with the profits and losses from his investments detailed, and it matches the one Dean provided when I first talked to him. Nothing looks amiss at first glance, but...."

Greta pressed her lips together, waiting for the other shoe to drop.

"As I'm guessing you deduced, the total sum listed on Dean's print-out is much higher than the actual amount in the accounts. I've cross-checked it with the statement we found on Franklin's property and the one the bank turned over after I got a warrant."

"So, Dean had a faulty statement?" Greta was certain it wasn't so innocent.

"More like Dean was creating a faulty statement. I don't see how else to explain it. Dean had to be fudging the numbers on Franklin's account.

There is no other reason the total on the statement he provided would be different than a copy from the bank."

The final piece of the puzzle fit into place. "Dean was ripping Franklin off."

"It looks like it."

"And if Franklin found out and confronted him, that would be motive." Greta squeezed her eyes shut.

"Hey, hey!" Josie's loud greeting had Greta's eyes popping open and the detective whirling around to see Josie and Iris walking through the main door.

"Hi!" Greta greeted her friends with so much energy Detective McHenry looked at her funny. Greta couldn't help it. She was overcompensating with cheer for how much she hated all of this, and now she didn't know the whole story, and there was no way to finish talking to the detective about what he was going to do next.

"Miss Plank, would you mind coming to my office and taking a look?" Detective McHenry asked.

"W-what?" Greta stuttered. What was he talking about?

"What do you need Greta for?" Iris set her purse on the circulation desk, shooting a coy smile in Greta's direction.

For once, Greta didn't care if her friend was teasing her about her relationship—or lack of—with Detective McHenry. At least it gave her a second to figure out how to proceed with the whole Dean situation.

"Miss Plank offered to help Lori with some sort of glitch with the receptionist's computer, didn't you?"

"Oh! Right, of course. Since Josie and Iris are back, I can definitely help. Right now." Greta hurried around the desk to follow Detective McHenry toward the police station. "I'll be back in a minute," she called over her shoulder.

"Take your time." Iris's voice held a teasing lilt, and Greta didn't miss the grin she and Josie exchanged.

Detective McHenry walked toward the back entrance of the police station offices. As they neared the door, he grabbed for Greta's arm and yanked her to the right. Greta stumbled as he pulled her into a small janitor's closet off the hallway.

"What are you doing?" Greta asked into the darkness. The bleached fragrance of cleaning supplies tickled her nose. Her toe connected with what sounded like a pail, sending a clang echoing through the space.

"Shh." Detective McHenry shut the door and flipped on the light. The yellow glow illuminated the small, cramped closet. There couldn't have been more than six inches of room between where she stood and where the detective leaned with his back against the door. "I didn't want anyone to overhear, not even Lori. This case is hanging in the balance. Based on the lengths he went to hurt you and Dolores, Dean is dangerous—especially if he thinks someone is on to him. What I didn't get a chance to tell you is I can't get a hold of him. He's not answering his cell, and when I called his office's phone number, Sidney said he's out for the day."

Greta covered her mouth and pressed her fingers against the bridge of her nose. "So, correct me if I'm wrong, but the hypothesis we're working under is Dean was stealing money from Franklin. Franklin figured it out and guessed he wasn't the only one being taken advantage of. He wrote up a list of all the people who were also Dean's clients and was going to talk to each of them. He started with Dolores. Somehow, Dean found out Franklin was on to him, so he killed Franklin before he could expose Dean to the rest of the town, or turn him in for fraud?"

"That about sums it up."

Greta combed her hands through her hair, wincing as she caught her finger on her stitches. "What do we do? What do I do?"

"That's why I needed to talk to you. I need you to keep Iris away from Dean, and if you see Dean, I need you to contact me immediately. I've got officers canvassing the area, and I'm going to work on getting a warrant for his computer, files, and his financial statements, and records. If I can track money being funneled to his accounts, my suspicions will be confirmed. I shouldn't have a problem getting a warrant now. However, that'll tip Dean off. What he might do is anyone's guess. I wouldn't be surprised if he tried to leave town, but we can't be too careful."

Greta shuddered. "Okay, keep Iris away from Dean and call you if I see him or know where he is. I can do that. Can I tell Iris and Josie what's going on?"

"I don't want Iris to know yet, at least not before the end of the day. We'll tell her when we have to for her safety, but right now, there's no telling what she'll do or if she'll tip Dean off...."

Greta opened her mouth, but the detective held out a hand to forestall her interruption. "Please, Miss Plank. Yes, this is hard, but it's for the best, and I need you to trust me. If Josie will be able to help with Iris or help us find Dean, fine, tell her. But I'm trying to keep control of this. Think about how news spreads in this town."

Greta couldn't argue with him there. "Okay. Let's be in touch."

Detective McHenry slipped out the door without another word.

"Be safe," Greta whispered to his back before taking a deep breath and stepping into the hallway.

Chapter Forty-Six

"Oh!"

Greta walked almost directly into Celeste Janowicki, one of Dolores's good friends.

"Greta, dear. What a surprise!" Celeste's gaze darted beyond Greta to the door to the police station. Greta suppressed a groan, sure Celeste had seen the detective exiting the same closet. The whole town would be buzzing about how the two of them were having some sort of torrid affair in no time. "I was coming to chat with the new, fine-looking detective. He called, and I missed it, but I had to swing by the library today anyway, so I thought I'd come to see him in person."

"I'm sure he's in his office." Greta unhooked her hair from behind her ears, letting it fall forward and hoping it hid the blush in her cheeks.

"Yes, I'm sure he is...now." Celeste chuckled, continuing her walk down the hallway. To herself, Celeste mumbled, "Kids these days."

Greta closed her eyes and summoned her resolve. She'd worry about the rumors after Dean was taken care of. For the first time in a long time, her reputation was the least of her concerns.

When she walked back into the library, Iris looked up from the desk. "Did you get everything figured out for Lori?"

"What? Oh, yes." Greta faked a smile. "She needed to reset her password." Greta hurried to change the subject so as not to prolong the lie. "Where's Josie?"

"She took Maren Charles over to show her our newest Young Adult titles. Her son can't seem to find a series to enjoy, so she's doing some leg work."

"Nice." Greta glanced to where Iris pointed and saw Josie between two shelves with a woman who appeared to be in her forties. She busied herself with logging on to her computer and shuffling paperwork around on the circulation desk. It was killing her not to tell Iris about Dean, but Detective McHenry had asked her not to, and, for now, she needed to defer to him.

Celeste strolled into the library ten minutes later. Her eyes danced when she looked at Greta, and Greta's ears burned. "Did you catch Detective McHenry?" she asked when Celeste approached the desk to check out her books.

At this point, Celeste had jumped to her own conclusions, so who cared if Greta came off like a lovesick teenager.

"I did. He was quite happy to see me. Though I'm sure not as happy as he is to see you, dear." Celeste winked, and Greta laughed an uncharacteristically high-pitched laugh.

"I'm not sure I was much help to that beau of yours, though." Her silvery hair danced back and forth as she tipped her head. "He asked me who I used for my services in town. Car repair. Hair care. Financial services. Housekeeping sorts of things."

"Oh?" Greta didn't want to press Celeste, but she was pretty sure the detective was couching his questions about Dean in general inquiries about Larkspur to avoid arousing suspicion. She had to hand it to him. He'd figured out how to deal with the town and its rumor mill—it was a smart strategy.

"Yeah, but what is my recommendation for Lou's Hair Salon going to do for Detective McHenry? It's not really his style."

Greta got a great mental image of the detective in the beauty salon surrounded by women who were gabbing away with their heads under dryers. She restrained her laughter and instead tried to be reassuring. "I bet he found your opinions very informative. Is there anything else you need while you're here?"

"No. No. I'll be going now. You tell the detective if he needs anything more, he can give me a ring. If he's not too busy with you," Celeste chortled.

"Will do." Greta cringed.

She turned to find Iris's eyes gleaming. "What was that all about?"

Josie arrived at the counter. "What was what about?"

"Celeste was teasing Greta about Detective McHenry."

Josie shot her a curious look.

The back of Greta's neck felt impossibly hot. "Celeste has her wires crossed. No biggie."

"If you say so." Josie threw Greta a bone and changed the subject, gesturing to the office. "We brought you lunch. It's on the desk in there."

"Thanks. By the way, what are you guys up to tonight? I could use a girls' night."

"I'm in." Josie bobbed her head.

"I'd love to, but I didn't leave things the best with Dean this morning." The quiver in Iris's voice betrayed her earlier sadness, hiding just beneath the surface.

"All the more reason for a girls' night." Josie stepped in front of Iris and placed her hands on her shoulders. "You guys need time to cool off, and you can't expect to reconcile without a little space."

Iris sighed. "I guess you're probably right."

Greta barely refrained from whooping with relief. Instead, she clapped her hands. "Jos, can we go to your place after dinner at the café?"

"Of course."

"I should let Dean know." Iris reached into her pocket to retrieve her phone.

"Have you heard from him today?" Greta asked.

"Radio silence."

"He must be busy with work."

"Maybe." Iris typed out a quick message before stowing her phone again.

Greta hurried into the office and downed her lunch in record time, barely tasting the turkey and avocado melt. Iris was right outside, but she still didn't like the thought of leaving her out of sight. What if Dean swooped in and snatched her? She would have failed Detective McHenry, and, more importantly, Iris could be in real danger. Greta tossed the sandwich wrapper into the garbage and hustled back to the front desk.

The afternoon hours passed methodically. Iris stole glances at her phone every five minutes, and, judging from the crease deepening between her brows, Greta assumed she hadn't heard back from Dean.

Mayor Collins stopped in and chatted briefly with Greta about her plans for the upcoming fall festival. She had managed to get Larkspur a spotlight feature in a travel publication, and she was buzzing about the prospective good press. Greta assured her she'd be happy to help in any way.

Greta's mom and dad showed up at four. Her dad leaned over the counter to plant a quick peck on her cheek. "How's the day been, sunshine?"

"Business as usual." Greta let out a nervous chuckle. It had certainly *not* been business as usual. She didn't ever want to consider shielding a friend from her potentially deranged boyfriend "business as usual."

Her mom studied her for a beat, undoubtedly catching on to Greta's false positivity. Before Louisa could ask her about it, Greta gave a slight shake of her head. "What are you two up to?"

"Actually," her mom said, taking the hint. "We were hoping to check out the Mexican restaurant in town with all the rave reviews online."

"Everything's Coming Up Tacos?" Greta asked, and her parents nodded. "It's delicious. You should definitely go. The girls and I"—Greta motioned to her fellow librarians—"are going to do dinner and hang out tonight, so that works out well."

Josie waved, and Iris's smile almost reached her eyes.

"You'll be well taken care of." Her mom pressed her hand over her heart. "It makes me so happy to see what a strong community you've built here, dear. Now, if we can just find you a—"

"Don't say it."

"—man." Louisa finished her thought anyway, pinning Greta with a *mother-knows-best* look. "Of course you and I both know you don't *need* a man, G. We raised you to stand on your own two feet. But wouldn't it be nice? The companionship?"

Greta let her head fall back. "Mom, nice or not, I don't *want* a man."

"Duly noted."

Greta spun around at the deep, even tone of Detective McHenry's voice.

He held her eye for just a moment, and a burst of heat scaled her cheekbones.

"Mr. and Mrs. Plank." Detective McHenry greeted her parents before glancing back at her. "Miss Plank, I hate to bother you again, but Lori has another computer question. Would you mind?"

"Sure, of course. You guys can cover for me?"

Iris and Josie wore matching Cheshire grins on their lips.

"Absolutely."

"Take all the time you need."

Greta shot daggers at them.

"We should get going, or we'll be late for our reservation." Her mom followed Detective McHenry and Greta out of the library's entrance. Once out of earshot of Josie and Iris, she leaned closer to the detective. "Any news to report?"

Detective McHenry cut a glance over his shoulder. Fortunately, the hallway was deserted. Greta was glad all four of them didn't have to wedge themselves into the janitor's closet.

"The warrant came through for Dean's accounts and computers. I'm headed over to his office." Detective McHenry kept his voice low.

Greta chewed her lip. "I don't know if you'll find anything at his office, though. It's been under construction, remember? They've been working out of pocket and from laptops since before Franklin died."

Detective McHenry clasped his hands behind his back, pulling his suit jacket apart enough for Greta to see his firearm clipped to his belt. Greta gulped, and frisson spread over her skin—the same sensation she'd experienced when the detective searched her house after they got home from the hospital. It was dread.

"I'll start there and get my hands on the computers somehow. Sidney should be able to give me access to what she has, at least."

Greta pinched her eyes closed. Poor Sidney. "What are you going to tell her? Sidney, I mean."

Detective McHenry shot her a hard look. "The truth."

Greta pulled her mouth into a frown but nodded. It was all coming to a head, and as much as she hated it, she was ready to turn the page.

"I still haven't been able to find Dean. We have an APB out on his car, and all my available officers are out canvassing. I wanted to ask you if he's made contact with Iris."

"Iris texted him around two to tell him we're planning to have a girls' night, but she's still in a pretty bad mood from their fight this morning. He hasn't gotten back to her yet."

"Let us know if we can be of any help, but for now, we should go." Her dad put his hand on the small of her mom's back and coaxed her out the front doors of the municipal building.

As soon as they were gone, Detective McHenry cupped Greta's elbow and steered her toward the police department.

"Does Lori really need something?" Greta took in the detective's serious profile as he hurried her along.

"No, but we're still within sight of Iris, and if we don't at least pretend to go to the police station, she'll be suspicious. I don't know if I can count on you to come up with a good cover story on the fly."

Greta sniffed. "I'll have you know I'm very quick on my feet."

Detective McHenry gave a disbelieving snort and opened the closet door, letting her walk in first. When he flipped on the light, Greta took a deep breath, which proved to be a bad idea. The particular scent of sandalwood she'd come to associate with the detective combined with the smell of Pine-Sol in the air and rendered her momentarily lightheaded.

"Did Iris tell Dean you were going to Josie's house?" The seriousness of Detective McHenry's voice forced Greta to focus.

"I-I don't know. I didn't see the actual text message."

Detective McHenry frowned and, after a second's thought, said, "It doesn't matter. If he knows you're having a girls' night, he'll assume it's either at Josie's, your place, or Iris's house. After I'm done at Dean's office, I'll be your escort for the night."

"Won't that be pretty obvious to Iris?"

"I'll be discreet, but I don't want you to leave the library until you see me come back. I'll keep my distance and follow you to make sure there's no trouble."

Greta was getting tired of being watched, but she liked the thought of being attacked again much less. And she certainly didn't like the idea of Iris or Josie getting hurt. "Alright."

"Good. Promise you'll come up with an excuse not to leave the library until I'm around?"

"I can do that." Greta studied the detective's face. There were bags under his razor-sharp eyes. His hair was more disheveled than usual, and Greta doubted he'd slept much since her forced swim a couple nights before. She reached up without thinking and was about to brush some of the loose strands from his forehead when she realized what she was doing and awkwardly dropped her hands. She looked down at her shoes to hide the fire licking her cheeks. "I-uh…" She swallowed and peered back up at him. "Take care of yourself, Detective."

Detective McHenry stared at her for a long second before blinking. "Don't worry about me, and don't leave until I'm around for backup."

"Wouldn't think of it." Greta flashed him a smile and tucked her hands into her pockets. Underneath her cardigan, her shirt stuck to her body from sweat pooling on her back.

Detective McHenry opened his mouth and shut it again. He cleared his throat and opened the closet door without a word. He motioned for Greta to go first. She stepped out into the fluorescent light of the hallway and closed her eyes.

"I'll see you soon." The detective's voice rang low behind her.

Greta listened to his shoes pad along the linoleum floors, willing herself to summon a fraction of the confidence and bearing Detective McHenry exuded. She opened her eyes and rotated toward the library to find Josie staring at her from the end of the hallway, her eyebrows so far in the direction of her scalp they were hidden by her blunt-cut bangs.

"Well, well, well—"

"Not. Now." Greta punctuated her words before quickly filling Josie in on what Detective McHenry had told her.

"Fine. You're off the hook until this whole disaster is behind us. You think Dean is dangerous?" Josie and Greta both glanced toward the library at the mention of Dean's name.

As soon as Greta saw Iris was out of earshot, she put her head together with Josie. "I'm afraid so. We'll see what Detective McHenry finds on his computer, but until then, we've got to keep Iris out of harm's way."

They resumed their positions behind the circulation desk as some families filed in.

June Adler, a young mom Greta recognized from her family's participation in the summer reading program, asked for help finding some beginner's chapter books for her daughter, so Greta walked with her and her kids to the children's section. She pulled several A to Z Mystery stories as well as *Ivy and Bean* and the latest installment of *The Puppy Place*.

"These are great." The mother smiled as she glanced at her daughter, who already had her nose stuck inside the pages of *Ivy and Bean*.

Greta smiled back. "The best part is that they're all part of a series, so if she likes them, there are tons more titles to choose from."

"You're a lifesaver."

"Not me. Books. Books are a lifesaver."

June laughed. "Touché."

Greta answered a couple more questions, found some titles for June's twin toddlers, and when all the kids had books in hand, she led them to the front of the library. The sight that greeted her stopped Greta dead in her tracks.

Chapter Forty-Seven

D ean was down on one knee, holding Iris's left hand in his, and placing a ring on her finger.

"You've got to be kidding me," Greta whispered. Of all the things she'd braced herself for today, Dean proposing to Iris in the middle of the library was not one of them.

"Aww! How exciting!" June peered around her to get a closer look.

Greta would have parroted the sentiment under different circumstances. Instead, she had to work to swallow an upsurge of vomit. Where in the world was Josie? Her question was answered as her friend appeared from the nonfiction section carrying several large books.

As Iris leapt into Dean's arms, Josie's panicked gaze shot to Greta's.

June applauded as Dean spun Iris around. Iris was laughing and crying at once, and when she spotted them, she held out her hand, showing off a sparkling diamond. "I didn't realize we had an audience. I'm engaged!" Iris cheered the last word, and her announcement propelled Greta into action.

"Iris, wow." Greta hurried to her friend's side and gave her a quick hug. "Let me check the Adler family out, and we'll celebrate."

Greta scooted behind the desk. She mechanically swiped books under the scanner. It was a good thing she could do this part of her job in her sleep because her mind was not on the task at hand. She kept one eye on Dean and Iris. Josie had rushed to deposit the books behind the desk and was now making her way over to the couple.

"There you go." Greta handed the receipt to June. "Due dates are listed. I hope everyone enjoys the books."

"I have no doubt they will. I can't thank you enough for your help." June smiled at Greta as her kids skipped out in front of her. "Congratulations to Iris."

Greta hoped her return smile looked more genuine than it felt. As the Adler family left, the clock struck five, and it was a small mercy that at least they could lock up for the day.

"You guys. What a surprise!" Greta walked around the counter and reached for Iris's hand to study the ring, if only to give herself something to focus on that didn't include Dean's face. His eyes were on her, and if she looked at him, she was afraid he'd be able to see right through her. "Gosh, this is gorgeous. Did you pick it out all on your own, Dean?" Greta kept her eyes zoned in on the ring, which was huge and blinding. *And likely bought with dirty money.* The thought made it difficult for Greta to suck in a full breath.

"I sure did. Sorry to ruin your evening plans by proposing, but I couldn't wait one more day. I wanted to do it at the library, where Iris and I met."

Iris pulled her hand away from Greta and flung her arms around Dean. "Oh, Dean, and here I was worried you were going to break up with me."

"No way. I was just afraid you'd be on to me if I said too much. I'm sorry for seeming so distant." Dean reached for both of Iris's cheeks and kissed her with passion.

Greta's skin itched as sweat beads formed, and her head felt impossibly heavy. For a moment, she thought she might pass out. She gulped in a cleansing breath, setting her mind to what she needed to do—get Iris away from Dean and get to her phone, which was frustratingly tucked in her bag on the other side of the circulation desk, to contact Detective McHenry.

Dean pulled away from the kiss and clamped Iris to his side. "I've got to take my fiancée out to celebrate tonight. I have other big news, too. I picked a property—the waterfront lot by Shadow Lake. We've got house plans to start considering!" Dean sounded thrilled with himself. He looked from Iris's radiant face to Greta and Josie. "I hope you two don't mind postponing your girls' night."

Josie's agitated expression had spiraled to frantic. "Uh—we—well—"

"Of course not." Greta raised her voice to cut off Josie's stuttering. They

245

had to keep up the charade in front of Dean. "We completely understand."

"I've got to go home and change." Iris bounced up and down, vibrating with happiness. "I'm so excited."

"Let Josie take you." Greta reached for Josie's arm and squeezed it, pulling her forward. "She has the best wardrobe."

Greta considered it a minor victory when Josie smoothed out her features. "It's true. I'll get you all ready for the big night. Do your makeup and everything. I can drop her off at your house in an hour or so. Sound good, Dean?"

"I don't know if I can be apart from you for so long." Dean pulled Iris in for another kiss.

Josie's face turned a putrid shade of green. Greta was right there with her, but they couldn't let Dean know their feelings. Not yet. She stepped gently on her friend's foot to snap her out of it, but Josie's neutral expression was gone. She looked at Greta, her eyes the size of bowling balls.

Their attention snapped back to the couple when Dean started talking again.

"Is that what you want, baby?" Dean asked.

Iris giggled and nodded.

"Then I'll see you in an hour. I guess I'll finish up some work here while I wait—"

"Actually, we're closed, so—"

"It's fine!" Greta said over the top of Josie. If she could keep Dean within her sights, she could get a hold of Detective McHenry, and this would all be over. "I can stay behind and lock up when you're done."

"Perfect. I'm going to grab my laptop quick." Dean kissed Iris one more time before turning on his heel and striding out the door.

"Ahhh!" Iris threw her arms around her friends and jumped up and down. "I'm so happy!"

And thank God for that, Greta thought. At the moment, Iris's happiness was blinding her to the fact that Greta and Josie were—to put it mildly—less than enthused.

Iris hurried to collect her coat and purse. "Let's go, Jos. I've got a hot date tonight."

"Take her to your house and stall. I'll call Detective McHenry," Greta muttered to Josie. She waited for Josie to nod her understanding. "I'll close up and meet you guys at Josie's," Greta said at full volume, forcing herself to sound like this was about to be the best night ever.

Iris hugged her before seizing Josie's hand, pushing open the glass exit door, and pulling Josie out with her.

As soon as they rounded the corner, Greta dove for her purse and yanked out her cell phone. She didn't know if she had time for a phone call, so she typed out a message to Detective McHenry as quickly as she could with fingers that felt about as functional as frozen pipes.

Greta: SOS. Call me ASAP or get to the library.

Pressing send, Greta slid the phone into the front pocket of her cardigan and forced herself to relax the muscles in her face. They were stiff from faking happiness, but she had to keep Dean occupied and unsuspicious for a little longer. She could do this.

The glass door clicked open behind her, and she summoned her resolve to greet Dean with the realest looking fake smile she could muster. When she faced the entryway, Greta started. "Sidney! Hi!"

Sidney didn't smile as she stepped farther into the library. The closer she came to Greta, the worse she looked. *Oh no.* If Sidney had talked to Detective McHenry and he told her about Dean, then she was going to be reeling. And now Dean was coming back into the library. If they hadn't crossed paths in the parking lot, they would here. There was bound to be a confrontation, and Greta doubted it would end well.

"I'm guessing you spoke to Detective McHenry." When Sidney didn't respond, Greta walked toward her and pulled her into a hug. The library door whooshed open again behind her and Greta stepped back from Sidney. Out of the corner of her mouth she said, "Stay calm and play along."

She turned to see Dean enter, and Greta dialed up her most cheerful expression. "There he is. Come in, Dean. I'm sure you're anxious to take care of your work so you can get to celebrating." Greta shot Sidney a look, willing her to go along with the act.

Dean turned his back to them and locked the library door from the inside. Warning bells sounded in Greta's head, and the ringing in her ears made it momentarily difficult for Greta to act like nothing was wrong. Next to her, Sidney's face was set.

At least she wasn't alone with Dean.

"You can keep the door open. I'm sure we won't have any walk-ins right now." Greta felt drenched with dread. If only Detective McHenry would get here.

Dean faced them again. "We need to talk."

"What about?" Greta babbled on, her voice rising to match her panic level. "Are you looking for a suggestion for a dinner spot? I know all of Iris's favorites, so I can definitely help you there. Or if you want to talk wedding venues, or florists, I have a lot of experience since I helped my cousin about a year ago. Or—"

"Cut the crap, Greta," Dean hissed. "That's not what I mean, and you know it."

"What do you mean, then?" Greta's voice shook. Her phone started to vibrate, and Greta reached into the pocket of her cardigan for it. *Detective McHenry!*

"Don't answer that."

Chapter Forty-Eight

Greta whipped around at the harsh directive from Sidney, and her blood changed to ice. "W-why not?" Greta stood petrified as Sidney told Dean to turn off the lights. "Sidney?"

"Be quiet, Greta. Don't answer the phone, or you'll be sorry. And keep your hands where I can see them."

Greta slowly dropped her phone down into her pocket and held up her palms.

"What's going on? Sidney!" Greta yelped when Sidney squeezed her upper arm and dragged her behind the desk.

"Move, Greta. I've had about enough of you. Get into the office right now."

"What? No. Get off of me." Greta tried to shake herself free. "Why are you doing this? Ow!" Greta winced when Sidney tightened her grip.

"We're tying up a loose end. Now go." Sidney shoved Greta forward.

Greta fought, tripping over her own feet, until Dean came up on her other side and pinned her arms behind her back, wrenching her upright.

Sidney let go and walked ahead. She jerked open the door to the office and waited for Dean to lug Greta inside.

Greta hardly recognized Sidney. Gone was the happy-go-lucky woman she'd seen at the library the past couple of weeks. Sidney's gaze darted all around like a diseased animal, and the lines in her forehead were severe. Her usually tidy hair was spilling from a messy ponytail. She looked positively terrifying.

"How am I a loose end?" Greta's voice came out as a squeak. "Dean, what's going on? You're engaged to Iris. You're supposed to be out on the town celebrating. I thought you were going to finish your work and wait at home for Josie to drop Iris off? They're going to wonder where you are."

"Shut up." Sidney closed the door to the office behind herself and spun around, cutting Greta with an expression of sheer disdain.

Greta's toe connected with the desk, and she stumbled forward, nailing her shoulder against the bookcase on the near wall. Disoriented, she looked around for a way to escape, but there wasn't a window in the office—no way to attract any attention. Dean had a firm grip on her arm. Greta pulled forward to test his hold, but his fingers dug through her cardigan, and she had to work not to cry out in pain.

"Dean, please." Greta tried to turn her face to him, but he ducked behind her while Sidney stepped in front of her, blocking the door.

"Everything was going perfectly, Greta." Sidney spat out her name as if it was rotten milk. A vein throbbed in her temple, her face was flushed, and her breathing was erratic. "Franklin was out of the picture. We'd avoided disaster...until you started poking your nose into things. I was worried about Franklin's new relationship with you. You"—she sneered—"who swept right in for him to treat as a pseudo-daughter. I wasn't sure what he had told you."

"Told me about what?" Greta gasped in an attempt to fill her lungs with air and quell the fear making the edges of her vision fuzzy.

"What he found out. About our scheme."

"He didn't tell me anything about you." That much was true. "I didn't even know Dean worked with him until after he died." *Until after you killed him.* She pressed her mouth together to keep the contents of her stomach in place. This wasn't good.

Sidney flicked her wrist. "Water under the bridge. It doesn't matter now. What matters is you figured things out."

"What did I figure out?" Greta wanted Sidney to say it. She knew what she thought, but she needed confirmation.

"That all the senile old people in this town who were too stupid to do their own financial planning and check their own portfolios and accounts online were helping me get rich." Sidney pinged a glare at Dean and scowled. "*Us,*

250

get rich. They were none the wiser. We've built up a nice little nest egg. Though Dean was more of a liability."

"Hey, now." Dean tightened his grip on Greta's arms, and she felt him stand up straighter behind her, coming to his own defense. "Don't forget I'm the financial expert here. Without me, you'd have nothing."

Sidney scoffed. "You're a pawn, Dean. I would have found another way to go after Franklin, with or without you. But I underestimated him and his background, and the whole thing blew up in my face sooner than expected."

"Franklin worked in finance before getting hurt." Greta looked to the ceiling. Of course he figured out Sidney and Dean's scheme. "Why did you target him, then?"

"Because he owed me," she said. "And Dean swore he had built up a solid enough relationship with Franklin and could pull it off."

"I *did* pull it off. For long enough, at least. Now I've got property farther up north. Iris and I will get out of town and put down some new roots. Things are getting a little too hot here in Larkspur."

Greta's stomach bottomed out. She forced herself to remain calm. She had to keep her wits about her if she was going to get the information she needed and get out of this mess. And she had to get out of there to save Iris from Dean. "What about you, Sidney? Why did you need the money?" Maybe she had a gambling problem? Or a sick family member she was trying to help. Greta racked her brain for some reason, something that would compel someone like Sidney to act this way.

"Because money is power, and if I'm smart enough to get a bigger piece of the pie, why not?"

Greta flinched. "But stealing is wrong."

Sidney clicked her tongue. "Greta, you're so naïve. I saw an opportunity and followed through on it. I've been doing it for years, jumping from town to town and getting out of dodge when suspicions were aroused."

The Bernie Madoff book in the library aisle popped into Greta's head. "It was you, here in the library that night, wasn't it? What were you doing?"

Sidney snorted. "I wasn't expecting you to come back, that's for sure. I was printing off some statements. Dean had snagged Iris's key and library card, so we could get in after hours and use the printer. No way to trace it back to us that way. When I saw you coming back inside, I had to hide out."

"But then why not wait until I left to make your exit? You could have locked up, and we would have been none the wiser."

"That was the plan." Sidney looked exasperated, "But that dumb book slipped out of my hands, and then you started looking for me. Because you can't seem to mind your own damn business. So I had to escape. Which I did. Which I always do."

"How have you not been caught before?"

Sidney cackled. "Because I'm intelligent enough not to leave a trail. I finally tracked Franklin down here in Larkspur, and I tapped into Dean. Sweet little Dean, an upstanding citizen. He made the perfect front for our arrangement. In this sleepy town, no one suspected a thing. When I moved here two years ago, I came to Dean with the plan, and he bought in, simple as that."

"What do you mean you tracked Franklin down?" Greta's mind was like sludge. "I thought he was just one of many whom you took advantage of."

"Franklin was my father. My absent, never made any contact, left me to the streets father."

Greta blinked. It was probably spurred by the panic of the moment, but her first thought in response to this bombshell was, *so Liam had managed to get Franklin's daughter to the will reading after all...he just didn't know it.* Somewhere Alanis Morissette was singing about the irony of it all.

Greta stared at the woman across the room, trying to see...something—some resemblance to Franklin, perhaps. But it was futile. Sidney didn't look like herself. Or maybe she looked exactly like herself, and Greta was merely getting a glimpse of her true colors for the first time. The level of her supposed friend's deception was chilling, and Greta trembled.

"I-I don't get it. If Franklin was your father, why didn't he say something? Why didn't you say something? You've lived in the same town for years."

"Yep, during which time I used his pathetic self to get rich. He didn't know who I was. At least not until I told him the moment before...well...." She smirked as she trailed off and started pacing.

Greta's head spun with this new information, but her brain was functioning at the speed of the library's computer systems and would only compute one thing at a time. "The baby picture," she said to herself.

"What are you mumbling about?"

"He had a baby picture. At his house. I'm guessing it was of you. He might not have known you were his daughter, but he knew he had a baby. How do you know he hadn't been looking for you? Trying to reconnect? Why assume he was a villain? Did you always plan to kill him?" The thought horrified her, but Greta kept her eyes on Sidney. She had to keep her talking. The longer she could draw this out, the closer help would be. She hoped.

Sidney stopped and pointed at Greta. "Franklin had his chances to support my mother and me while he was alive, and he did nothing. I deserved the money I was taking from him. It was payback for all the years he'd neglected me. I never planned to kill him. Just to milk him for all he was worth. But then the bastard figured out we were stealing from him and threatened to expose Dean unless he came clean, so Franklin took a little fall."

Indignation flared through Greta's entire body like a lightning bolt. "More like you strangled him and pushed him off his deck. Your own father. How could you?"

Sidney's gaze was cold. "Franklin was already dead to me."

"I had nothing to do with killing him," Dean piped up. "I didn't want it to go down that way. I wasn't even there."

Sidney rolled her eyes so hard Greta could hear them squish in their sockets. "Nobody cares, Dean. The fact of the matter is, I handled it." Greta clenched her jaw as Sidney aimed her sly grin at her. "I would have handled you, too, Greta, if someone hadn't pulled you from the lake."

Greta's mind flashed to Richard. She'd hunted him down, thinking he could have killed Franklin, but how wrong she'd been. The whole time it was someone right under her nose. "Why'd you come after me, though? What did I do?"

"I could tell at the will reading you were getting close to unearthing our scheme. I figured if I killed you or scared you, either way, you'd be out of the picture."

Greta swallowed her panic and forced herself to try to stay focused. "You pushed Dolores, too. Why?"

"Actually, Dolores' little accident *was* Dean's doing," Sidney admitted. "Granted, I sent him after her after we overheard her tell you she might be able to help with your pathetic investigation. I panicked and thought Franklin might have let her in on something that would incriminate us. Something she might not have realized, but you would have fleshed out."

"So, you tried to kill her?"

"Who cares? Obviously, she doesn't know anything, or it would have come out." Sidney stopped pacing and faced Greta. "Now I have to figure out what to do with you, so I can move on with my life. It's only too bad I won't be able to claim Franklin's inheritance." Sidney made two *tsk* sounds with her tongue. "No matter, though. After years of wondering where my deadbeat Dad was, I finally found him, and I got the last word and the revenge I deserved."

Greta tried to wriggle free, hoping Dean had loosened his grip on her, but she stilled when Sidney dug into her purse and retrieved a gun.

"You can stop fighting it, Greta. This is it."

Everything started happening in slow motion. A bead of sweat dripped from Greta's hairline and trickled behind her ear, and she felt the entire trail it made. She had to work to unstick her tongue. "How is this going to end well for you, Sidney?" Greta carefully formed each word. Her heart hammered painfully against her ribs as if trying to escape her chest. She was running out of time, but, like any good librarian, she did what came naturally. She asked more questions.

"What are you going to do, shoot me here and now? And then what? Where will you go with my body? How do you expect to hide a crime scene in a public library? Someone at the police office is sure to recognize the sound of a gunshot." Greta ticked off all the things she wasn't sure Sidney was in the right mind to have thought through, buying herself every second she could.

Sidney's face turned crimson red. "Do you think I'm stupid?"

"No, but I'm not sure how you expect to walk away from this free and clear.

Even if you off me, someone will figure out what you've done." *Someone like Detective McHenry.*

Sidney waved the gun around dismissively. "No one will figure this out. I sent that good-for-nothing detective on a wild goose chase for Dean when he called me and told me about the warrant for our computers. He's probably an hour out of town by now. If I were you, I'd be worried less about me and more about how you're about to die." Sidney tipped the gun toward her and clicked the safety mechanism off. "Get out of the way, Dean."

"Sidney, let's not do anything rash." Dean's hollow voice sounded weak and pitiful. "She's not wrong. Won't doing this here be...messy? And what are we going to do with her body? How is this not going to get back to us?"

"It's not going to get back to *me*."

The insinuation hung in the air. Behind Greta, Dean took a sharp breath and dropped her arms. Greta held in a gasp of relief. She wasn't out of the woods yet—not while Sidney wielded a gun. She kept her hands tucked behind her and stayed where she was, afraid any sudden movement could startle Sidney into shooting.

Dean stepped forward. "What are you talking about? We're in this together."

Sidney laughed again. "You're dumber than I thought. If you would have paid any attention to what we were actually doing, you would have seen I hid my role entirely, just like I always do. No one has suspected or will suspect me of anything. Greta didn't until just now, did you, Greta?" Sidney pointed the gun at Greta.

Greta bit her lip, shaking her head.

With a victorious look, Sidney jabbed the gun in Dean's direction. "The detective is looking for you, Dean. Not me. No one has given me a second thought. That's how it's always been, and that's how it's going to stay. I'll stage a perfect murder-suicide. I'll leave a note and everything. How you shot Greta and couldn't live with yourself. I'll play the role of the horrified assistant who found her boss and her friend dead in the library. Greta, do you have any tips for making a murder scene look accurate? You've been the witness to a decent amount of crime scenes lately."

Bile rose in Greta's throat as Sidney laughed manically.

"You're not going to shoot me." Dean pulled himself up to his full height.

"You bet I will." Sidney raised the gun until it was level with his chest.

With all of Sidney's erratic pacing, she'd moved away from the door. Greta inched toward the room's only exit as Dean and Sidney continued arguing.

"You're not going to get away with this." Dean's voice was strained as he tried to reason with Sidney.

"Watch me."

Greta tripped over the corner of the desk and froze when Sidney faced her again. She reached behind herself, and her hand connected with the doorknob.

"Don't move another muscle, Greta."

Greta held up her hands at the same time as she leaned back against the door, which pushed open behind her. She stumbled backward, but, by some miracle, kept her footing. Sidney let out a strangled cry and lunged at Greta.

Greta sidestepped her and reached for one of the huge nonfiction books Josie left on the desk. She whirled around and smacked Sidney, the force of the blow reverberating up Greta's arms. Unfortunately, it wasn't enough to get Sidney to drop the gun. Greta let the book tumble to the floor and dove around the corner of the circulation desk, certain at any minute, Sidney would catch up to her and shoot. Greta squeezed her eyes closed and thought of her parents. Of Josie and Iris, who would still be in harm's way. Of Kelly.

At least she'd see her sister again.

"Freeze, Sidney. This is the Larkspur Police Department." Detective McHenry's voice boomed, calm and steady.

Hope soared, and Greta cracked an eye open. The detective was crouched behind the research table, near the printer station, with two uniformed police officers positioned on either side of him. Greta's gaze connected with his as he scanned the area. He held up his free hand, motioning for her to stay put.

Greta peered around the backside of the circulation desk to where she assumed Sidney was hiding. Sure enough, Sidney was bent behind the high desk with Dean a couple feet to her right. Dean's expression was one of a sheep being led to slaughter.

"Sidney, you're surrounded. It's over. Come out with your hands up."

"Don't come any closer, or I'll-I'll shoot someone." Sidney's voice wavered.

"No, you won't, Sidney." Detective McHenry seemed almost bored.

Greta moved her gaze so she could see both the detective, squatting behind the printer station in the center of the library, and Sidney, crouched behind the circulation desk. All at once, the detective abandoned the cover of the table and slunk forward.

Sidney must have sensed the movement. She poked her head up from behind the desk and pointed her gun at Detective McHenry.

Greta didn't think. She charged around the desk and tackled Sidney. Together, they hit the ground hard, with Greta landing on top of Sidney as her gun discharged.

At the same time, Detective McHenry catapulted himself over the circulation desk to where Greta and Sidney lay wrestling on the library floor.

"Get off of me, Greta," Sidney screamed. "You ruined everything."

The detective kicked Sidney's gun out of arm's reach and grabbed for her as Greta landed a punch to Sidney's nose. Josie would be so proud.

Sidney swore in pain, and her nose started gushing blood.

Detective McHenry had Sidney on her belly and handcuffed in less than five seconds, and Greta toppled backward, landing on her butt against the exterior wall of the office. Dean took off for the library's exit, only to be stopped by a uniformed officer. He held up his hands, surrendering, as Greta scrambled upright.

It was over.

Detective McHenry hauled Sidney to her feet and rattled off her rights as officers closed in. One took Sidney off the detective's hands. More officers swarmed the library, and Greta closed her eyes.

"What in the name of all that is holy were you doing?"

Greta's eyelids snapped open. Detective McHenry was standing directly in front of her, hands on his hips.

Greta relaxed and mirrored his pose. "Well, I wasn't going to let her shoot you. So, I figured I'd better act quickly."

Detective McHenry looked her up and down as if assessing for injury and checking to see if she was in her right mind. He shook his head slightly. "You are something else, Miss Plank."

Greta searched the detective's face, recognizing a look she now determined was a mixture of admiration and exasperation. *That* she could work with. "Call me, Greta, Detective. After all this, we ought to be on a first-name basis."

Chapter Forty-Nine

Later that night, Greta sat ensconced in a booth at Mugs & Hugs. Her parents had rushed home from Everything's Coming Up Tacos, forfeiting their authentic flan dessert in favor of getting back to be with her. Now they sat playing gatekeeper for Greta as all the town's folk came up to their table, trying to get firsthand information. No one could believe Sidney was behind Franklin's death, or that Dean was corrupt, but Greta assured them, like it or not, it was the truth.

Cindi Fields sat with some of her friends at a table across the café. Her nose stuck so high in the air it was obvious she was working very hard not to make eye contact with Greta. Cindi's name had been on Franklin's list, so Greta figured she'd been taken advantage of by Dean and Sidney, as well. Greta half hoped that her role in uncovering the fraud would endear Cindi to her, but judging from the woman's aloof posture and sour expression, that wasn't going to happen anytime soon.

Oh well. One problem at a time. There would be many an opportunity to go toe-to-toe with the Library Board chairwoman, she was sure. Right now, Greta was tired.

She had gone with Detective McHenry to give her statement and called Josie and filled her in from the detective's office. Josie had already started telling Iris what was going on. Iris was in denial, but Josie promised to explain as best as she could and stay with Iris for the night. Greta was thankful she didn't have to face Iris yet. Her friend would need her, but she didn't have enough energy for the tough conversation at the moment. Her own experience as a jilted lover was poking dangerously at the surface, and

259

Greta needed to get her head on straight before she could put on a brave face for Iris.

Allison approached the table. "Here you go, G." She set down a refilled cup of piping hot green tea. "Extra honey, just how you like it."

Greta took a tentative sip but stopped before she burned her tongue, instead picking up a buttery shortbread cookie Allison had added to her plate. The cookie dissolved in her mouth, not too salty and not too sweet. Just right.

The bell on the door of the café jingled behind her, and her parents looked beyond her. Greta's mom smiled. "Detective McHenry. Would you care to join us?"

The detective appeared in Greta's peripheral vision. "I thought you might appreciate an update."

"Please, sit." Her dad motioned to the spot next to Greta, and she scooted over.

Detective McHenry slid into the booth.

"Well?" Greta's mom leaned forward. "Is everything tied up?"

The detective nodded. "I informed Sidney of everything we had on her and Dean, thanks to your intel." He tipped his head toward Greta. "It was brilliant of you to answer my call, by the way. I was able to tell what was going on. I called for backup and got there as soon as I could."

Greta allowed herself a moment of pride and a smug smile at Detective McHenry's praise. She had blindly clicked the "answer" button as she slid her phone back into the pocket of her cardigan. "I'm glad you could still hear what was happening through my sweater."

Detective McHenry ran a hand through his mussed hair. "Fortunately, I thought to grab the master key for the building from the police station. I would have hated to have to shatter the glass library door to get in. It would have made entering undetected a bit more of a challenge."

Greta pressed her lips together and considered how many things could have gone horribly wrong this evening, but she was saved from dwelling on the what-ifs when Detective McHenry kept talking.

"Sidney confessed to everything in less than fifteen minutes. Franklin's murder. The investment fraud. Your attempted murder. Everything.

"After killing Franklin, she deleted his email account using hacking skills she's honed over the years. She guessed he'd been communicating with the bank, and she wanted to buy herself some time to cover her tracks. We're lucky Franklin had the foresight to print his email correspondence and hide it."

Greta swallowed another sip of tea. She wished Franklin had said something to someone rather than trying to handle it all himself. He must've been suspicious and worried enough about what Dean and Sidney were capable of if he'd gone to such lengths to preserve evidence of the fraud. Thank goodness he had, or they might not have figured out what happened until it was too late, but it still hurt Greta to know that she wasn't able to be there for her friend when he needed her. Because he hadn't let her in.

Detective McHenry shifted next to her, stirring Greta from her thoughts. "I figured you'd also want to know that Sidney said she chucked the copy of *Crime and Punishment* down the stairs after shoving Franklin. Called it poetic justice." The detective side-eyed Greta. "I don't think she's ever read the book."

If Greta had been standing, she might have staggered back, shocked and not a little impressed that Detective McHenry was familiar with the tale of Raskolnikov.

"This isn't her first foray into criminal behavior," he continued. "When we ran her prints, we got hits from three other states. She's wanted all over the Midwest, but she's been using an assumed name. The woman Larkspur knows as Sidney Lawrence is actually Susan Olson. And this was her MO. She would latch onto a financial representative, employ her fraudulent scheme, and then let the other guy take the fall when it all went south. Her partners have all turned on her, but by the time the police have tried to hunt her down, she's been in the wind. As she tells it, she's been searching for Franklin to enact her revenge for years. She finally found him, and in taking him down, she went up in flames."

Greta bit her lip. She was still stunned by the revelation of Franklin and Sidney's relationship. It would take some serious time to unpack. Perhaps

Franklin was a morally gray character, like those in some of her favorite books. Heathcliff came to mind. Severus Snape, too. In any case, his history would remain a mystery to her, as would his motives for not asking for help at the first signs of trouble with Dean and Sidney. But she refused to let that taint the good memories she had with him.

Greta's mom leaned back. "So, it was all Sidney, or Susan, as it were, and not Dean."

"She was the mastermind, yes." Detective McHenry readjusted his position in the booth, and his arm brushed Greta's. "Dean was complicit, though. He attacked Dolores to keep her from talking. He'll face charges for assault and reckless endangerment, on top of fraud, withholding evidence, and tampering with a police investigation. He won't be living anywhere but a jail cell for many years to come. How's Iris?"

Greta stopped circling her mug with her finger. She looked up at him to see his dark eyes looking softer than usual, more charcoal gray than granite black. Greta cleared her throat. "She's not great from the sounds of things, but she'll be okay eventually. We'll make sure of it."

The bell over the café door rang again. Greta sipped her tea but nearly choked when, out of the corner of her eye, she spotted Richard approaching the table.

His gaze roved nervously around until it landed on Greta. "Um, excuse me, I don't mean to interrupt."

"No problem at all. Mom, Dad, this is Richard Bennings, Franklin's half-brother and the man who fished me out of the lake the other night."

Her dad stood and clasped Richard's hand, his voice thick with emotion. "We can't ever express enough gratitude to you for saving Greta."

"I'm glad I was in the right place at the right time."

Her dad sat back down, and Richard shot a look to Detective McHenry.

"What's up?" Greta stared between Richard and the detective as Richard pulled out a book from his jacket. Greta caught sight of the title, and her mouth dropped open.

"I reckon you'll be wanting this back, Miss Plank." Richard held out the first edition copy of *Live and Let Die*. "Like I told the detective here, I'm sorry for taking it."

Greta took the book, letting her fingers run over the plastic wrapper protecting the slightly worn dust jacket. It was a beautiful book. "Why did you take it?" She wasn't super acquainted with Richard, but he didn't strike her as a burglar.

"Actually, Franklin told me he wanted me to have it. Like I said to you and Josie when you came to visit, we had plans to reconnect."

Detective McHenry snorted next to her. "And when did you go and see Richard, Miss—Greta?"

"That's neither here nor there at this point, right, Detective?" Greta smiled sweetly before turning her attention to Richard. "Please go on."

"Franklin talked about sharing more of his collection with me the next time we got together, so he didn't give me the book at our initial meeting. My relationship with my brother was complicated. We weren't close growing up, but I'm a medical assistant. When Franklin had his accident, I called him and told him I'd be happy to be his live-in aid. He shut me down. Hurt my feelings pretty good. But he was a proud man and rarely let people in, so I guess I understood. Anyway, slowly but surely, we'd been rebuilding our relationship. He asked me to leave Mumsy's photo albums with him last month after we'd gone through them. He was warming to me, I think. Though he never told me he was a father." Richard seemed as stunned by that news as Greta had been. "Anyhow, I returned to the cabin for the book because I wanted something to remember my brother by, but it was wrong of me to steal it. And it's your collection now, so I want to return it."

Greta stared down at the book and handed it back to him. "I want you to have it."

Richard held up his hands. "No, I couldn't. Besides, I promised Detective McHenry I would return it. It was the condition of him not arresting me."

Greta shoved the book at Richard. "Well, you held up your end of the bargain. Detective McHenry isn't going to arrest you. Right, Detective?" Before he could get a word in, Greta went on. "I insist you take it. Consider this a gift. In fact, I've been thinking about what I want to do with Franklin's collection, and I want to lease it, free of charge, to the Larkspur Library."

Greta scanned the table. Everyone's wide-eyed gazes were on her. Her mom beamed, and her dad looked thoughtful.

"That's very generous of you," Detective McHenry said.

Greta brushed off the compliment. "I want everyone to be able to enjoy the books. And it'll be a cool tourist destination, too. We'll have to petition the town to add on to the library or reconfigure it and use some of the current space to create a rare books room, but it'll be worth it. I'm going to talk to the mayor about it so we can tease it at the fall festival." Greta leaned back in the booth, excitement at the prospect of a rare books room coming to life in the Larkspur Library warming her from the inside out. "You know, Richard, once we get the room up and running, we'll need a part-time curator. Would you have any interest?"

Richard's jaw dropped. "Are you serious?"

"Very serious. You'd have to interview, but I know the hiring coordinator for the library." She pointed at herself.

A small smile spread over Richard's face. "I'd like that very much." He wished the four of them good night and had a pep in his step as he walked out.

Greta took a deep and satisfied breath as her parents launched into a conversation with Detective McHenry about Chicago and the many landmarks they were all familiar with in the city.

Greta was content to let the conversation swirl around her as she sipped her tea and scanned the café. All these friends and neighbors. They had their own stories. Their own secrets. And that was just the way it was, wasn't it? People were messy. Life was, too. She'd take her chances with life in Larkspur, though, because, while the events of the past month might not have had the happy ending Greta expected, there was nowhere else she'd rather be.

Acknowledgements

All glory to God, now and forever.

Thank you, dear readers, for taking a chance on my debut cozy mystery. If you're reading these acknowledgements, then I think we're kindred spirits! Getting to share this story with you has been such a gift. I hope you enjoyed your visit to Larkspur. I hope Greta and the gang made you smile. I hope you had a fabulous time piecing the clues together and solving the crime. And I hope I see you right back here in the next book's acknowledgements section!

To my editor, Shawn. You are a rock star. I'm so thankful for all your work and for the time you spent polishing my manuscript and making sure it was ready to launch as a real, live book. To everyone at Level Best Books, thank you for your support and kindness. I'm very proud to be on the LBB team.

To my agent, Dawn. You made this happen. Thanks for believing in my story and seeing its potential. Thank you for encouraging me and working with me to make it better. Thank you for answering countless emails and questions. I am truly grateful for your knowledge, expertise, and to be a part of your agency.

To the writing community as a whole, with extra thanks to Kate, Sarah, Christina, Jackie, and Heather, the authors who took time out of their busy schedules to read an early copy of *Death Checked Out* and provide blurbs. I'm humbled by your willingness to champion my book. Thank you.

To the librarians in Kimberly. You are my favorite! I wrote this story as a love letter to libraries, and it's people like you who have made me a library lover. Thank you for everything you to do to raise up readers and to make our community great. A big thanks to Holly for reading a proof copy and telling me you enjoyed it (you have no idea how much I massively exhaled upon hearing that!). And to Tracy. I cannot tell you how much your thoughtfulness means to me. From answering my questions in detail to inviting me to the library during off hours to show me how things work, you helped me to bring the Larkspur Community Library and Greta's character to life.

To the Dobrinskas. Thanks for loving me as one of your own and telling everyone you know that you have an author in the family while gently shoving my books in front of their faces.

To my extended family. Thanks for giving me great ideas for Greta's assumptions of Detective McHenry's hobbies. That text string still makes me cackle. Shout out to Sam for naming Mugs & Hugs so perfectly. Shout out to Samantha, Clare, Rachael, and Ashley for your endless cheerleading. Shout out to you, Aunt Anne, for reading an early draft of this book years ago and being excited about it ever since. To the entire Cottage crew. The memories we made in that place are sprinkled throughout these pages. I hope you loved finding them. I love you!

To my family. Mom, Dad, Luke, Bailey, and Ben. Words won't ever be enough. I'm so grateful for you. Thanks for supporting this dream and all my dreams, forever and ever. Dad, thanks for always believing in me. Mom, thanks for the last minute editing help and inspiring me to write. Luke and Ben, I wrote something that's not a romance…you're welcome! Bailey, you're the best sister a girl could ask for and one of the best humans I know. All my love, you guys.

To my kids, Miriam, Lyla, Ellen, and Francis. This one's for you! At the heart of all mystery novels is an innate sense of curiosity and a quest for truth. I hope you stay curious, keep asking questions, and pursue what is true. I am so proud to be your mom. I love you.

Finally, to Nick. I always save you until the end, thinking I'll come up with something profound to say. But here we are again. Just thank you…for everything. I love you madly. Always.

About the Author

Leah Dobrinska is the author of the Larkspur Library Mysteries, a cozy mystery series set in the Wisconsin Northwoods, and the Mapleton novels, a series of standalone small town romances. She earned her degree in English Literature from UW-Madison where she was awarded the Dean's Prize and served as a Writing Fellow. She has since worked as a freelance writer, editor, and content marketer. As a kid, she hoped to grow up to be either Nancy Drew or Elizabeth Bennet. Now, she fulfills that dream by writing mysteries and love stories.

A sucker for a good sentence, a happy ending, and the smell of books—both old and new—Leah lives out her very own happily ever after in a small Wisconsin town with her husband and their gaggle of kids. When she's not writing, handing out snacks, or visiting local parks, Leah enjoys reading and running. Find out more about Leah, join her newsletter community, and connect with her through her website, leahdobrinska.com.

SOCIAL MEDIA HANDLES:
  Facebook: facebook.com/whatleahwrote
  Instagram: Instagram.com/whatleahwrote
  TikTok: tiktok.com/@whatleahwrote

AUTHOR WEBSITE:

268

Also by Leah Dobrinska

Love at On Deck Café

Good To Be Home

Together With You